SINS OF THE FATHERS

SINS OF THE FATHERS

Sally Spencer

This first world edition published in Great Britain 2006 by
SEVERN HOUSE PUBLISHERS LTD of
9–15 High Street, Sutton, Surrey SM1 1DF.
This first world edition published in the USA 2006 by
SEVERN HOUSE PUBLISHERS INC of
595 Madison Avenue, New York, N.Y. 10022.

British Library Cataloguing in Publication Data

Spencer, Sally
      Sins of the fathers
      1.   Woodend, Charlie (Fictitious character) - Fiction
      2.   Police - England - Fiction
      3.   Detective and mystery stories
      I.   Title
      823.9'14 [F]

      ISBN-13: 978-0-7278-6395-9 (cased)
      ISBN-10: 0-7278-6395-9   (cased)
      ISBN-13: 978-0-7278-9181-2 (paper)
      ISBN-13: 0-7278-9182-0   (paper)

All Severn House titles are printed on acid-free paper.

Typeset by Palimpsest Book Production Ltd.,
Grangemouth, Stirlingshire, Scotland.
Printed and bound in Great Britain by
MPG Books Ltd., Bodmin, Cornwall.

Prologue

The English Lake District – January 1962

From the moment the shivers had taken hold of him, Jeremy Tully had been convinced that he was dying.

Now, several hours later – if it *was* hours, rather than minutes or days, both of which seemed equally possible – the shivering had almost stopped.

Tully took no consolation from this fact. He knew enough about hypothermia to understand that rather than indicating that his condition was improving, it was a sign it was getting much worse. What had happened was that his body – independent of his mind – had decided, in a desperate attempt to preserve its glucose, to partly shut itself down.

But the attempt wouldn't work.

Nothing would work.

He was dying. That was the end of it – the end of him.

There were three of them on the ledge – Tully himself, Bradley Pine and Alec Hawtrey.

Of the trio, Alec was easily in the worst shape. He was the oldest member of the party – the least physically fit from the beginning – and when he had fallen and broken his leg, it had only served to stack the odds even further against him.

Every time the other two had attempted to move the injured man, he had screamed with agony.

But it was now a long time since Alec had even had the strength to express his pain.

So he would probably go first.

Then, Tully thought, it would be his turn.

But Bradley would not follow them down the route to oblivion. He wouldn't die – however intense the blizzard grew,

1

however long it took the rescue party to find them – because he was a survivor.

More than that – Bradley Pine was a planner, who always thought three steps ahead. So that while his *body* might be trapped on this mountainside, his mind was already back in Whitebridge, making its next move.

The snow no longer seemed to be lashing them quite as fiercely as it had been. Perhaps the blizzard had finally decided to let up, Tully thought. Perhaps he would live through the experience after all.

He uncurled a little from the foetal position that his battling body had instinctively taken. His muscles did not want to co-operate, but he forced them to, because he had to see for himself if it were really true that the weather was getting better – that there was finally some faint glimmer of hope.

What he *did* see, through the swirling snow, was that Pine had shifted position, so that now he was bent over Alec Hawtrey.

What he *did* see was the large sheath knife in Pine's hand.

He wanted to shout out to Pine that he should put the knife away. Wanted to tell him that Alec was probably past the point of conscious suffering, and it would be no act of kindness to rob him of what dignity he had left by killing him now – that he should just be allowed to die of natural causes.

But the words would not come – not as a shout, not even as a whisper.

And perhaps, he thought, with a mind half-turned to ice, it wouldn't have mattered even if the words had come. Because perhaps what he was witnessing wasn't a *mercy* killing at all.

Whitebridge Evening Courier – 6th April 1965

The sudden death of Seth Johnson, Member of Parliament for the Whitebridge Constituency since 1945, has created turmoil in both the leading political parties.

Labour has been losing ground for a number of years, and, in the considered opinion of many political observers, has only maintained the slim majority it now holds because of Seth Johnson's personal prestige. The Labour candidate selected to fight for Johnson's seat in the coming by-election will, therefore, have an uphill struggle.

The Conservative Party is currently deciding between two strong candidates.

The first, Henry Marlowe, has been Chief Constable of Central Lancashire for the last three years, and was Deputy Chief Constable before that.

The second, Bradley Pine, is a local businessman, whose company (Hawtrey-Pine Holdings) is one of Whitebridge's most successful manufacturing firms. Many of our readers will remember the tragedy which occurred three years ago, when, despite Bradley Pine's heroic efforts to save him, Alec Hawtrey lost his life in a mountaineering accident.

The election promises to be one of the liveliest in quite some time, and you may rest assured that the Courier will be covering it in the greatest possible detail, every step of the way.

One

Henry Marlowe stood at the very back of the Sleaburn Village Hall, watching the man on the small stage as he addressed an audience which had dragged itself out on a densely foggy evening, just for the privilege of hearing him speak.

Bradley Pine looked good, Marlowe thought reluctantly. Better than good. He looked sharp. He looked caring. He looked like a man who was confident of winning the coming by-election.

And the bastard probably *would* win!

'For nearly twenty years, this constituency has been in the hands of a party which hates individual freedom and individual responsibility with a passion,' Pine was telling his eager listeners. 'A party which wants to reward the scrounger for his idleness – and will do it at your expense. Well, my friends, it's time to draw a line in the sand – time to show them, with this election, that we won't stand for it!'

The audience applauded enthusiastically.

'It should have been me standing on that platform,' Marlowe said softly to himself.

He deserved it, he thought. Nobody had worked harder to win the selection committee's approval than he had. *Nobody* had bought more drinks, slapped more backs or done more favours. And it had all been for nothing!

Now this jumped-up little creep had been handed the mantle that he – the upholder of law and order throughout the county – had been denied.

It didn't seem right.

It didn't seem fair.

And Marlowe found himself wondering if – even at this late stage in the proceedings – there was anything he could do to seize back what was properly his.

* * *

Bradley Pine opened the door of the village hall and stepped out into the chill night air. He supposed that instead of making such a rapid exit, he could always have stayed longer – shaking a few more hands, making a few more personal promises. But, on the whole, he felt that would have been running an unnecessary risk – because the more time the glittering star spends among his acolytes, the greater the danger that some of the glitter will begin to flake off.

The fog had thickened while he'd been making his speech, and his car – which was conveniently parked in the country lane behind the hall – was no more than a vague shape. Even so, he could not fail to notice, as he drew closer to it, that a man was standing beside the vehicle.

'Who's that?' he asked.

'It's me,' said a voice that he recognized instantly as belonging to Henry Marlowe.

'I saw you standing at the back of the hall, Henry,' Pine said. 'It was very good of you to put in an appearance.'

'I didn't have much choice, did I?' Marlowe growled. 'I couldn't have people saying I was a sore loser.'

'No, of course you couldn't,' Pine agreed. 'Especially since such an assumption on their part would have been so patently unfair.'

'What's that supposed to mean?' Marlowe demanded. 'Is it meant to be some sort of joke?'

'Certainly not,' Pine assured him.

'Then what's your point?'

Pine sighed. 'I suppose I was just giving you the opportunity to show that you could accept defeat gracefully.'

'You could have supported my nomination, you know,' Marlowe said, showing no desire to do anything of the kind. 'You could have dropped your own candidature and given *me* your backing.'

'I seriously thought about doing just that,' Pine said, with the kind of sincerity that only a politician can ever truly manage.

'Did you? Well, you didn't show much sign of it!'

'But, ultimately, I had to base my decision on what I thought would be best for the Party, Henry. I knew I could win the seat, you see, and I very much doubted that you could.'

'In the current political climate, we could have put up a

turnip as our candidate and it would still have romped home,' Marlowe said.

'Perhaps you're right,' Pine conceded.

'You know I'm right.'

'But you still shouldn't look on this as a rout, Henry. You should see it more as a postponement.'

'Should I?'

'Of course. It won't be long before you're selected for another constituency. And think what an advantage it will be for you to have a friend in Westminster, speeding the process along.'

'Throwing me crumbs from his table would be closer to the truth,' Marlowe said bitterly.

'That's a little harsh,' Pine said. 'Listen, Henry, I'm very grateful for what you've done for me—'

'And so you bloody-well should be!'

'—but even gratitude must eventually have its limitations. You can rely on my help in the future, there's no question about that – but you can't keep drawing on debts from the past, as if they were some kind of bottomless well.'

'I could destroy you, you know!' Marlowe said.

'Not without destroying yourself,' Pine countered.

'So what?' Marlowe asked defiantly. 'It might almost be worth it!'

'You know that's not true,' Pine told him. He glanced down at his watch, though given the combination of night-time darkness and swirling fog, he knew he would be unable to read it. 'I'm afraid I really do have to go now, Henry. I'm due at St Mary's Church.'

'Oh, so you've suddenly found your religion again, have you?' Marlowe asked aggressively.

'I never lost it,' Pine said mildly. 'It's simply been in moth balls all these years – and now I'm taking it out for an airing.'

'You're a cynical bastard,' Marlowe said.

'And you are perhaps not quite cynical enough, Henry,' Pine responded, opening the door of his Cortina and climbing in. 'You see things far too much in terms of black and white. The politician's art is to be able to distinguish the various shades of grey, and it's an art you'll have to learn if you're ever to start climbing the political ladder yourself.'

He turned the ignition key and, despite the dampness in the atmosphere, the Cortina fired first time.

Henry Marlowe stood and watched as the vehicle's tail lights were swallowed up by the fog.

If ever a man was asking to get himself topped, he thought, that man was Bradley Pine.

The three people – two men and a woman – who were sitting in the corner of the public bar of the Drum and Monkey that night were regulars, not only of that particular boozer but of that particular table.

The older of the two men, Chief Inspector Charlie Woodend, was in his early fifties. He was what people in Whitebridge would call 'a big bugger', which meant that even violent drunks would think twice before taking a poke at him. He was wearing a hairy sports jacket and a pair of cavalry twill trousers, both items selected at random that morning from a wardrobe containing half a dozen similar jackets and several pairs of trousers which were almost identical.

The younger man, Constable Colin Beresford, was in his early twenties. He was wearing a blue suit which looked like it should have been reserved for Sundays. Occasionally, he would take a surreptitious glance at his watch, for while he felt honoured to be sitting in the company of the others, he was also conscious of the fact that it had been quite some time since he'd last checked on the state of his poor, demented mother.

The woman, Detective Sergeant Monika Paniatowski, was around thirty, and a blonde. She was smartly – though not expensively – dressed in a two-piece check suit, the skirt of which was short enough to reveal that she had rather sensational legs. Her largish nose suggested that she might be Central European in origin – and the nose did not lie. She could not have been called a beautiful woman, but to label her as merely 'attractive' would not have done her justice, either.

The barman, who had been watching them – and waiting for a signal which would indicate they required two more pints of best bitter and one vodka without ice – turned to the landlord, who was polishing beer glasses.

'Have you noticed that though there's not been a major crime for weeks, "the usual suspects" are in here again tonight,' he said jokingly.

The landlord placed the pint mug which he had been shining down on the counter.

'You've got it arse-over-backwards, haven't you, lad?' he asked. 'Since they're the bobbies, they'd have to be "the usual *suspectors*".'

The barman chuckled. 'Which would make Cloggin-it Charlie the *Chief Suspector*, I suppose,' he said. 'Chief Suspector Woodend! I rather like the sound of that.'

'I think we've gone quite far enough with that particular line of whimsy,' the landlord cautioned.

'It's only a joke!' the barman protested.

'It's always a mistake to take the piss out of the customers,' the landlord told him gravely. 'They're our bread an' butter, in case you need remindin'.'

'I know that, but—'

'An' Mr Woodend alone spends enough in here to keep us in puddings an' all.'

It was Father Taylor who greeted Bradley Pine at the door of St Mary's. He was a young priest, who had been in the parish for less than three years, and thus presented a marked contrast to Father Kenyon, who had served this particular flock for so long that there were now very few of the communicants of the church under the age of forty who had not been personally baptized by him.

'Welcome, Mr Pine!' the young priest said, full of enthusiasm. 'It's good to see you.'

'It's good to be here, Father,' Pine replied.

He was speaking no more than the truth. Though he might have glibly told Henry Marlowe that he had put his religion in moth balls, that had never really been the case, and recently he had found it a great source of comfort and a great source of strength.

'Are you here for a moment of quiet prayer?' Father Taylor asked. 'If so, I'll leave you to it.'

'No, I . . .' Pine began. 'I'd rather like to make my confession. I know it's not the normal time, but . . .'

Father Taylor laughed. 'This is a church, not an office with fixed opening hours,' he said. 'If you wish to confess your sins, I'm more than willing to hear them at any time.'

'That's . . .er . . .very kind of you, Father, but Father Kenyon is my usual confessor,' Pine said awkwardly.

'So he is,' Father Taylor agreed. 'But we in the priesthood are all God's instruments. Each and every one of us serves as no more than a telephone line to the Almighty.'

Pine frowned. He knew the young priest meant well – and it couldn't have been easy, coming into a parish in which the other priest was already an established figure – but he was not sure he was quite comfortable with the casual, modern way that Father Taylor talked about his religion.

'If you don't mind, Father, I'd prefer to make my confession to Father Kenyon,' he said.

A look of disappointment flickered across Father Taylor's features, and then was gone.

'Of course I don't mind,' he told Pine. 'Father Kenyon's in the vestry. I'll go and fetch him.'

Pine watched the young priest cross the church. He supposed he could have confessed to him rather than to Father Kenyon – they *were* both God's instruments, as the priest had pointed out – but he had a feeling that Father Taylor was perhaps a little too unyielding for his taste.

Father Kenyon, on the other hand, was almost as much of a politician as he was himself. Father Kenyon would give him the absolution he needed, even though the old priest would probably have a pretty shrewd idea of where he was going when he had made his confession – and even what he would do once he got there!

There was some truth in what the landlord of the Drum and Monkey had said earlier about Charlie Woodend's drinking habits. The chief inspector liked pubs, especially his local. He claimed that best bitter was nature's way of lubricating the brain, and given his success rate in clearing up cases, there were very few people – at least, few below the rank of chief superintendent – who were prepared to dispute it. That night, however, Woodend hadn't gathered his team together to discuss an investigation. Instead, he planned to make an announcement about what was potentially a very delicate situation. And now – having been in the pub for over two hours, and with four pints under his belt – he supposed he'd better get on with it.

He cleared his throat, looked from Monika Paniatowski to Colin Beresford and back again.

'Inspector Rutter was given his final clearance from the police shrink the day before yesterday,' he said. 'Which means that he'll be reportin' for duty again tomorrow mornin'.'

There was an awkward pause.

Then Constable Beresford said, 'Well, sir, I must admit that certainly *is* good news.'

Good news? Woodend repeated silently.

It all depended on who you were – and how you looked at it.

It was good news for Bob Rutter, certainly – he'd been saying for some time that he'd finally got over the nervous breakdown he'd suffered as a result of his wife's murder, and was eager to climb back into the saddle.

It was good news as far Woodend himself was concerned, too. He'd worked with Rutter since his days down in Scotland Yard, and had come not only to trust him absolutely, but almost to regard him as the son he'd never had.

But what about Monika – Bob Rutter's one-time lover, his co-conspirator in the adulterous affair carried on behind Rutter's blind wife's back? She'd been wracked with guilt when Maria was murdered, even though the affair was long over by then. How would she feel about having to work closely with Rutter again?

Not that any of these considerations were on young Beresford's mind at that moment, Woodend realized. He was much more concerned about the effect that Rutter's return would have on *him*.

The landlord leaned out over the bar counter. 'Phone call for you, Mr Woodend,' he called out.

Woodend rose to his feet and walked over to the bar.

'Do you think there'll still be a place for me on the team when Inspector Rutter gets back, Sarge?' Beresford asked Paniatowski, the moment the chief inspector had gone.

Paniatowski took a sip of her vodka. 'You know, Beresford, the question you should really be asking yourself is not whether you'll be *allowed* to stay on the team, but whether you *want* to.'

'Why wouldn't I want to?'

'Because, if you do stay, you'll be working directly under the man who's at the very top of Mr Marlowe's Shit List. And some of that shit is bound to stick to you eventually.'

10

'Maybe you're right, but it doesn't seem to bother you too much,' Beresford pointed out.

'It bothers me a great deal,' Paniatowski corrected him. 'I'd like to be the first female chief inspector in the county, but I'll never get promotion as long as I'm Cloggin-it Charlie's bagman.'

'So why don't you put in for a transfer?'

'I've given that possibility serious consideration,' Paniatowski admitted. 'But in the end, I just can't bring myself to do it.'

'Why not?'

Why not indeed, Paniatowski wondered.

Because, she supposed, she owed Woodend.

Because a couple of times when she'd been in danger of drowning in a sea of her own neuroses, he had kept her afloat.

Because there was a bond between them that . . . that she didn't even want to start trying to analyse.

'He's very good at what he does,' she said, knowing full well she was copping out of really answering the question – and not giving a damn. 'I'm learning a lot from him – more than I think I could learn from any other senior officer on the Force.'

'I think *I* could learn a lot from both of you,' Beresford said seriously. 'And if that means joining the Shit List myself, it's a price that I'm more than willing to pay.'

Woodend returned from the bar, looking thoughtful.

'What's happened?' Paniatowski asked.

'It seems there's been somethin' of a blip in the normally smooth an' democratic process of electin' ourselves an MP,' Woodend told her.

'Sorry, sir, I'm not sure I quite understand what you're getting at?' Beresford said.

'He means one of the candidates has been murdered,' Paniatowski translated. 'Which one is it, sir?'

'Off-hand, I'd have to say it was the one who'd *really* pissed somebody off,' Woodend replied.

Two

There was very little traffic moving on the dual carriageway which ran between Whitebridge and Accrington that night, and the few drivers who had chosen to brave the thick fog did so with all the hesitation and timidity of an old lady negotiating an icy puddle.

'I can remember when this road was first opened, in the early fifties,' Woodend said, peering through the windscreen of his battered Wolseley into the swirling confusion. 'The local press made such a noise about it that you'd have thought it was the newest wonder of the world, beside which the Great Pyramid at Giza and the Coliseum in Rome shrank to mere insignificance.' He paused for a moment. 'Do either of you remember all the fuss?'

'No, I can't say that I do, sir,' Beresford replied – truthfully – from the back seat. 'I was only a little kid, back then.'

'And I'm not *that* much older than the constable,' Paniatowski said, from the front passenger seat.

'Babies!' Woodend said, in mock disgust. 'I'm workin' with babies. I'm more like a nanny to you than a boss.'

'And a very good nanny you are, sir,' said Paniatowski, who actually *did* remember the opening of the dual carriageway quite well, but had learned from previous experience that when Woodend was in the mood to blow off steam about 'the modern world', as he somewhat disparagingly called it, the easiest thing was just to let him get on with it.

'At long last, accordin' to the *Evenin' Courier*, two of the great mill towns of Lancashire had a connectin' road that was worthy of them,' Woodend continued. 'Aye, an' where do you think they found the space from to make this modern wonder?'

'They pulled down houses and despoiled the countryside,' Paniatowski said, deadpan.

'They pulled down houses an' despoiled the countryside!'

12

Woodend agreed. 'Bloody good houses, some of them. Houses that had stood for two hundred years, an' would have stood for *another* two hundred if they'd been left alone. New houses went, an' all – houses that had only just gone up. An' I don't even want to talk about the huge bleedin' gash they tore through the fields and meadows!'

'Well, that's progress for you, sir,' said Beresford, who had not been with the team long enough to have learned any better.

'Progress!' Woodend repeated, derisively. 'The road hadn't been opened for more than a few months before them same newspapers were complainin' that traffic was movin' along it at a snail's pace, an' sayin' that what Central Lancs really needed was a new dual carriageway to take some of the pressure off the old dual carriageway. An' what's the next step after that? A new-new dual carriageway to take the pressure off the old-new dual carriageway?'

He stopped speaking, not because he had run out of things to say on the subject but because of the flashing orange lights which had suddenly – and somewhat eerily – appeared out of the fog.

'We've arrived, an' to prove it, we're here,' Woodend told his team.

The lay-by was long enough to accommodate half a dozen parked lorries, but there was only one there at that moment – a twelve-wheeler with the name 'Holden Brothers Transport, Carlisle' painted on its side in large blue letters. Most of the rest of the available space was taken up by several police patrol cars, an ambulance and a Land Rover.

'I see Dr Shastri's already here,' Woodend said approvingly as he parked behind the doctor's Land Rover. He turned his head to address the constable in the back of the car. 'Have you met our esteemed an' intrepid police surgeon yet, Beresford?'

'Can't say I have, sir.'

'Then you've a real treat in store for you, lad. You're bound to fall in love with her – she could bring a statue out in a sweat – but however tempted you might feel to go romancin' her, I'd appreciate it if you'd curb the urge.'

'I beg your pardon, sir?'

'She's the best police surgeon that we've had in a very long while, so I don't want her fallin' for a handsome young bobby, getting' hitched to him, an' leavin' the job.'

Beresford felt himself starting to blush. Sergeant Paniatowski seemed to appreciate when Mr Woodend was joking and when he wasn't, the constable thought, but so far it was not a skill he had entirely mastered himself.

A uniformed inspector walked over to the Wolseley. 'I've secured the site, sir,' he said.

Woodend winced.

Secured the site!

Why was it that so many bobbies now felt the need to talk like that, he wondered. At what point had good straightforward policing become tangled up in jargon?

'Who found the stiff?' he asked aloud.

'The driver of that lorry. He pulled in because the fog was getting thicker. He noticed the body straight away, but thought it was just a tramp lying there at first. It was only when he got right on top of it that he could see there'd been foul play.'

'An' where is he now?'

'I got one of the lads to drive him into town. I thought he could use a good hot cup of tea.'

Now that *was* good policin', Woodend thought – an' not a hint of jargon in sight.

'Right, well, I suppose we'd better go an' look at the corpse,' he said.

Emergency spotlights had been set up in a rough circle around the dead man, and kneeling next to the body was a woman wearing a heavy sheepskin jacket over a colourful silk sari.

'How's it goin', Doc?' Woodend asked.

Dr Shastri looked up from her grisly work, and favoured him with one of her more radiant smiles.

'My dear Mr Woodend,' she said warmly. 'What a great pleasure it is to see you.'

'The feelin's mutual,' Woodend told her. 'What can you tell me about the body?'

Dr Shastri clicked her tongue disapprovingly.

'Always so eager to get down to business, with not even a hint of polite chit-chat first,' she said. 'You are completely bereft of social skills, aren't you, you poor fellow?'

14

Woodend grinned. 'Completely,' he agreed. 'Now what about my stiff, Doc?'

'He was killed by a blow to the back of the head.'

'How hard was it?'

'Very violent indeed. If you wish to replicate the effect for yourself, I suggest you get a packet of crisps – any flavour will do – place it on a flat surface, and bring the palm of your hand down on it, as hard as you can.'

Woodend grimaced. 'So whoever delivered the blow almost certainly meant to kill him?'

'Undoubtedly. Especially in the light of the injuries the killer inflicted on his victim *after* he had delivered it.'

'An' what might they have been?'

Dr Shastri straightened up, and moved away from the body.

'See for yourself, my dear Chief Inspector,' she invited

The corpse had been placed on to a large plastic sheet. It was dressed in an expensive blue lounge suit, and since it was lying on its front, the wound to the back of the head was clearly visible.

The killer must have used *massive* force to stove in his skull like that, Woodend thought, letting his eyes travel slowly from the wound itself to the shoulders of the jacket, which were stained bright red.

'He was not killed here,' Dr Shastri said conversationally, 'so although pieces of his brain will have been spattered everywhere, I have very little hope of being able to recover any of them.'

Behind him, Woodend heard Beresford gulping for air.

'Easy, lad,' he said over his shoulder. 'Think of it as no more than a piece of dead meat.'

He turned his attention back on the corpse. There had been real anger – real *hatred* – behind the attack, he thought.

'Where are the injuries which were inflicted after he was dead?' he asked Dr Shastri.

'Ah, I must turn him over in order for you to see the results of the *post-mortem* attack,' the doctor said, crouching down again. 'It might be wiser for you to leave now, Constable.'

'I'll be all right,' Beresford said, unconvincingly.

'Very well, that is your choice,' Shastri said, and expertly rolled the corpse over on to the other end of the plastic sheet.

It was the victim's mouth that Woodend noticed first – or

rather, the place where the mouth had been. All that remained now was a mush of bone, muscle and flesh.

'Jesus!' Woodend said.

'I think I have managed to find most of the teeth,' Dr Shastri informed him. 'Not that I expect them to tell us anything that we don't already know. I should have thought it would be fairly obvious to anyone what had happened to him.'

'Aye, you don't need a medical degree to see he's been given a right good hammerin',' Woodend agreed.

'But it is the other wound which truly fascinates me,' Dr Shastri continued. 'I do not think I have ever come across an attack quite like that before.'

'The other wound?' Woodend asked.

Dr Shastri laughed. 'Tear your eyes away from his face for a moment and examine his mid-section,' she suggested.

The chief inspector shifted his gaze downwards. Pine's jacket was open and largely undamaged, but his shirt had been slashed by the same cut which had ripped through the flesh and muscle it had been covering.

The incision had opened up the dead man from just below his sternum right down to his pelvis, and exposed most of his stomach and a great deal of his intestines, thereby turning what had once been an ingenious biological machine into no more than a pile of bloody offal.

'It must have been very messy work to carry out,' Dr Shastri said, clinically. 'To tear through someone else's stomach in this way, you need a fairly strong stomach yourself.'

Yes, that was exactly what you would need, Woodend thought, as behind him, he heard the sound of Constable Beresford throwing up.

Three

Woodend stood in the reception room outside the chief constable's office, waiting for the green light (set into the door-frame) to flash and buzz, as a signal that he was now permitted to enter the inner sanctum.

He was anticipating a long wait, since this was the style of the man he had been summoned to see. Henry Marlowe measured his own importance by the fact that he *could* keep his subordinates waiting, and Woodend had no doubt that even once he was inside the office itself, the chief constable would prolong the wait by pretending to study whatever documents – however irrelevant to the matter in hand – that he happened to have on his desk at that particular moment.

The chief inspector looked out of the window. The fog which had plagued Whitebridge the previous day had almost completely lifted, and the late spring sun was making its first appearance in nearly a week. Birds were swooping and diving in the air over the police car park, and squirrels were busy scuttling around the bases of the nearby trees.

Life was renewing itself everywhere, Woodend thought fancifully, though – thanks to a person or persons as yet unknown – Bradley Pine would most definitely not be taking part in that particular process.

The green light buzzed.

It was probably a technical fault, Woodend thought, glancing down at his watch and noting that he had been standing there for no more than a couple of minutes. Or perhaps it was human error – a case of Marlowe pressing the button accidentally. Whichever it was, the chief constable couldn't be willing to see him already. But since the light undoubtedly *had* flashed – and his was not to reason why – he knocked on the door, then turned the handle and stepped inside.

Marlowe looked up from his paperwork immediately –

another first! – and said, 'I'd like a progress report on the investigation into Bradley Pine's murder, Chief Inspector.'

Woodend scratched his ear. 'There hasn't *been* any progress to speak of,' he admitted. 'The patrol cars have been alerted to look out for Pine's vehicle, but since the body wasn't discovered until most people were gettin' ready for bed, there wasn't much more we could do.'

This was the point at which the bollocking should come, Woodend thought. This was the point at which Marlowe should tell him that any halfway decent chief inspector would already have had the murderer under lock and key.

But that didn't happen. Instead, Marlowe said, 'Being the first senior officer at the scene of the crime does not automatically give you the right to be put in charge of the investigation, you know.'

'I appreciate that, sir,' Woodend replied.

'However, after having given the matter due consideration, I *have* decided to assign the case to you,' Marlowe continued, 'though naturally, taking into account both the prominence of the victim and the particularly gruesome manner of his death, there will be some conditions attached.'

'What sort of conditions?' Woodend wondered.

'I want this murder cleared up as soon as possible.'

'Which means?'

'Within the week.'

'I can't promise that,' Woodend told the chief constable. 'Conductin' a murder investigation's isn't like runnin' a bus company, where you know the route you goin' to have to cover, an' you can draw up some kind of timetable for how long it should take you.'

'Well, of course I realize that, but—'

'In fact, it's much more like gardenin'.'

'Gardening!' Marlowe exclaimed. 'How could it possibly be like gardening?'

'Because you can do all kinds of things to encourage the seeds to begin sproutin', but until they actually do, you can't even think of beginnin' to think of harvestin' them.'

The chief constable shook his head – slowly, and almost despairingly. 'There are times when you don't sound at all like an officer working in a modern police force,' he said.

'There are times when I don't *feel* much like one, either,'

Woodend admitted. 'Listen, sir, you've often enough made it quite plain that you don't have a lot of confidence in my ability to lead an enquiry—'

'And you've often enough given me ample grounds for that belief—'

'—so why don't you simply assign the case to somebody you *do* have confidence in?'

Marlowe swallowed hard.

'It's true that there have been times when your approach has made me seriously doubt your competence,' he said, 'but there have also been times – especially in dealing with crimes of a bizarre nature – when you seem to have been able to solve cases which have quite baffled most of your colleagues.'

It was not a wise move to grin at his boss's obvious discomfort, but Woodend did it anyway.

'Thank you, sir,' he said. 'That means a lot to me – especially comin' from you.'

'I don't know *why* you should have been so successful in those cases,' Marlowe continued, hurriedly. 'Perhaps, after all, it was no more than a matter of luck.'

'Aye, that might explain it,' Woodend agreed.

'Or perhaps, when the crime *is* bizarre, your brain is better attuned to the insane mind behind it than those of more *professional* officers.'

'So it's a case of set a nutter to catch a nutter, is it?' Woodend asked innocently.

'I wouldn't have put it quite in those terms, Chief Inspector,' Marlowe said frostily, 'but you will concur with me that Bradley Pine's murderer is a dangerous lunatic, won't you?'

'Murderers are pretty much dangerous by definition,' Woodend agreed, 'an' slittin' open another man's stomach is not somethin' I'd normally associate with a well-balanced feller.'

'Precisely!' Marlowe said. 'So, in this particular investigation, there'll be no real need to delve very deeply into the victim's background, will there?'

'I'm sorry, sir,' Woodend said, 'I think I must have missed a step in the logic of that argument.'

Marlowe sighed. 'Bradley Pine was killed by a madman, so it is certainly worth looking closely at any madmen who he might have had dealings with in the past,' he explained.

'On the other hand, it would be a complete waste of time to dwell too much on the dealings he had with people who were perfectly sane.'

'It doesn't work like that,' Woodend said.

'What do you mean?'

'There was real rage behind the attack on Bradley Pine, an' maybe that rage had taken the killer to the point of madness. But the *cause* of the rage may have been perfectly understandable an' perfectly sane.'

'You're splitting hairs,' Marlowe said dismissively.

'People sometimes kill simply because they've been taken beyond the point of endurance,' Woodend argued. 'An' what's got them to that stage is often somethin' that happened a long time ago.'

'You will not waste time and resources looking too closely into Bradley Pine's background,' Marlowe said firmly. 'That is a direct order, and though I will not personally be here to see that it is enforced—'

His mouth snapped shut like a steel trap, as if he'd suddenly realized he'd said too much.

'What was that, sir?' Woodend asked.

'I will not be supervising you directly in this investigation, but whoever assumes that responsibility will be working to the remit that I have given him,' Marlowe said, attempting to blur his previous statement.

'You'll be replacin' Bradley Pine as Conservative candidate, won't you?' Woodend asked.

'The idea has been mooted,' Marlowe admitted, 'but that is really no concern of yours, Chief Inspector. *Your* task is to track down the brutal and insane killer who may well yet turn out to have had no connection with Bradley Pine at all, but merely selected him because he was in the wrong place at the wrong time.'

Woodend said nothing. If Marlowe was prepared to accept that particular theory as a possibility, he thought, then persuading him that the moon was made of green cheese should be a doddle.

'And speaking of Pine's movements, I might be able to point you in the right direction, there,' Marlowe continued.

'Oh aye?'

'Indeed. I attended a meeting that Bradley addressed

20

yesterday evening, and at the end of it he came up to me for advice.'

'What kind of advice?'

'Nothing that could possibly have any relevance to the case. He wanted to know how I thought his speech had gone down, and wondered if I could make any suggestions to improve his performance in the future.' Marlowe paused. 'I think he was beginning to realize he was completely out of his depth, you know. I think he was starting to regret accepting the nomination at all, when there was another – clearly more able – candidate available.'

'An' that candidate would be?' Woodend asked.

'That candidate would be *me!*' Marlowe said, not quite sure whether or not he should take offence.

'Of course it would, sir,' Woodend said.

'But that's neither here nor there,' Marlowe ploughed on. 'The important point is that he happened to say to me that when he left the village hall he intended to drive straight to St Mary's Church. Bradley was a Roman Catholic, you know, though you shouldn't hold that against him.'

'I won't,' Woodend said, wisely concealing what would have been his second broad grin of the meeting. 'Us Buddhists tend to be very tolerant of other religions, sir.'

'Are you a *Buddhist* now?' Marlowe asked.

'I am,' Woodend lied.

Marlowe shook his head. 'Extraordinary – though not really all that surprising,' he said.

The chief constable glanced involuntarily at the telephone, then at his watch, then at the telephone again.

He was on tenterhooks, Woodend thought. He knew he was almost certain to be contacted by the Conservative Party Selection Committee, but he wouldn't really be at ease until the call had actually been made.

'Can I go, sir?' the chief inspector asked.

'Yes, yes, by all means,' Marlowe said impatiently, as if the murder case were now no more than an annoying distraction.

Woodend turned and walked to the door. He was already turning the handle when he heard Marlowe say, 'You will remember what I told you, won't you, Chief Inspector?'

'I'm sorry, sir?'

'You are not – under any circumstances – to carry out a detailed check on Bradley Pine's background.'

'Oh yes, I'll remember that,' Woodend assured him.

'Good, because if you don't . . .'

'You've no worries on that score, sir. Us Buddhists have memories like elephants. It's part of the trainin'.'

Woodend stepped out in the reception room and closed Marlowe's door behind him.

I'll remember it, all right, he thought, *but that's a long way from sayin' I'll pay any attention to it.*

Four

Whenever the chief constable was holding one of his press briefings – and how he *loved* to hold his press briefings – he would describe the room in which Woodend was now standing as 'The Incident Room'. Once the briefing was in full flow – and his normally high opinion of himself was inflated even further – he would go so far as to talk about it as 'The Nerve Centre of Our Investigation, Located in the Very Heart of Police Headquarters'.

It wasn't a description that DCI Woodend found it easy to subscribe to. The nerve centre of any investigation that he took part in was, as far as he was concerned, in his head.

Beside, whilst he was willing to admit that he had – in common with most other Northern men from a working class background – an almost complete ignorance of the subject of human biology (that sort of thing was best left to the women, who made a sort of hobby out of it) he was pretty sure that the heart did not reside in a person's feet, whereas the 'Incident Room' was quite clearly in the basement.

In fact, the Incident Room *was* the basement. Or rather, the basement *became* the Incident Room whenever a major crime had been committed, but otherwise served as a repository for junk which didn't seem to particularly belong anywhere else.

The junk which had built up since the last major case had been cleared away overnight. Now the basement contained a dozen desks, set out in a horseshoe pattern so that the detective constables manning them could see both each other and the large blackboard which had been erected at the broad end of the horseshoe.

Woodend studied the young DCs for a moment.

Every one of them was talking energetically on the phone, and taking copious notes as he went.

Yesterday, they had all been based in small stations dotted

23

throughout Central Lancashire, the chief inspector thought, and the caseloads they had been handling involved such crimes as burglary, car theft, wilful damage and arson. Now they had been trawled into headquarters, and suddenly found themselves in the middle of a real murder inquiry. All of which meant that they were as excited as little children who'd discovered, on Christmas morning, that Santa had brought them *exactly* the toys that they'd wished for.

Woodend nodded to Detective Sergeant Dix – a grey-haired veteran who was supervising the initial phases of the operation – then positioned himself by the blackboard.

He cleared his throat. 'For the benefit of those of you who don't already know me, I'm Chief Inspector Charlie Woodend, an' I've been put in charge of this investigation,' he said.

The detective constables looked up from their tasks with interest. They all *did* know him – if only by reputation.

'Finish the calls you're makin', then listen up to what I've got to tell you,' Woodend told them.

The detective constables galloped through their calls and replaced the receivers.

'Let's get one thing out of the way immediately,' Woodend said. 'There is absolutely nothin' glamorous about a murder investigation. It's hard work, an' it's frustratin' work, but if we all pull together, we just might get a result.' He paused to light a cigarette. 'At the moment, you've got only one task in front of you, which is to find out where Bradley Pine went last night an' what happened to his green Cortina once he'd been killed. Is that clear so far?'

The detective constables nodded enthusiastically.

Kids! the chief inspector thought, with a mixture of concern, affection – and envy.

'It's not actually *necessary*, in operational terms, for you to be told the precise details of the murder,' he continued. 'Strictly speakin', all you need to know in order to do your jobs is that, as the result of actions by a person or persons unknown, Bradley Pine is dead. But I've always believed that if you're part of a team you should be kept informed – as much as is practicable – about what's goin' on. That's why I've asked Sergeant Dix to tell you exactly what happened to Pine last night, even though that same information is still bein' withheld from the press.'

The constables looked pleased – as well they might.

'But before you're briefed, let me give you one word of warnin',' Woodend said. 'When you go off duty tonight, there'll be loads of people – wives, girlfriends an' mates – who'll be itchin' to be filled in on the gory details. An' there'll be a great temptation to tell them, because everybody likes to be the centre of attention an' interest – everybody likes to reveal secrets. But it's a temptation you must resist. Is *that* clear?'

The detective constables nodded earnestly, as if to say that *of course* the secret was safe with them.

'Good!' Woodend said. 'Because if word *does* get out – an' I find it came from any of you – I'll get the offender's balls between a couple of Accrington bricks an' crush them to a pulp.'

The young constables – for whom a surging in their loins was still a recent enough experience for it not to have lost its novelty value – grimaced.

Woodend paused again to allow time for their scrotal sacs to return to their normal positions.

'Your team leader will be Detective Inspector Rutter,' he continued. 'At the moment, he's travellin' up from London, but he managed to ring me while he was changin' trains at Crewe, an' I've filled him in on most of the details.' He turned to the grey-haired sergeant. 'You've worked with Bob Rutter before, haven't you, Sergeant Dix?'

Dix nodded. 'I have, sir. He's a good man.'

'He's a *very* good man – one of the best – an' he has my full confidence,' Woodend said.

But was that entirely true any more, he wondered. Could Bob Rutter handle so much stress on his first day back on the job?

Well, there was only one way to find out.

'If you study the way DI Rutter works, you should learn a lot from him,' he continued. 'But one more word of warnin' – mess with him, an' what he'll do to you in return will make bein' fed through a meat grinder seem like a holiday by the seaside.'

He'd done all he could to smooth Rutter's passage back into the job, he thought.

Now it was up to Bob.

* * *

The man stepping down from the train which had just pulled in at the main platform of Whitebridge Railway Station was in his early thirties, carrying a suitcase, and dressed in a smart blue suit.

He looked – to anyone giving him a casual glance – like a successful businessman. A closer examination, however, revealed quite a different story. The lines etched into his face told a tale of worry and strain – possibly even of despair – and any observer would have been forced to conclude that if he *was* a businessman, he had not been so successful recently.

There were other signs that all was not well. He seemed ill at ease, and instead of heading briskly for the exit – as any businessman with a tight schedule would – he remained on the platform, looking back longingly at the train from which he had just disembarked.

The truth was that Bob Rutter was far from sure it had been a good idea to return to Whitebridge at all – and now was fighting the very strong urge to get back on the train and let it take him where it would.

The train guard was walking along the platform, checking that all the doors had been properly closed. Satisfied that they had been, he returned to the guards' van, blew his whistle, and climbed aboard.

Rutter watched the train pull out of the station, then picked up his suitcase and walked towards the exit.

The station occupied an elevated position above the town, and once clear of the ticket gate, a panoramic view of Whitebridge opened up before Bob Rutter.

There were the cathedral and the bus station; there the old cotton mills, many of which had now been converted into other more-or-less viable businesses; there the canal, along which large barges had once carried the spun cotton cloth to the seaport of Liverpool.

He remembered the first time he had come to Whitebridge, three years earlier. Then, he had been following in the wake of his boss, who had transferred from Scotland Yard – who had been *ejected* from Scotland Yard – and was about to take up a new posting in the Central Lancs CID. Then, he'd had a wife who was just learning to cope with blindness and motherhood. Then, he had yet to meet Monika Paniatowski and

26

embark on an affair with her which he bitterly regretted – but could not quite bring himself to wish undone.

Was it *only* three years? Bob Rutter asked himself.

It felt like a hundred.

He felt a hundred.

He walked over to the taxi rank.

'Where to?' the cabbie asked.

Where to, indeed, Rutter wondered.

He had in his pocket the key to the house that he and Maria had lived in – the house in which she had been murdered. The murderer had set a fire to cover his grisly crime, but the insurance company had informed Rutter, by letter, that all the damage had been repaired, and the house was once again perfectly habitable. So he could always go there, if he wished.

'Where to?' the cabbie repeated, with a slight edge of impatience entering his voice.

'Whitebridge Police Headquarters,' Rutter said.

Five

Constable Beresford and DS Paniatowski were already in the office when Woodend arrived, and from the evidence of the poisonous cloud of cigarette smoke which hovered above them, it was clear they'd been there for some time.

'So how have you two been keepin' yourself amused while I've been addressin' the troops?' Woodend asked, taking his customary seat and lighting up a cigarette of his own to add to the general fug.

'We've been researching into Bradley Pine's background,' Paniatowski told him.

Woodend chuckled. 'Our Mr Marlowe won't like that, Monika. He won't like it one bit.'

'He won't?'

'Definitely not. He's given me specific instructions that we're not to delve too deeply into Pine's past.'

'Why would he have done that?' Paniatowski asked.

'I'm assumin' it's because he doesn't want us diggin' up anythin' with even the whiff of scandal attached to it.'

'But why should that matter, now that Bradley Pine's dead?' Beresford wondered.

'Because while *he's* dead, there are other people – possibly includin' our esteemed chief constable – who might also be involved in the scandals, an' are still very much alive,' Woodend explained.

'What scandals are you talking about, sir?' Beresford asked.

'I've no idea,' Woodend admitted.

'Then how can you be sure there are any scandals?'

'Because it's in the nature of the beast.'

'I don't understand,' Beresford confessed.

'Then listen carefully, lad, an' you just might. You can vote for who you like at the local elections, but all the important decisions about the town are made over drinks in the bar of

28

the Golf an' Country Club. The fact is that Whitebridge is controlled by a group of fellers who've never even thought of standin' for election – because they've never seen the need.'

'I still don't see it,' Beresford admitted.

Woodend shook his head, half-pityingly. 'Ah, to be young an' innocent again,' he said. 'The Whitebridge Establishment runs this town like a well-oiled machine, an' what keeps the oil flowin' is favours an' mutual back-scratchin'. So Mr A will do somethin' for Mr B, and Mr B will do somethin' for Mr C, et cetera, et cetera. Of course, none of this comes free, an' eventually the favours will have to be paid for. But the payment won't necessarily be made to the person who granted you the favour in the first place. You see what I mean?'

'I'd be happier if you'd spell it out a bit more,' Beresford said.

'Let's say Mr W wants a favour from Mr A. Now Mr A doesn't owe him a thing, but Mr N does – an' Mr A owes Mr N. So Mr W gets Mr N to put the pressure on Mr A.'

'But that's nothing short of municipal corruption!' Beresford said, outraged. 'That's *illegal*!'

'Maybe it would be, if it was all carried out as crudely as I've just described it,' Woodend agreed. 'But it isn't. I doubt money ever changes hands. I doubt anythin's ever put down in writin'. A wink an' nod is all they need. An' sometimes not even that – because they share the same values, an' they understand each other perfectly. So even if you could pin down the details of some of their deals – an' that would take a lot of effort, an' a lot of luck – the best you're goin' to end up with is somethin' that's a bit morally questionable.'

'That's better than nothing,' Beresford said.

'Is it?' Woodend asked. 'Who to? Them buggers up at the Golf Club don't care what people like *you* think of them. All they need is the approval of their mates – an' they get that readily enough, because all their mates are wallowin' around in the same trough of shit that they are.'

'But then—'

'But then, occasionally, your opinion *does* matter, like when they're runnin' for Parliament. So what I think Marlowe is worried about is that I might find a skeleton in Pine's cupboard which is busily engaged in scratchin' the back of a skeleton

29

in his.' Woodend turned to Paniatowski. 'Wouldn't you agree about that, Monika?'

'Yes, I would,' Paniatowski said cautiously. 'But surely Mr Marlowe must know that whatever instructions he gives you, you'll go your own way – just like you always do.'

'He does know that,' Woodend agreed. 'But he's gamblin' on the fact that what he's said will cause me to rein myself in just a *little* bit.'

'Why run even that risk?' Paniatowski wondered. 'Why not put one of his normal lapdogs in charge of the investigation?'

'Ah, that's because he's badly in need of a result on this one,' Woodend said.

Paniatowski nodded sagely. 'Yes, I can see that,' she said.

'Can you see it, Beresford?' Woodend asked.

'I think so,' the constable said.

'Then explain it to me.'

'Mr Marlowe will be running his campaign on the basis that if he was a good chief constable, he'll make a good MP.'

'But?'

'But he won't look as if he's been much of a chief constable at all if he can't come up with Bradley Pine's killer.'

'Exactly. You're only as good as your last arrest, an' the last arrest Marlowe has to have before polling day is the arrest of Bradley Pine's killer. So that's why I'm on the case, because – as much as he hates to admit it – he thinks I'm the man most likely to get him his result.'

'But if you don't – and he loses the election because of it – he's going to hold you personally responsible!' Beresford said.

'Which would be totally unreasonable, but perfectly in character,' Woodend agreed.

'And if he loses the election because of something you've uncovered about him, it'll be even worse,' Beresford said, with growing horror.

Paniatowski smiled. 'Now do you understand why I said you should think twice before trying to join this team?' she asked the constable.

There were no fields in the Greenfields area of Whitebridge. No fields, no trees, no municipal gardens – no signs whatever of the natural world.

In the old days, when the mills had all been working at full steam, the inhabitants of Greenfields had been spinners and tacklers. They had been poor, but they had also been honest and hardworking. They kept their two-up-two-down terraced houses freshly painted and scrupulously clean, and even though each house was separated from its neighbour in the next street by no more than two small back yards and a narrow alley, the residents had some justification for regarding their homes as little palaces.

All that had changed since the mills began to close down. The mill workers had sought fresh occupations and left the area, and the houses had been taken over by folk whose main concern was to avoid work of *any* kind.

The bobbies who had to walk the Greenfields beat all hated it. The crime they came across there was petty but often very unpleasant, and was perpetrated by people who were both vicious and unimaginative. It was a slum. It was a dump. The current residents would rather spend their money on boozing and betting than on feeding and clothing their children.

It was certainly not an area in which anyone would expect to find a two-year-old Ford Cortina, but that was exactly what the motor patrol found at ten forty-seven that morning.

The fug in Woodend's office was getting thicker by the minute, and Beresford, who hadn't been smoking for anything like as long as the others, was starting to find it hard to take.

'So tell me what we know about Bradley Pine, Monika,' Woodend said, before adding to the pollution by lighting up yet another Capstan Full Strength cigarette.

'We know that he was what you call a self-made man,' Monika Paniatowski replied.

'Interestin' label,' Woodend said. 'A self-made man. What exactly does that mean?'

'What it says. He was brought up in Holy Trinity Orphanage over in Brinsleydale.'

'It's a Catholic orphanage, isn't it?'

'I should think so, with a name like that. Anyway, when he left the orphanage, at the age of fifteen, he went to work as an apprentice in Hawtrey's Mattresses—'

'Which is now Hawtrey an' Pine Holdings?'

'Correct.'

31

'So how did a penniless orphan eventually get to be a partner in the business?'

'Through being clever and inventive.'

'How so?'

'He came up with an idea which is now widely used in the production of interior sprung mattresses, and for which he holds the patent. It didn't exactly make him a multimillionaire, but it did give him sufficient cash to buy his way into the company.'

'An' this would have been when, exactly?'

'About fifteen years ago.'

The chief inspector did a quick mental calculation. 'So Pine would have been in his early-to-middle twenties at the time?'

'That's right.'

Woodend whistled softly. 'I see what you mean about him bein' self-made. I seem to remember readin' somewhere that the other half of the company – Hawtrey – is dead now. Is that right?'

'Yes, it is. But you're wrong to assume that Pine owned half the company. Alec Hawtrey held on to just enough of the stock to make sure he remained the majority shareholder.'

'Remind me what happened to Hawtrey,' Woodend said.

'He died in a mountaineering accident up in the Lakes, a couple of years ago.'

'How old was he when this happened?'

'In his mid-fifties.'

Woodend sniffed. 'Seems a bit long in the tooth to be buggerin' about climbin' mountains,' he said. 'So what happened to Alec Hawtrey's shares after he died?'

'They went to his widow, Thelma.'

'So she's the one who's actually in charge?'

Paniatowski shook her head. 'She makes slightly more money out of the company than Pine did, but she doesn't take any active part in running it.'

'An' the business is healthy, is it?'

'More than healthy. It's fighting fit. It posted record profits last year, and had to take on a lot of extra staff in order to meet demand.'

'You've done very well to come up with so much on the feller in such a short time, Monika,' Woodend said approvingly.

'Thank you, but I can't really claim much personal credit for it,' Paniatowski told him. 'I got most of the material out of his political manifesto.'

'So now let's get on to the really big questions,' Woodend suggested, taking a deep drag of his cigarette. 'What was the motive behind Bradley Pine's murder, and – perhaps even more importantly, in terms of openin' up the investigation – why did the killer mutilate him once he was dead?'

The other two looked him blankly for a moment.

Then Paniatowski said, 'I've no idea. I've never come across a case of murder and mutilation before. Have you, sir?'

'Only once,' Woodend told her. 'It was while I was at the Yard. The victim had been beaten to death, then his killers had cut off his genitals an' stuffed them in his mouth.'

Beresford shuddered, and put his hand protectively – and instinctively – over his lap.

'Did you ever find out the reason for the castration?' Monika Paniatowski asked.

'I did. It turned out that the dead man had raped the sister of the two fellers who murdered him. I can't say I was entirely surprised by the result. I suspected it might be somethin' like that right from the start, because what they'd done made a twisted kind of sense, you see. But this is a different matter altogether. Whoever killed Pine smashed in his mouth an' slit open his stomach. What kind of message was that meant to send?'

'Smashing in his mouth could have signified that he talked too much,' Paniatowski said.

'An' slittin' open his stomach signified that he *ate* too much?' Woodend asked.

'Probably not,' Paniatowski agreed.

'I suppose that sex could have been involved,' Beresford suggested, tentatively.

'In what way?'

'Well, I'm not entirely sure,' admitted Beresford, who was still a virgin, but would have died rather than admit it to the other two. 'Maybe he treated a woman very badly, and this was her revenge.'

'Fair point,' Woodend agreed. 'What have we found out about his love life so far, Monika?'

'Not a lot,' Paniatowski admitted. 'There hasn't been time.

But we do know that he wasn't married, nor ever had been – which is quite unusual for a man in his late thirties.'

'Aye, it is,' Woodend said. 'Is there any indication that he might have been inclined the other way?'

'There's no record of him ever having been arrested for loitering outside public lavatories, if that's what you mean,' Paniatowski said.

'Not that that rules out the possibility of his bein' homosexual,' Woodend said. 'Still, there's no point in just sittin' here an' speculatin', is there? It's time we got diggin'.'

'Into his past or his present?' Paniatowski asked.

Woodend grinned. 'He doesn't have a "present",' he said. 'He's bloody-well dead.'

'Into his recent past, or into his more distant past?' Monika Paniatowski amended.

'Into both.'

'In spite of what Mr Marlowe said to you?'

'Aye, we can't let a dickhead like him get in the way of us doin' our job properly, now can we? So how shall we divide it up?' Woodend thought for a moment. 'Beresford, you can go up to the mattress factory an' see what you can find out about Pine's rise to fame an' fortune.'

'You want me to go on my own, sir?' the constable asked, sounding somewhat alarmed.

'Why not on your own? Do you want me there beside you, holdin' your hand?'

'No, but—'

'It's about time you learned that there's a lot more to bein' a detective than just wearin' your best suit to work. Don't worry, lad, you can do it. I've got confidence in you.'

Beresford either blushed with embarrassment or glowed with pleasure – and very possibly both.

'Thank you, sir,' he said.

Woodend turned to Paniatowski. 'You're still a Catholic, aren't you, Monika?'

'Not exactly,' the sergeant said, with some show of reluctance.

'But you do know more about the mysteries of the faith than either me or Beresford?'

'I suppose so.'

'Then you get to go to St Mary's, which is where, accordin'

34

to our beloved chief constable, Pine was headin' when he left the village hall meetin'. See if he arrived at the church as he expected to, an' if he *did* arrive, how long he stayed an' who he talked to.'

'And what will you be doing, sir?' Paniatowski asked.

'Me? I shall be descendin' into the Heart of Darkness.'

'I'm sorry, sir?' Beresford said.

'He'll be going where no man with honest working class credentials would ever normally dream of showing his face,' supplied Paniatowski, who was well tuned in to Woodend's mind.

'I still don't get it,' Beresford admitted.

'First, I shall be poppin' into the morgue – which *isn't* the Heart of Darkness – to have a quick word with Dr Shastri,' Woodend explained. 'Then I'll take myself over to the Whitebridge Golf an' Country Club – which is.'

'Where they'll kill the fatted calf, and welcome you with open arms, like a long-lost brother,' Paniatowski said.

'I somehow doubt that,' Woodend replied. 'But since I *am* a police officer engaged in a murder inquiry, they won't be able to actually bar the door to me, either – however much they'd like to.'

Six

St Mary's Roman Catholic Church had stood at the crest of Woodstock Hill for over five hundred years.

In its early days, when Whitebridge was no more than a small village in which a collection of downtrodden peasants scratched out a meagre existence, the gothic spire and sturdy square tower must have been a truly formidable sight. Even in the modern Whitebridge – a city that had recently begun to experiment with high-rise buildings – it was still the most impressive structure around, eclipsing the Anglican cathedral which the Protestant ecclesiastical planners had foolishly decided to construct on the flat ground in the town centre.

The edifice's history was chequered, as most history is. Though it was originally built as a Catholic church, there had been a period – a little over three centuries, in fact – when it had fallen into the hands of King Henry VIII's breakaway movement, the adherents of which had smashed the statues and stripped away all other signs of Papistry. But the world turns – as it inevitably will – and in the mid-nineteenth century, Catholic cotton money had been used to purchase the church and re-consecrate it into the old faith.

Monika Paniatowski could have left her bright red MGA right in front of the church – there were parking restrictions in force there, but what did that matter when you were the law? – yet instead she chose to park at the bottom of the hill, even though that meant subjecting herself to a long, steep climb.

The reasoning behind her decision was simple. Her sporty car was one of the most distinctive vehicles in Whitebridge, so people seeing it parked outside the church might be forgiven for assuming she had gone inside to pray.

And that was an assumption she really did not want *anyone* to make.

Ever!

That was an assumption it was worth climbing the highest and most gruelling *mountain* to avoid.

As she toiled up the steep gradient, Monika found herself thinking about her past in general, and her mother in particular – and with these thoughts came an involuntary physical reaction which made her feel as though her bowels were slowly turning to water.

Her mother had been a devout Roman Catholic. It had been Agnieszka Paniatowski's faith that had sustained her during those long, terrible, years while she and her daughter had criss-crossed war-torn Europe as refugees on the run. Never once – despite all the hardship they had endured, despite all the horrors they had seen – had that faith of Agnieszka's wavered.

And neither had her little daughter's. Even as a small child, Monika had understood that she was both a Pole and Roman Catholic – and that the two things were so intertwined that she could no more separate the one from other than she could separate her mind from her body, or her heart from her soul.

It was only later, in the supposed safety of this English mill town where they had come to live, that she had finally lost her faith – and even then she had not so much *lost* it as had it *torn from her* by what was said from the other side of the confessional grill.

Monika is thirteen years old. Her body is beginning to fill out, and the boys at school have started to notice her.

And not just the boys.

Not just at school.

She is sitting in the confessional of St Mary's Church. Her church. On the other side of the grille sits her priest.

'Bless me, Father, for I have sinned,' she says. 'It has been a week since my last confession.'

For a moment, she can say no more, but when she does speak again, the words spill out of her and feel like they will never stop. She tells how her stepfather came to her room, late at night and smelling of drink, and put his hand on her shoulder. She describes how that hand – that big, beefy, demanding, hand – burrowed its way under the blankets and found its way to her young breasts. With tears streaming down her face, she recounts what happened next – how he climbed

37

into her bed, how he forced her legs apart, how he . . . how he . . .

'Do you think perhaps you led him on, my child?' the priest, Father O'Brien, asks.

She is not even sure she knows what that means.

'Led him on?' she repeats.

'Man is but an imperfect being, prone to temptation,' the priest intones. 'Did you tempt him, Monika? Did you cause him to think that his attentions would be welcomed?'

'No. I didn't. I swear I didn't.'

'But did you, deep within yourself, want him to do it to you, my child?' the priest persists.

She feels like yelling at the top of her voice that of course she didn't want him to do all those terrible things to her.

She wants to scream out that the priest must be a bloody fool for even thinking to ask that.

But she is in a confessional, talking to a holy man who represents Mother Church, and all she says is, 'No, Father, I didn't want him to do it.'

There is a long silence from the other side of the grill, then the priest says, 'But did you enjoy it, my child?'

Enjoy it! Did she enjoy it? Can't he even begin to imagine how soiled she felt when it was all over?

'No, Father,' she says, almost in a whisper. 'I didn't enjoy it all.'

'Then you have done nothing wrong, my child, and there will be no penance to pay. You may continue with your confession.'

'Is that it?' she asks herself. 'I've done nothing wrong? And that's the end of the matter?'

She leaves the confessional with her faith sorely tested – but still intact. And then, a week later, as she is walking past the Catholic Club, she looks through the window and sees Father O'Brien and her stepfather drinking pints of Guinness together.

And, fool that she is, she takes comfort from that!

She actually believes that the priest is telling her stepfather that he must stop molesting her.

But later that night she wakes up to find the familiar hands making their familiar demands of her body, and knows that nothing has changed – that, despite the priest talking to her stepfather, no change has even been suggested.

38

She has been to her last confession. She has lost her belief in the priesthood, and with it, her belief in God.

Monika had reached the level of the church. She was finding it hard to breathe, though it was her memories, rather than the steep climb, which were the source of her difficulties.

She studied the main doorway, with its vaulted Gothic arch and its stone statue of the Madonna and Child.

She did not want to walk through the heavy oak door – did not want to hear it slam closed behind her, like a baited trap.

This is stupid! she told herself angrily.

She wasn't a frightened little girl any more. She was a police officer. *Other* people were frightened of *her*. And since she had a job to do, she'd better start bloody-well doing it.

Her breathing was more regular now. She took a resolute step forward, turned the handle, and pushed the door open. Then, after only the slightest of hesitations, she stepped through the gap and allowed the church to swallow her up.

Woodend hated the morgue. Not because it was full of dead people – that was, after all, why it was there – but because of the chemicals.

For days after he had made a visit to it, he was convinced that he stank of formaldehyde. It wasn't a rational conviction – he accepted that, just as he accepted the fact that when he met Dr Shastri outside her grisly kingdom, he could detect no odour of death clinging to her. Yet still he would scrub and scrub at his flesh, and still the all-pervading smell would not go away.

He could almost taste the chemicals that morning – swooping down on him through the air like kamikaze swallows, mingling with the acrid smoke from his Capstan Full Strength and being drawn into his lungs – but, as usual, the delightful Dr Shastri seemed blissfully unaware of them.

'I have cut up our little friend in accordance with your wishes, Oh Master,' the doctor said, bowing like the pantomime genie in *Aladdin*. 'Even so, I am afraid that I'm unable to tell you much more than I told you last night. The blow to his head was inflicted with considerable force, as is fairly obvious from the extent of the injuries sustained. Death would have been almost instantaneous.'

'Do you think that a woman could have delivered the blow?' Woodend asked.

'A strong woman, most certainly,' Dr Shastri replied. 'A very angry woman, quite possibly. What would have caused a woman more problems would have been moving the body. Dead weight, for that is what he had become: our little friend would have been quite heavy.'

'An' you're certain he *was* moved?'

'Oh, yes. Wherever it was that he was killed, it was certainly not in the lay-by.'

'Any idea what weapon was used?' Woodend asked.

'The proverbial blunt instrument,' Dr Shastri told him.

'No more than that?'

'I found tiny slivers of metal in the wound, but certainly no single piece large enough for me to be able to tell you with any confidence that they came from a set of eighteenth century candlesticks which can be found only in Doomlock Manor, the home of the mad and dangerous Lord Homicide.'

Woodend grinned. 'What can you tell me about the post-mortem injuries?' he asked.

'Again, not much more than you have seen for yourself. His mouth was smashed in, his stomach was slashed open.'

'But was the mutilation to the stomach done with any kind of medical precision?'

'Now why would you ask that?' Dr Shastri wondered. 'Could it be that you have already decided, Chief Inspector, to "fit up" one of my esteemed colleagues for the murder?'

'As a matter of fact, I was thinkin' of pinnin' the whole business on you,' Woodend said.

'A good choice,' Dr Shastri told him. 'I would certainly be a more colourful and interesting defendant than most of the drab, sad men you usually bring to trial. But in answer to your question, I would have to reply that this particular murderer was not in any way precise. I would almost say that our little friend was butchered, but that would be being unfair to butchers, many of whom know more about anatomy than half the surgeons currently operating in our great hospitals.'

'Now that *is* a cheerful thought,' Woodend said. 'Why did he make such a bloody mess of the mutilation? Was it simply because he had no idea what he was doing?'

'Perhaps,' Doctor Shastri said cautiously. 'But it is equally possible that the killer *wanted* to make a bloody mess.'

'Why would he have wanted to do that?'

'I am no psychologist, but it seems to me that the attack which ended the victim's life – and the mutilation which followed it – were both spurred on by very deep emotion. The aim of mutilation, I think, was to humiliate Bradley Pine – even in death.'

'Why?'

'I don't know,' the doctor confessed.

'But you could make a guess?'

'Perhaps. Did you know that when the British pulled out of India, and my poor country was partitioned, I was living there myself?'

'No, I didn't,' Woodend admitted.

'The sectarian violence which broke out, once your soldiers and policemen had withdrawn, was terrible to behold. Moslems massacred Hindus, and Hindus massacred Moslems. No one was spared – not the old, not the young, not the crippled and infirm. And in some cases, the massacres were followed by mutilation of the corpses. I saw some of those mutilated bodies. The outrages committed on them were not a perfect match with what was done to Mr Pine, but I sensed the same kind of rage at work.'

'So our killer was a very angry man?'

'Our killer, I believe, felt an anger such as you and I have never experienced – and hopefully never will.'

Seven

Her mind and emotions firmly back in the present – though still deeply scarred by the events of the past – Monika Paniatowski took up a strategic position next to the font and – even though she knew that Father O'Brien was long dead – found herself scanning the church for signs of the old enemy.

Not a member of the clergy in sight, she noted. In fact, the only people in the church at that particular moment were several old ladies – and one old man – who were knelt stiffly in prayer in the pews in front of the high altar.

She felt the urge to smoke – partly to calm her nerves, partly as an act of defiance – but then she remembered something that Charlie Woodend had told her early on in their working relationship.

'Whatever you do, don't go rubbin' up potential witnesses the wrong way, Monika,' Woodend had said.

'Never?'

'Never!' Woodend had confirmed sternly. Then he'd chuckled, and continued. *'Unless, of course, you think you can squeeze some advantage out of makin' them lose their rag.'*

But there was no advantage to be gained from rubbing up the priests of this church the wrong way.

At least, not yet!

She found herself wondering how Woodend would have reacted if he'd been the priest sitting on the other side of that confessional grill of her childhood.

Would he have sat back, and done nothing to save her?

Would he have gone out and drunk a few friendly pints of Guinness with her abuser?

Of course he wouldn't. He'd have been more likely to take the man round the back of the church for a few quiet words, and when they returned, the abuser would have both a black eye and a pronounced limp.

Yes, that was how Charlie Woodend would have handled it if he'd been that priest. But then, Charlie would never have contemplated becoming a priest in the first place.

She heard a set of heavy footsteps approaching from her left, and turning, saw that a youngish priest – certainly not more than thirty or thirty-one years old – was walking towards her.

He smiled warmly. 'I am Father Taylor,' he said. 'And who might you be, my child?'

'I'm far too old to be your child,' Monika said, thinking, even as she spoke, that she was certainly *sounding* childish.

'I didn't mean to offend you,' the priest told her, his smile still firmly in place.

'And, as regards your question, I *might* be any number of people,' Monika continued, trying to sound more adult – trying to sound more *sophisticated*. 'But, as it happens, I'm a detective sergeant from Whitebridge CID.'

The priest did not even look at the warrant card she was holding out to him, nor did he seem the least put off by her deliberate rudeness.

'What's your name?' he asked gently.

'It's on the card.'

'I'm sure it is, but I haven't got my reading glasses with me.'

'I'm Sergeant Paniatowski.'

'Do you have a Christian name?'

'Not being a Christian, I'd have to say that I don't. But I do have a *first* name.'

Why was she acting like this, she asked herself. Father O'Brien had been an ugly old man with bad teeth, a squint and a wart on the end of his nose. Father Taylor had fine white teeth, and the nose and eyes of a Hollywood leading man. They had nothing in common – except, of course, that once you'd learned to detest one priest, it was very easy to learn to detest all of them.

'So what's this *first* name of yours?' Father Taylor asked.

'It's "Sergeant"!' Paniatowski said, still refusing to soften to this man of the distrusted cloth.

The young priest laughed easily. 'Now that is an unusual name, whether you're a Christian *or* a heathen,' he said. 'So let me see if I've got this straight – you're Sergeant Sergeant Paniatowski, are you?'

43

Paniatowski laughed too, despite herself. 'No, not really,' she said. 'I'm Monika.'

'And my Christian name is Fred,' the priest told her. 'You may call me Father Fred, if you wish.'

'How about if we forget the "Father" business and I simply call you Fred?' Paniatowski asked.

'That would be fine,' the priest conceded. 'Though most Catholics do normally put a "Father" in front of it.'

'I've already told you I'm not a Catholic,' Paniatowski said.

The priest laughed again. 'Of course you are,' he insisted. 'I spotted you as belonging to the True Faith the moment you walked through the door. And I'm never wrong.'

'You are this time,' Paniatowski insisted.

The priest slowly shook his head from side to side. 'You may deny it – you may not even know it to be true – but you're tied to Mother Church by bonds of faith as strong as steel.'

'I'm investigating a murder,' Paniatowski said.

The smile drained from Father Taylor's face, and was replaced by a troubled expression.

'Ah yes, poor Mr Pine,' he said. 'But I've already told the other policemen everything I know.'

'*What* other policemen?'

'The ones your Inspector Rutter sent to talk to me, after I'd phoned the police station and told him Mr Pine had been here last night.'

Oh God, with everything that had been going on, she'd almost forgotten that Bob was back, Paniatowski thought.

But he *was* back, and she'd have to see him later – however much she might dread the prospect.

'Is something wrong?' Father Taylor asked.

'No. Why should there be?'

'You've suddenly gone rather pale.'

'Maybe that's because I don't like churches,' Paniatowski said aggressively. 'Would you mind going over the same ground with me that you probably went over with them?' she continued, a little less harshly.

'Not in the slightest,' Father Taylor replied. 'I want to do everything I can to help.'

'Did you notice anything odd about Mr Pine last night?'

'We're all odd in our own ways. It's the way God made us.

But I certainly wouldn't say that Bradley Pine was any more than his "normal" odd – which is to say, just about as odd as you or I.'

'How well did you know him?'

'Not well at all, I'm afraid.'

'Because he's not a regular church-goer? Because he didn't start putting in appearances at this church until he'd clinched the Conservative nomination and worked out he'd need the Catholic vote?'

'I wonder if you can really be as cynical as you seem?' Father Taylor asked, looking pained. 'I pray that you aren't.'

'You still haven't answered my question, *Fred*,' Monika Paniatowski said flatly.

'You're right, of course. The answer that you're looking for is that I didn't know him well because he chose not to know *me* well.'

'I understand every word in that last sentence, but put them all together and I'm still not sure you've actually told me anything I wanted to know,' Paniatowski said.

'Then I'll explain it in another way, which hopefully you'll find clearer,' Father Taylor said. 'Most of our parishioners have one particular priest with whom they feel especially comfortable, and Mr Pine felt especially comfortable with Father Kenyon.'

'Why is that? Don't you have much pull with the older parishioners? Are you here mainly to attract the younger set?'

Father Taylor laughed good-naturedly again.

'It's nothing like as simple as that, Monika,' he said. 'As you can plainly see for yourself, I'm a priest, not a pop star. Some of the older parishioners prefer to talk to me, and some of the younger ones are much happier with Father Kenyon. I like to think that each makes his or her own choice, although, of course, we are *all* guided by God.'

'So how long would you say Bradley Pine was here?' Paniatowski asked briskly.

'I wasn't keeping a record, but I would guess it was a little more than half an hour.'

'That's an awful lot of praying,' Paniatowski said.

'Do you think so?' Father Taylor asked, with just a hint of reproach in his voice. 'It seems to me that since we're all such miserable sinners, we can never have too much prayer.'

45

'After he'd prayed, did he go to confess his sins?' asked Paniatowski, who was starting to feel uneasy – and was not quite sure why.

'Yes, he did.'

'To Father Kenyon?'

'To God. Although Father Kenyon was certainly there in the confessional with both of them.'

'Do you know where I'll find Father Kenyon at the moment?' Paniatowski asked.

'I saw him go into the vestry about five minutes ago.'

'And do you think it will be all right if I disturbed him?'

'I don't see why not. I think he only went in there for a smoke. He's a terrible slave to the weed.'

'I think I could use a cigarette myself,' Paniatowski told him.

'I've no doubt you could. It's always a strain.'

'What is? A murder investigation?'

'I wouldn't know about that. But I *do* know it's a strain setting your feet on the right path again.'

'The only path I'm looking for is the one that leads to the vestry,' Paniatowski said tartly. 'Which way is it?'

'Straight through that door,' Father Taylor said, pointing.

'I'll see you again, Fred,' Monika said.

'Yes, I rather think you will,' Father Taylor agreed.

Paniatowski was halfway between the priest and the vestry door when she heard Father Taylor call out, 'Oh, Monika, one more thing.'

She stopped, and turned around. 'Yes?'

'I just want you to know that when you *do* return to the Church, I won't take offence if it's Father Kenyon whom you choose to welcome you back.'

Eight

The green Ford Cortina, which had belonged to the late Bradley Pine, was parked in the alleyway which ran between the backs of the houses in Gladstone Street and the backs of those on Palmerston Row.

The car, like its late owner, had been put through some very unpleasant and disfiguring experiences. It no longer had its windscreen wipers or indicator lights, and was resting wheel-less on piles of old bricks. The boot had been forced open, and whatever it might once have contained had been removed. And a quick glance under the bonnet revealed to Bob Rutter that the car no longer had an engine.

'Round here, they'll nick *anything* that's not actually nailed down,' Sergeant Dix said in disgust. 'In fact, even if it *is* nailed down, these buggers will find some way to prise it up.'

'Do you think this could be the spot where Pine was killed?' Rutter wondered.

'I doubt it,' Dix replied.

'Why?'

'Well, for a start, what reason would he have had for even *being* here in the first place?' the sergeant said.

Then he chuckled to himself.

'What's so funny?' Rutter asked.

'I was just thinking – a posh gentleman like Mr Pine wouldn't be seen *dead* in a place like this.'

Dix had a point, Rutter thought. Policemen came to Greenfields. Debt collectors came to Greenfields. But anybody who didn't actually *have to* visit it steered well clear of the area.

Besides, it was over two miles to the lay-by where Pine's body had been found, and it seemed improbable that the killer would have taken him from here to there, and then driven the car back to the scene of the crime. It was much more likely that abandoning the car in the alleyway was no more than the last in the chain of events which began with the actual murder.

The vandals who had wrecked most of the car had kindly left the door handles in place, so Rutter was able to open the back door and look inside.

'Do you think that's blood?' he asked, pointing to a brownish, half-moon shaped stain on the back seat.

'Certainly looks like it to me,' Dix said.

Rutter glanced up, first at the back bedroom windows in Gladstone Terrace and then at the ones in Palmerston Row. As his gaze fell on several of the windows, the curtains twitched.

He was being watched from nearly every one of those bedroom windows, he thought.

'What do you think are the chances that, even though there was a thick fog last night, a few of the people who are watching us now also saw the killer abandon the Cortina?' he asked Dix.

'Very high,' Dix told him. 'It's almost a racing certainty. A decent car like this one couldn't go a hundred yards through this area without being spotted. And once it *had* been spotted, it would be tracked. It was probably being dismantled within a minute or two of the killer abandoning it.'

'So we'd better organize a house-to-house,' Rutter said.

'I suppose we might as well,' Dix agreed. 'But it won't do us any good at all, sir.'

'No?'

'Definitely not. As far as this lot are concerned, seeing something is one thing, but telling *us* about it is quite another.'

'Even though they'll know that it's a murder investigation that we're working on?'

The sergeant shrugged. 'If it's not one of their own who's been topped, they couldn't care less about it. There was a young social worker raped in this very alley, not more than a few weeks ago. It was broad daylight when it happened, and the poor girl was screaming blue murder throughout the entire attack. Yet when we started asking questions, there was nobody from Greenfields who was willing to admit they'd heard or seen a bloody thing.'

Father Kenyon was the sort of priest who was much beloved by the makers of sentimental black-and-white Hollywood movies based around the life of New York parish churches.

He was in his early sixties, and had silver hair, a roundish red face and a kindly smile. True, his clothes smelled strongly of cheap cigarettes, and the hint of whisky on his breath suggested he had already taken at least one drink that morning, but these were both permissible weakness in a man who had voluntarily signed away his right to other pleasures of the flesh.

'I'd like to ask you a few questions about Bradley Pine, Father Kenyon,' Paniatowski said.

The priest nodded sagely. 'I can well imagine that you would, and I'll answer them as honestly as I feel I'm able to.'

'As you *feel you're able to*?' Paniatowski repeated. 'And what exactly does that mean?'

'You must understand that there are certain matters of which I have knowledge that I must keep to myself.'

Even if that does mean a mother will never learn her daughter has been molested by her husband, Paniatowski thought savagely.

But aloud, all she said was, 'How long had Mr Pine been coming to this church?'

'I've known him for over twenty years. He contacted me when he first arrived in Whitebridge, just as Father Swales, the director of Holy Trinity Orphanage had asked him to.' Father Kenyon paused. 'You did know that he was an orphan, didn't you?'

'Yes, I did.'

The old priest sighed. 'It is a terrible thing to lose a parent, but from what Father Swales told me, the death of his father was something of a merciful release for Bradley.'

'Why? Was his father a bad man?'

'We should not judge lest we ourselves be judged,' the priest said, with a note of caution creeping into his voice, 'but, by all accounts, the boy led a miserable life. His father was both a drunkard and a very violent man. Though Bradley never talked about it to me himself, I have seen the cigarette burn scars on his arms with my own eyes.'

Paniatowski felt a wave of sympathy for the dead man sweep over her, then found herself brushing it angrily aside.

'Yes, well, a lot of us had fairly difficult childhoods,' she said. 'Did Bradley Pine attend Mass regularly in the last few weeks of his life?'

49

'Yes, he did.'

'And before that?'

'Not to attend Mass is, as you are probably only too well aware yourself, a mortal sin.'

'Which he was guilty of?'

'Next question,' Father Kenyon said.

'You heard his confession last night?'

'Yes, I did.'

'Did you talk to him outside the confines of the confessional?'

'Yes.'

'And when you talked to him *outside* the confessional, did he seem worried or disturbed about anything in particular?'

'I can't answer that.'

'But surely, if it wasn't under the seal of—'

'Let me ask *you* a question,' the priest interrupted.

'All right,' Paniatowski agreed.

'Are you able to divorce what goes on in your interview rooms from what goes on outside them?'

'I think so.'

'And *I* think you are almost certainly deluding yourself, my child. What you encounter in that interview room must be much like what I often encounter in the confessional.'

'And what is that?'

'People who are so unsure of themselves – or so terrified – that the mask they normally wear slips off, and the disguise with which they seek to clothe themselves is quite stripped away. We have penetrated their secret selves. We have seen them naked.'

'I'm not sure I—'

'And later, when we meet them again – outside the confessional or outside the interview room – we may hear them say the same words as other people hear them say, but we will interpret them differently. Because we understand them better – because we have been given the *key* to them.'

'Perhaps you're right about that,' Monika Paniatowski conceded. 'But so what?'

The priest laughed. 'It doesn't bother you. And why should it? You're a police officer, and those you question have no choice in the matter. But my parishioners do have a choice. They come to me because they trust me. They *give* me the key, rather than my having to seize it from them. And that means that though I may physically leave the confessional, there is a sense in which I will always take it with me.'

'I'm not asking any of these questions just to satisfy my own idle curiosity, you know,' Paniatowski said, experiencing a rising frustration. 'I'm doing it because I'm trying to catch a murderer.'

'Yes, I quite understand that.'

'Some people would consider that a worthwhile aim.'

'*Most* people would. And they would be quite right to. It undoubtedly *is* a worthwhile aim.'

'Then why won't you help us to achieve it?'

'Because I am restrained from doing so. And those restraints go far beyond the single issue of catching your murderer. Even if, by speaking out, I could save other lives—'

'Are other lives in danger in this case?'

'Not as far as I know. But if they were, I would still maintain my silence, because nothing can justify breaking the seal of the confessional.'

'Not even the needless suffering of a young child?'

'Not even that.'

'But would you go drinking with the man who had made her suffer – the man who continued to make her suffer?' Paniatowski demanded angrily.

The priest looked suddenly troubled. 'I'm sorry, but I'm afraid I have no idea what you're talking about,' he admitted.

Paniatowski took a deep breath. 'No, of course you don't,' she said. 'Did Bradley Pine say where he was intending to go after he left the church last night – or don't you feel able to tell me *that*, either?'

'I can see no reason why I wouldn't be able to reveal that particular piece of information if I had it,' the priest replied. 'But I don't. Bradley didn't tell me where he was going.'

A lorry had arrived to transport the battered and violated Ford Cortina to the police garage, where it would be given a detailed forensic examination, but Dr Shastri – who arrived just before the car was about to be loaded – had insisted that nothing should be moved until she had made a thorough search of the area.

'If it were women in charge of removing the car, I would

have no qualms about letting them go ahead,' she told Bob Rutter, 'but men are, by their very nature, such clumsy creatures, don't you find?'

'Yes, I do,' Rutter agreed.

They *were* clumsy, he thought to himself – in oh-so-many ways.

Dr Shastri gave the area around the battered car a brief inspection.

'Well, on with the show,' she said, in a tone not unlike that of a music hall compère.

It would have been generous to describe the floor of the alley as merely unsavoury – the council felt no strong urge to do anything about improving the environment of tenants who rarely paid either their rent or their rates – but the filth and squalor did not seem to deter Dr Shastri in the slightest. She produced a rubber mat from the back of her Land Rover, and was soon kneeling down on it and examining the grimy cobblestones.

A few minutes had ticked by – and she had shifted the mat around several times – before she looked and said, 'The murderous attack did not take place here, my dear Inspector.'

'You're sure of that?' Rutter asked.

'Absolutely positive. It is true that if Mr Pine had been killed on this spot, the local rats would have removed much of the evidence – a piece of the human brain is to them what a fine pork roast would be to you or I – but there would still have been bloodstains left behind.'

'There would have been a lot of blood, wouldn't there?'

'A veritable fountain of it. And however diligently the killer had tried to clean it up, he would inevitably have left some traces.'

'Would you mind taking a look inside the car?' Rutter asked.

Dr Shastri smiled. 'Of course not,' she said. 'I am willing to do anything at all which will contribute – even in a small way – to making my second-favourite police officer happy.'

She opened the car door, and examined the stain Rutter had spotted on the back seat.

'Now that *is* blood,' she said. 'And if it is not our little friend's blood, I would be most surprised.'

'Shouldn't there be more of it?' Rutter asked.

'Not once the heart had ceased to pump. What we have here is mere seepage.'

'And you're as sure that he *was* mutilated in the lay-by as you are that he *wasn't* killed here?'

'Indeed.'

'I wonder why the murderer waited until he reached the lay-by before he finished off the job,' Rutter mused. 'Do you think it was because it would have been too messy to have done it earlier?'

'Perhaps,' Dr Shastri said, cautiously.

'You're not convinced that's the case at all, are you?' Rutter asked. 'You've got a theory of your own.'

'I have,' Dr Shastri admitted. 'But as I have already pointed out to your superior, the admirable Chief Inspector Woodend, I am more of a plumber than a brain doctor, and my theory may well not be worth a bag of acorns.'

'I'd like to hear it, anyway.'

'Even though you run the risk – if you take it seriously – of being sent off on a wild goose hunt?'

'Yes.'

'Very well, on your own head be it. I believe that, initially, the murderer thought that whatever torment was driving him to distraction would be assuaged by simply *killing* his victim. But by the time he had reached the lay-by, he had realized that was not enough to bring him the relief he needed, and he would have to do more. That is, I believe, when he decided to inflict the final humiliation by mutilating the corpse.'

'Let me see if I've got this straight,' Rutter said. 'You think that the idea of mutilation didn't occur to him until he reached the lay-by?'

'Essentially. Although, I suppose, it is possible that the urge came over him while he was still en route to it.'

'So the reason he made the decision to go there *wasn't* simply because he needed somewhere quiet where he could finish his work?'

'That seems unlikely, don't you think? The lay-by was not *so* secluded, even in a thick fog. The lorry which drove on to it *after* the mutilation had been concluded could just as easily have arrived whilst it was still in progress. If what the killer had wanted was total privacy to carry out his grisly task, he would surely have driven the body out on to the moors.'

'So if that wasn't the reason he took the body to the lay-by, what *did* make him choose that particular spot?'

Dr Shastri smiled again. 'That is a very interesting question,' she said. 'An intriguing, infuriating question. And one that, as a simple doctor, I am happy to leave in your much more capable hands.'

Nine

Elizabeth Driver was sitting in the First Class carriage of the local train from Manchester to Whitebridge. Her eyes were taking in the countryside through which the train was passing, but her mind was fixed very firmly on what was awaiting her at the end of the journey.

As the chief crime reporter for a salacious national newspaper which sold copies by the million – but which very few people would actually *admit* to reading – she was a true queen of her dubious profession. But being a queen could have its drawbacks. To stay at the top required a very delicate balancing act, and she only had to make one little slip – one tiny mistake – to come toppling down. On her good days, she told herself this was no problem, that she could go on for ever. On her bad days, she wondered how much longer she could continue to cap the last sensational story that she'd filed with one which was even more outrageous.

The story she was on her way to cover was a good case in point. For most reporters, the murder of a parliamentary candidate would provide them with all the copy they needed. They had only to report the facts to keep their editors satisfied. But when you were Elizabeth Driver, your editor and readers wanted – and expected – much more.

The death of Bradley Pine held out the promise of more. Driver's source in the Whitebridge Police had hinted that there were macabre aspects to the killing which had not yet been released to the press.

But that was all her source had done.

Bloody hint!

It was all he *could* do. He was far too low on the totem pole to give her any of the juicy details she needed if she were to keep ahead of her rivals.

She had a serious problem with the Whitebridge Police, she

admitted – and that problem was called Charlie Woodend. Their relationship had got off to a bad start when he had still been with Scotland Yard, investigating the Westbury Manor Murder – and it had pretty much gone downhill since then.

She had tried to mend fences – God alone knew how hard she had tried. She'd done her best to charm him, and he'd been distinctly unimpressed. She'd promised to write him up favourably in her articles, and he'd told her where she could stuff it. She'd even said she'd have sex with him – had offered him, on a plate, the body that half the hacks in Fleet Street fell asleep in their lonely beds lusting over – and been rebuffed.

The low point had come when Woodend had realized that it was she who had told Maria Rutter – a few days before her murder – that her husband Bob had had an affair with Monika Paniatowski.

There was no climbing out of that particular hole, she thought. Woodend would never – ever – forgive her for what she had done. But Bob Rutter, if handled right, just might. And while that wasn't as good as having Woodend himself on her side, it was *almost* as good.

The Whitebridge Golf and Country Club had been closely modelled on the mock-Gothic palaces that many rich men with no taste had built for themselves towards the end of the nine-teenth century. It was located on the north side of the city, far away from the dark satanic mills which had financed its construction. It was a pleasant enough place, Woodend admitted, if you happened to like manicured lawns and flower beds laid out with almost military precision, but for him it came nowhere near matching the savage grandeur of the moors.

There were only a few club members in the bar when he arrived and they looked at him with suspicion, for while there *were* chief inspectors in the Central Lancs Constabulary who they – at a push – would have regarded as *almost* their social equals, Woodend was definitely not among that number.

Woodend walked across the room to the bar counter. The blank-faced steward, standing behind it, watched his progress carefully, yet somehow managed to appear as if he were looking right through him.

'A pint of best bitter, when you've got the time, lad,' the chief inspector said.

The steward blinked. So apparently, while Woodend might be invisible, he was not quite inaudible.

'I'm terribly sorry, sir, but we're not allowed, by law, to serve non-members,' the steward said.

'Fair enough,' Woodend replied. 'I'm all for obeyin' the law myself, which is why – if I was you – I wouldn't go out on my bike after dark again without first checkin' my lights very carefully.'

To his left someone chuckled, then a voice said, 'That sounds like a threat to me.'

Woodend turned. The man who had addressed him was in his fifties, and was wearing a blue blazer with the club's badge on its pocket.

'A threat?' Woodend repeated. 'You've got it all wrong, sir. What you've just heard me offer was advice – kindly meant, an' purely in the interest of road safety.'

The man chuckled again, and held out his hand. 'Tom Carey, the club secretary. And you're Chief Inspector Woodend, aren't you?'

'That's right,' Woodend agreed, taking the hand.

'Henry Marlowe phoned me earlier, and said I should be expecting you,' Carey said.

'Aye, he would have done,' Woodend said. 'Normally, he'd move heaven an' earth to stop me pokin' my nose around in places like this, but since he really needs a result on the Pine case, he's had to compromise.'

'Compromise?'

'Aye. He's givin' me a bit of rope, but he's also put a few of his minders in place to make sure I don't tug on it too hard. You've been nominated as his minder here.'

Carey smiled. 'I can see you know our Henry quite well,' he said. He turned to the barman. 'A gin and tonic for me, and a pint of bitter for Mr Woodend, Donald. Put it on my account.'

The two men took their drinks over to a table.

'So how can we help you, Mr Woodend?' Carey asked.

'I'm tryin' to build up a picture of what Bradley Pine was like,' Woodend told him.

'Is *that* how the Central Lancs Police conduct their investigations?' Carey asked, sounding more curious than censorious. 'I thought that these days it was all fingerprints and

57

blood samples. Very scientific and modern, of course – but perhaps a little boring.'

'There are fellers on the Force who rely on forensics to do their job for them,' Woodend admitted, taking an exploratory sip of his pint and quickly deciding that the golf club's beer had more than earned its fine reputation. 'But that isn't the way I work.'

'So what *do* you do?'

'I try to get inside people's heads.'

'And, at the moment, you want to get inside Bradley Pine's?'

'That's correct.'

'Well, maybe I can help you there,' Carey told him. 'Bradley was a pillar of the community, who constantly strived to improve the conditions of those less fortunate than himself.' He winked. 'That's what it says in his political manifesto, anyway.'

'But what would *you* say?' Woodend wondered.

'I'd have say that I quite admired him, but never really knew him,' Carey replied, after a moment's thought. 'I admired him because he came from nothing, and made no bones about it. He was an orphan, you know.'

'Aye, I had heard,' Woodend agreed.

'Some of the less socially secure members of this club try their damnedest to hide their origins. They spend small fortunes searching their family trees for some trace of nobility, and even have family crests commissioned. Bradley never did anything like that. Ask him about his family, and he'd admit quite openly that his father was a drunkard who had no one to blame for his early death but himself. And it must say something for the man, don't you think, that despite his refusal to put on any airs and graces, he still managed to get himself elected to the committee?'

'If he was on the committee, then you, as club secretary, must have worked quite closely with him.'

'I did.'

'An' yet you say you never really knew him?'

'None of the members really knew Bradley. He was friendly with all, but a *close* friend of no one. He didn't seem to need the assurances of support that most people do. I suppose that might have something to do with being brought up in an orphanage – you have to learn to rely on yourself alone.'

'Can you think of anybody who might have held a grudge against him?' Woodend asked.

'You'd have to be a saint for there to be nobody who held a grudge against you,' Carey said.

'An' even then, there'd be some bugger who'd find a way to pick holes in you,' Woodend agreed. 'But I'd still like an answer to my question.'

'I'm sure there were people who resented the fact that Bradley was on the committee and they weren't,' Carey said. 'I'm sure there are those who think they would have made a better parliamentary candidate. But I certainly can't think of anyone who disliked him enough to kill him.'

'Business rivals?' Woodend prodded. 'Jealous husbands?'

The question seemed to amuse Carey. 'When you're the undisputed king of the interior sprung mattresses in central Lancashire, you *have* no business rivals,' he said.

'It was a two-part question,' Woodend reminded him.

'So it was,' Carey agreed. 'Bradley's been a member of this club since soon after he registered his patent. Back then, there probably were a few jealous husbands around. After all, Bradley was young, unattached and rather good looking, so naturally there were rumours that his relationships with some of the other members' wives were perhaps a little too close.'

'Were they *just* rumours?' Woodend asked.

'Since he was not actually caught *in flagrante*, we'll never actually know for sure, but I have to say that it wouldn't surprise me if there'd been a little fire to go with all the smoke.'

'You've been talkin' in the past tense,' Woodend said. 'Haven't there been any recent rumours?'

'No. In fact, there have been none at all for a good few years now.'

'Why? Did he suddenly lose all interest in sex?'

'No, I wouldn't quite say that.'

'Then what *would* you say?'

Carey hesitated for a second, then said, 'I'm not entirely sure I should say anything at all.'

'The man's dead,' Woodend pointed out.

'Yes,' Carey agreed, 'but *she* isn't.'

'She?'

'This is all pure speculation,' Carey said cautiously.

59

'I'll bear that in mind,' Woodend promised.

'I think he fell in love.'

'Who with?'

'I really have no idea.'

'Come on, Mr Carey,' Woodend urged.

'I mean it, Chief Inspector. I have no idea.'

'Then how do you know that he fell in love *at all*?'

'I was in love once,' Carey said. 'It was a long time ago, but I still recognize the signs.'

'What signs?'

'The look in his eyes, sometimes. The far-away expression on his face, as if he'd suddenly started thinking about the best thing that had ever happened to him. The fact that he no longer seemed anything like as interested in other women as he had once done. It's not something you can put your finger on, but then love's like that, isn't it?'

'But you have no idea who this woman – if she exists – is?'

'None at all.'

'So she could be the wife of one of your members?'

'Given that Bradley seemed to have virtually no social life outside the confines of this club, I'd be very much surprised if the woman in question *wasn't* a member's wife.'

'There's a pretty good motive for murder, then,' Woodend said.

'I don't think so,' Carey countered.

'Why not?'

'But if she is a member's wife, then the member himself certainly doesn't know about it.'

'How can you be so sure of that?'

'I've already said that it's not hard to spot a man who's suddenly fallen deeply in love, haven't I?' Carey said.

'Yes.'

'But doing that is rocket science compared to spotting a man who suspects he's been cuckolded. That's as easy as falling off a log.'

Ten

Though a little of the skill and ball control of a professional football match may have been lacking from the lunch-time match that was being played on the cinder pitch behind Hawtrey and Pine Holdings, the players themselves more than made up for it with their ferocity and enthusiasm – and Constable Beresford, a large mug of tea in his hand, had been watching the game with pleasure for over ten minutes when it suddenly occurred to him that he wasn't actually there to enjoy himself.

He forced his gaze away from the pitch, and on to the old man in the flat cap and boiler suit who was standing next to him and had told him earlier that his name was Harry Ramsbotham.

'I'm surprised they're playing a game at all on a day like this, Harry,' Beresford said, conversationally.

'Are you now?' the old man replied. 'An' why might that be?'

'Well, when all's said and done, your boss has just been brutally murdered, hasn't he?'

'That's true enough.'

'And I would have thought they might have abandoned the game as a sign of respect.'

'Mr Pine wasn't that kind of boss,' Harry Ramsbotham said.

'Wasn't *what* kind of boss? Are you saying you all hated him? That you're all glad he's dead?'

The old man shook his head. 'You young lads,' he said, almost despairingly. 'Everythin's got to be either one extreme or the other with you, hasn't it? No, we didn't hate Mr Pine—'

'Well, then—'

'—but he wasn't like family to us, either. He was the boss. He paid reasonably fair wages, we put in a reasonably fair day's work for them. By an' large, we had no real complaints

61

about him, an' he had no real complaints about us. But nobody's goin' to break into floods of tears now that he's gone.'

'I see,' Beresford said.

'Of course, it was different in the old days,' Harry Ramsbotham continued, wistfully. 'When old Mr Hawtrey died – that's Mr *Samuel* Hawtrey, I'm talkin' about, Mr Alec's dad – they closed down the factory for the day of the funeral, an' every man-jack who worked here went to it. An' there was a funeral tea afterwards, with enough booze flowin' for all his workers to drink to his memory. But like I say, them days are gone forever.'

'I expect you're right,' Beresford agreed.

'I *am* right. Old Mr Hawtrey knew the first name of everybody who worked for him. Even Mr Alec knew most of them. But the only people whose names Mr Pine knew were the managers.' Harry Ramsbotham paused for a moment. 'No, that's not quite fair,' he continued. 'He did know the names of most of the lads he'd worked with while he was makin' his own way up the ladder to the top.'

There was the sound of cheering from around the cinder pitch, and Beresford turned to see what was happening. A young apprentice had just artfully dribbled the ball around two of his older, slower opponents and was now facing an open goal mouth.

'Take your time, lad!' Ramsbotham called out. 'Don't just kick it! *Think* about it.'

The apprentice paused for a moment, perhaps as a result of the old man's advice, then slammed his foot into the ball with tremendous force. The goalkeeper made a desperate dive, but it was a wasted effort and the ball flew into the back of the net.

'He's good enough to turn professional, that lad,' Ramsbotham told Beresford.

'Did Alec Hawtrey own the whole business before Bradley Pine became a partner?' Beresford asked.

'He most certainly did. Mr Samuel left it to him in his will – lock, stock an' barrel.'

'So how *did* Bradley Pine become a partner?'

'Bought his way in, with the money he'd made from that invention of his, didn't he? He always was a clever chap.'

'Yes, I know that,' Beresford said. 'What I don't understand is why Alec Hawtrey would *want* to sell part of his family business.'

'He didn't want to. He needed the money.'

'Why was that?'

'Ah, thereby hangs a tale,' Harry Ramsbotham. 'An' not just a tale – but a lesson to us all.'

'Go on,' Beresford said, encouragingly.

'You'd have thought Mr Alec had the perfect life. He was happily married – at least, as far as anybody knew – an' he had two lovely children, one son an' one daughter. Then one of the lasses in the typin' pool caught his eye, an' he lost all reason.'

'That can happen,' Beresford said sagely.

Harry Ramsbotham laughed. 'How would you know?' he asked. 'You're nowt but a lad.'

Beresford blushed. 'I'm sorry, I didn't mean to—'

'No, I'm sorry,' the old man said kindly. 'You can't help bein' young, an' I shouldn't take the mickey out of you for it. Now where was I?'

'He lost all reason.'

'He did. He was a man in his thirties, an' she was a slip of a girl who hadn't even reached her majority, but it made no difference to him. He started knockin' around openly with her, as if he didn't care who saw them. Well, it was only a matter of time before his wife found out, an' once she did, she started divorce proceedin's on the ground of adultery. An' this was fifteen or sixteen years ago, mind, when it was a much more serious matter than it is now.'

'Was it really *so* different then?' Beresford asked.

'Bloody right it was different. There wasn't all that much of this here promiscuity around in them days – which is not to say that everybody back then behaved like little angels.'

'No?'

'Definitely not! A lot of fellers *did* have their bit of fluff on side, an' most of the people who knew about it chose to look the other way. But if you got caught out, that was another matter entirely. If you got caught out, you were in deep trouble an' nobody decent wanted anythin' to do with you.'

'So Alec Hawtrey's sin was letting himself get caught.'

'Exactly. Couldn't have put it better myself. An' when the divorce case got to court, the judge told Mr Alec that as a leadin' light in the community, he should have been settin' a much better example for the rest of us to follow. So it didn't really come as a surprise to anybody when, in announcin' the settlement, he gave Mrs Hawtrey half the factory. It was his way of punishin' Mr Alec for behavin' so disgracefully, you see.'

'So am I to assume that Mrs Hawtrey still owns half the factory?'

'You can assume what you like, lad, but you'd be wrong on both counts.'

'I beg your pardon?'

'First of all, she wasn't Mrs Hawtrey any more. She'd got divorced an' gone back to her maiden name.'

'Yes, but—'

'An' secondly, she didn't want anythin' more to do with the factory – or even with the town. She accepted on a big wodge of cash in return for her shares, an' she moved. But in order to raise that big wodge of cash, Mr Alec had had to saddle himself with a huge debt, you see.'

'Yes, he must have done.'

'Well, despite that, the company did manage to struggle on a few more years, but in the end the debt got so cripplin' that he had no choice but to take on a partner who could put some more money into the business. An' the partner he chose was Bradley Pine.'

'What happened to the young girl from the typing pool, the one who Mr Hawtrey had been having an affair with?' Beresford asked.

The old man grinned. 'What are you expectin' me to say, lad?' he asked. 'That she couldn't live with the shame of bein' a home-wrecker, so she drowned herself in the river?'

'Well, no,' replied Beresford.

And it was quite true that he hadn't been expecting it. In fact, he couldn't really conceive of a time in which women *would* have acted like that.

'She didn't drown herself,' the old man said. 'She married him. She became the second Mrs Hawtrey. And now she's his widow.'

There was another roar from the cinder pitch as the young apprentice scored again.

'He could have a great future, that lad,' Harry Ramsbotham

told Beresford. 'But then you could say that of most of us – until we put a foot wrong.'

Elizabeth Driver strode into the most expensive hairdresser's salon Whitebridge could offer with the air of someone who knows quite well that she's slumming it, but really has no choice in the matter.

'I want you to dye my hair,' she told the young assistant, who was already unnerved by her imperious manner. 'I want it blonde.'

'Any particular shade?'

'Well, of course I want a particular shade!' Elizabeth Driver snapped. 'Get me the colour card, and I'll show you.'

The assistant presented her with the card, and Driver immediately pointed to a colour. 'That's the one.'

'But that seems to be your natural colour anyway,' the assistant said, parting her hair and examining her roots.

'Oh really? And I never even realized it,' Elizabeth Driver said with heavy sarcasm.

'The thing is, Madam, if you let the dye grow out, you'll get your own colour back naturally,' the assistant explained.

'That's something else I hadn't realized,' Driver said. 'Do you want my business or not?'

'Yes, but—'

'But what?'

'Before I can dye your hair, I'll have to bleach it.'

'Naturally.'

'And that could damage your hair.'

'I'll risk it,' Driver said.

'But if you'll just let nature take its course—'

'That would be fine if I'd got the time – but I haven't!' Elizabeth Driver snapped.

'Could I . . . could I ask what all the hurry is, Madam?' the assistant asked bravely.

Elizabeth Driver sighed. 'I'm doing it for the same reason that any woman changes her appearance in a hurry,' she said. 'And even a dim mind like yours should be able to guess what that is.'

'You want to impress a man,' the assistant said.

'That's right,' Elizabeth Driver agreed. 'I'm doing it because I want to impress a man.'

65

Eleven

Woodend and Paniatowski arrived at the door of the Drum and Monkey at exactly the same time. They hadn't arranged for that to happen, but neither was it a surprise to either of them that it had.

This was how they meshed when they were working on a murder case together. Each of them anticipated the other's actions. Each had at least a glimmering of what the other was thinking. It was as if they developed some special kind of telepathy which would continue to transmit for the whole course of the investigation, and whilst they were not quite sure how it worked – or even *why* it worked – they were always extremely grateful when it did.

'The whole problem with this case, as far as I can see, is that I've not been able to get a proper handle on it yet,' the chief inspector told his sergeant as they sat down at their table. 'An' to be fair to myself, I don't think that's entirely my fault.'

'Then whose fault is it?'

'Bradley Pine has to take some of the blame. He seems to have been a bit of a secretive bugger even *before* he turned politician.'

'In what way?'

'In all sorts of ways. For example, the secretary of the golf club, who's a sharp feller called Carey, is convinced that Pine's been carryin' on an affair for years, an' yet nobody can put a name to the woman he's involved with. An' as you know yourself, it's almost impossible to . . .'

He stopped speaking, horrified that he'd allowed himself to wander blindly into this particular emotional mine field.

'As I know myself, it's almost impossible to keep an affair hidden, however hard you try?' Paniatowski supplied.

'Yes,' Woodend agreed. 'Sorry.'

'There's no need to apologize,' Paniatowski told him. 'We

can't keep on pretending that the past never happened, especially now Bob's back at work as a walking, talking reminder that it did.'

Woodend nodded. 'Shall we get back on to the subject of Bradley Pine?'

'I think it would be a good idea if we did.'

'It's the very fact that he was so secretive himself that's makin' his murderer into such a shadowy figure. We know so little about Pine as a person that we can't even begin to guess who could have hated him enough to not only kill him, but also to mutilate him.'

'Or why the killer, once he'd done the deed, would have wanted to move his body,' Paniatowski said.

'Well, exactly!' Woodend agreed. 'He was runnin' a terrific risk takin' the corpse to the lay-by – but why take him to a lay-by *at all*? Why *do* killers move the bodies of their victims?'

'Sometimes they do it to hide them.'

'But in this case, the killer did just the opposite. He dumped the corpse in a spot where it was bound to be discovered – an' sooner rather than later.'

'Sometimes killers leave their victims in a specific place as a way of sending a message – a warning – to other people.'

'Like leavin' thieves hangin' on the gibbet for days on end? Or killin' a member of a rival gang, an' then dumpin' his body in front of that gang's headquarters?'

'Yes, that kind of thing.'

'But if the killer was sendin' a message here, who the bloody hell was he sendin' it to? Lorry drivers? Speedin' motorists? There has to be another reason why that lay-by has a special significance. But what sort of special significance could a bloody lay-by *possibly* have?'

The bar door opened, and Bob Rutter walked in. Though they were expecting him, it still somehow took them by surprise that he had actually arrived, and for a moment both Woodend and Paniatowski froze.

Then Woodend pulled himself together, stood up, and held out his hand to Rutter.

'It's good to have you back with us, Bob,' he said.

'It's good to *be* back, sir,' Bob Rutter told him, taking the proffered hand and shaking it.

67

Oh my God, he looks so thin, Monika Paniatowski thought. *He looks so* haunted.

But what had she been expecting, she asked herself. Had she thought he would waltz in as if he hadn't got a care in the world – as if all the terrible things which had happened to him were now no more than a distant memory?

She noticed that Rutter was looking down at her. 'I'm glad you're back, too, Bob,' she said.

But was she?

Was she *really*?

Wouldn't Bob's return do no more than open old wounds? Might she not find – despite knowing how pointless it was – that she was still very much in love with him?

Rutter sat down, and the landlord brought an unordered – but much appreciated – pint across to the table.

With one hand Rutter grasped the drink as if it were a lifebelt, while with the other he searched in his jacket pocket for change.

The landlord shook his head. 'I won't take your money, Mr Rutter,' he said. 'This one's on the house.'

'So how did your first mornin' back go, Bob?' Woodend asked, when the landlord had returned to the bar. 'Do you think you're gettin' anywhere?'

He had been aiming to sound as normal as possible – without any evidence of the awkwardness and lack of ease he was actually feeling – and listening to his own voice he decided he'd *almost* achieved that.

Rutter shrugged. 'It's been pretty much like the start of most of our investigations, sir,' he said. 'We haven't got anything like enough information yet to know where to find the leads we need, so we just have to look everywhere we can possibly think of.'

'Is Pine's car likely to tell us anything?' Woodend wondered, noting that his voice was still sounding somewhat strained.

'I doubt it,' Rutter replied. 'The thugs who stripped it down in the alley are likely to have destroyed any forensic evidence there might have been.'

The phone at the bar rang, and the three people at the table jumped as if they'd heard a shot.

The landlord picked up the phone and listened for a second, then called out, 'It's for you, Sergeant Paniatowski.'

'Who is it?'

'She wants to know who's calling,' the landlord said into the telephone receiver.

Rutter picked up his pint and drained half of it in a single gulp.

None of them were finding this easy, Woodend thought.

'The feller on the phone says he's a colleague of yours, Sergeant,' the landlord shouted, across the bar. 'He says it's been quite a while since you've spoken to one another.'

Monika Paniatowski rose to her feet slowly, as if her legs had suddenly turned to lead.

'Could you transfer the call through to the phone in the corridor for me?' she asked.

'I suppose so,' the landlord replied. 'But wouldn't you be much more comfortable taking it in here?'

'The corridor!' Paniatowski said firmly.

The landlord shrugged. 'If that's what you want, Sergeant, it's no problem at all.'

Jesus, what was going on now, Woodend wondered, as he watched his sergeant walk heavily over to the door, like a condemned woman on the way to her execution.

He became aware that Rutter had been talking to him, but had no idea what he'd been saying.

'I'm sorry, lad, but could you just run that by me again?' he asked the inspector.

'As I said, I don't think the car itself will turn out to be of much use to the investigation,' Rutter told him, 'but I think that, in leaving it where he did, the killer may have given more away than he ever intended to.'

'Go on,' Woodend said, doing his best to take his mind off Paniatowski and re-focus it on the investigation.

'He abandoned the Cortina there because Greenfields was close to home – not too close, but close enough.'

'What do you mean by that?'

'It was close enough for him to make the journey home on foot without running too much of a risk of being spotted by anyone else. But it was not *so* close to his base that if we carry out blanket interviewing in the area around Greenfields, we'll be bound to end up talking to him.'

Woodend scratched his head, then took a sip of his pint. 'You just might be on to something there,' he admitted.

* * *

69

The phone call – coming in those awkward moments after Bob Rutter's arrival – should have felt like a godsend, Paniatowski thought, as she closed the corridor door firmly behind her. It should have seemed like the emotional equivalent of being untied from the railway tracks just before the express train arrived.

But it hadn't.

Instead, it had filled her with dread.

And though she didn't quite know why a call from Chief Inspector Baxter – for who else could it be? – should have done that, she was convinced that she would soon find out.

She lifted the phone off its cradle, and heard a click as the landlord hung up the one in the bar.

'Monika Paniatowski,' she said.

'It's me,' Baxter replied.

'I wasn't expecting you to call,' Paniatowski told him, thinking – even as she spoke the words – that it seemed an inadequate response to a man who was, after all, her lover.

'Can we meet?' Baxter asked.

'When?'

'If you don't mind, I'd rather like it to be some time within the next day or so.'

She needed time to get over seeing Bob Rutter again, Paniatowski thought – and a couple of days just wasn't enough.

'Actually I do mind,' she said. 'As things are here at the moment, it might be rather difficult to arrange.'

'Oh?'

'You see, we're in the first twenty-four hours of a new murder inquiry – and you know from your own experience what that's like.'

'So are you saying that you can't spare me even half an hour of your valuable time?'

Damn him! Why was he being so persistent?

'Half an hour?' Monika asked, stalling. 'Yes, I suppose I could spare that. But it wouldn't *be* half an hour, would it?'

'Wouldn't it?'

'Of course it wouldn't. You're not living just around the corner from me, you know. It's a couple of hours drive up to Dunethorpe – and a couple of hours drive back.'

'If that's the only problem you can see, I could come across to Whitebridge,' Baxter suggested.

Paniatowski glanced into the mirror over the phone. The last time she'd looked at herself – which couldn't have been more than an hour earlier – she'd thought she was presentable enough, but now she was a complete wreck.

'You know what I'm like when I'm all wrapped in a case,' she said. 'I'm just not fit to know. So I really would rather leave meeting you until we've got a result on this one.'

'Maybe you would,' Baxter agreed. 'But I wouldn't.'

'Well, we can't always have what we want in this life,' Paniatowski said, trying her best to sound light-hearted.

'Ain't that the truth,' Baxter agreed grimly. 'We can't always have it, although sometimes – for a little while at least – we can talk ourselves into believing that we've got it.'

'You've lost me,' Paniatowski admitted.

'I never had you. That was the whole problem,' Baxter countered. 'Listen, Monika, I didn't want to do this over the phone, but—'

'Do *what* over the phone?'

'I've met a woman.'

'Really? I've met *dozens* of women since the last time we spoke. Dozens of men, too.'

'You know what I mean.'

'Yes,' Monika admitted. 'I rather think I do. I expect she's very pretty, is she?'

'She's pleasant enough, but she's nothing compared to you in the looks department. Hasn't got any of your brains, either. But at least I know where I am with her.'

'I see,' Paniatowski said flatly.

'You've no reason to sound like you think you've been badly done by,' Baxter said, with just a hint of aggression starting to appear in his voice. 'You're the one who's always insisted that there should be no firm commitment given – from either of us.'

'That's true,' Paniatowski admitted. She paused for a second. 'So is this goodbye then?'

'I wouldn't put it in quite those terms,' Baxter said. 'We still like each other, don't we?'

'Yes, I suppose we do.'

'So there's no reason why we still can't meet up now and again for a drink, is there?'

'No reason at all,' Paniatowski agreed. 'But we won't, will we?'

71

For several seconds, Baxter was silent, then he said, 'No, I don't really think we will.'

'So we might as well just say our goodbyes to each other now, and have done with it.'

'Goodbye, Monika,' Baxter said – and she thought she could hear a slight catch in his throat.

'Goodbye,' Monika replied. 'And thanks for trying so hard.'

'To do what?'

'To make things between us work.'

She was crying as she hung up the phone, but she was not entirely sure why. She had never loved Baxter, and though she had enjoyed the sex life they had shared, she'd known the earth to move much more with other men.

So why the tears, she wondered.

She supposed it could be for no other reason than that she was suddenly feeling very, very alone.

'So you think the killer is almost certainly a Whitebridge man?' Woodend asked Rutter.

'Yes. Or if he's not, he's at least *living* in Whitebridge at the moment.'

Woodend took a drag on his cigarette, and then nodded.

'I think I'd agree with you on that,' he said. 'If I wanted to kill somebody who lived in another town, I certainly wouldn't wait till there was a thick fog before I drove over there to do it.'

'The question is, how *far* would he be prepared to walk before he reached his safe haven,' Rutter said. 'Half a mile? A mile? I suppose it would depend on how strong his nerve was and what calculations he'd made about the risks . . . about the risks . . .'

Rutter stopped speaking, and gazed with horror in the direction of the corridor.

Woodend turned his own head, and immediately understood his inspector's reaction.

Monika Paniatowski was standing framed in the doorway between the bar and the corridor. It was obvious from the expression she'd forced on to her face that she was trying to appear to be her normal self – but she looked totally destroyed.

Twelve

The three men leaning against the factory wall had all been enthusiastic players in the cinder pitch football match earlier in the lunch break, but now they seemed content to merely look on while others grabbed the glory.

Well, that wasn't really very surprising, was it, Beresford asked himself. When you were getting on in years – and these men, he guessed, must be somewhere in their late thirties – you simply didn't have the stamina any more.

One of the men had a shock of red curly hair. The second was completely bald, and his pink head gleamed in the early afternoon sun. The third had a duck-tail quiff which was held in place by an impressive amount of grease, and made him look a little like Elvis Presley might have done if Elvis had been wearing a boiler suit, smoking a Woodbine, and working in a mattress factory.

Separately, the trio would probably have passed largely unnoticed and unremarked, but standing together as they were, they looked like some kind of a comedy act – the Three Stooges of Whitebridge, or Hawtrey-Pine Holdings's answer to the Marx Brothers.

Beresford ambled over to them in the casual way he thought a detective, totally at ease with the situation, probably would.

'Mind if I join you?' he asked.

'Why, are we comin' apart?' said the ginger-haired man, then laughed loudly, as if he'd cracked the most original joke in the world.

Charlie Woodend would have come back with a clever line instantly, Beresford told himself, but all he could think to say was, 'No, I just thought you might be willing to answer a few questions for me.'

'What kind of questions?' the ginger man asked. 'What's the capital of Russia? I can tell you that. It's Moscow! What's the longest river in the world? Easy! It's the Nile. Who really runs Hawtrey-Pine Holdings? Another absolute doddle! The Vatican!'

'The Vatican?' Beresford repeated.

'Ignore him,' the bald man said wearily. 'That's the only thing to do when he starts ridin' that particular hobby horse.'

'Hobby horse, is it?' the ginger man asked, aggrieved. 'Well, just look at the facts, will you? Mr Hawtrey was a Roman Catholic, Mr Pine was a Roman Catholic. Mr *Tully* was a Roman Catholic.'

'Leave off,' the bald man said. 'This is *supposed* to be our break. We're *supposed* to be havin' a good time.'

'An' I'm just *supposed* to stand here an' listen to you hintin' that I'm some kind of nutter, am I?' the ginger man asked. 'Well, you don't need to take my word for anythin', because the facts speak for themselves. You can go right through the payroll an' find the same thing – anybody with a cushy job belongs to the Church of Rome. It's a wonder to me that the Pope's not got a job here.'

'Maybe he has,' said the Elvis impersonator, in what was probably an attempt to defuse the situation by making a joke of it. 'Perhaps the only reason we don't see him ourselves is because he works the night shift.'

'Was Mr Pine a good boss?' Beresford asked, doing his best to steer the conversation towards something more fruitful.

'He was all right – as bosses go,' the Elvis impersonator said.

'An' as bosses go, he went,' the ginger man said, chuckling.

The bald man shook his head, rebukingly. 'Let's have a little decorum, shall we?' he suggested. 'The poor bugger's not even cold yet.'

'Which is more than you can say for the state Mr Hawtrey was in, when they took him off that mountainside,' the ginger man said, still laughing.

'Now that's *not* right,' the bald man said sternly. 'Mr Hawtrey was a bloody good bloke, an' even if you've no respect for Mr Pine, you could at least show a little towards him.'

'Don't get all high an' mighty with me,' the ginger man said. 'It wasn't me what killed Hawtrey – it was Pine.'

'Pine *killed* Hawtrey?' Beresford asked, shocked.

74

'You'll be givin' the lad the wrong impression if you're not careful,' the bald man said hastily.

'That I won't,' the ginger man countered, totally unrepentant. 'Pine didn't stick a knife in him, or blow his head off with a shotgun – or do anythin' at all like that – but he still killed him, right enough.'

'What he means to say, is that he thinks Mr Pine should never have persuaded Mr Hawtrey to go on that mountain climb with him an' Mr Tully,' the bald man explained to Beresford. He glared at the ginger man. 'Isn't that right?'

'More or less,' the ginger man agreed, reluctantly. 'Pine an' Tully were in their thirties – fit young men who could handle it when things went wrong. But Mr Hawtrey was the wrong side of fifty – an' he couldn't.'

'You can't go puttin' all the blame on Mr Pine's shoulders,' the Elvis impersonator said. 'From what I heard, there was originally supposed to be just the two of them on the climb – Pine an' Tully – an' the only reason that Mr Hawtrey ended up accompanying them was because he invited *himself* along.'

'Why would he have done that?' the ginger man demanded.

'You *know* why he did it. It was because he wanted to impress his wife!'

'So now you're sayin' *Thelma* wanted him to climb that mountain?'

'Course I'm not. Why should she want him to? It's not a woman's thing, is it? But he thought that by goin' on the climb with them, he could prove to her that he could keep up with men who were much closer to her age than he was himself.'

'I still think it was all Pine's fault,' the ginger man said.

'You would,' the Elvis impersonator responded. 'But sooner or later you'll have to face the fact that the way Mr Pine tried to keep Mr Hawtrey alive on the mountain makes him nothing less than a bloody hero.'

'If he *did* try to keep him alive,' the ginger man said. 'We've only Pine's own word for it.'

'As a matter of fact, you couldn't be wronger about that,' the Elvis impersonator said. 'Mr Pine said very little about what went on up that mountain. Nearly everythin' we do know about it came from Mr Tully.'

'Well, he would stick up for Pine, wouldn't he? He's another bloody Catholic.'

'An' I suppose the committee of inquiry – which decided that Pine did more than could have been expected of any man – was made up of Catholics as well, was it?' the mock Elvis asked.

'Wouldn't surprise me at all,' the ginger man said. 'Anyway, I wouldn't put a lot of faith in anythin' Tully said, if I was you. He was a bloody wreck when they brought him down.'

'So would you have been, if you'd damn near died of exposure,' the bald man said. 'But you are right about one thing – he was never the same man again.'

'Didn't even seem to know where he was, half the time,' the Elvis impersonator agreed. 'Makin' a clean break was the best thing he could have done, if you want my opinion.'

'Making a clean break?' Beresford repeated.

'A few months after it all happened, he resigned from the company,' the bald man explained. 'He said he wanted to leave the past behind him and make a new start.'

'So he left Whitebridge, did he?'

'Left Whitebridge?' the ginger man repeated. 'He did a bit more than that. He left the country! In fact, he left the bloody continent! He's livin' somewhere in Australia now.'

A large-scale map of Whitebridge had been pinned to the frame of the blackboard in the basement, and Rutter studied it for a moment before turning to address his team of fresh-faced detective constables.

'Some of you – especially the ones who've never been involved in a murder inquiry before – may be starting to think that we're getting nowhere,' he said. 'But if that *is* what you're thinking, you're wrong. Police work is largely a matter of elimination. The more places we can rule out, the fewer there are left where the murder could have taken place.'

He paused, to let his words sink in.

What the hell was the matter with Monika, he found himself wondering in the space the silence had granted him.

She hadn't looked exactly great when he arrived at the Drum and Monkey – and given what they'd been through together, he hadn't expected her to – but after that phone call, she looked like *death*.

A constable at the far end of the horseshoe coughed, and

Rutter remembered where he was, and what he was supposed to be doing.

'I've marked three spots on the map,' he said, tracing them out with his finger. 'Here in the middle of town is Point A, St Mary's Church. A bit further out is Point B, Greenfield. And right up there, at the edge of the map, is Point C, the lay-by. But we still have to find Point D – the place where Pine was killed. What I want to know from you is where you think we should be looking for that point – and where you think we *shouldn't*.'

'It's unlikely he was killed anywhere outside the city boundaries,' one of DCs suggested.

'Is it? Why?'

'He left the church at around nine o'clock, and his body was discovered a little after ten. He wouldn't have *time* to drive far, especially in a thick fog like there was last night.'

'Good point,' Rutter agreed. 'Where else?'

'He couldn't have been attacked anywhere very public,' another DC chipped in.

'Why not?'

'If he had have been, somebody would have come across the bloodstains by now.'

Rutter nodded. 'Sound thinking. So what have we just ruled out?'

'The streets. The bus station. The railway station. Pub car parks. Anywhere a lot of people go.'

'So what does that leave us with?' Rutter said.

'The murderer could have killed him somewhere indoors,' a third detective constable speculated. 'Maybe he got Pine to visit his house on some pretext or other, and did it there.'

'We'll ignore that possibility for the moment,' Rutter said.

'But, sir—' the DC protested.

'And the *reason* we'll ignore it is not because it's a bad idea. It isn't. But if that *is* what actually happened, then the only way we're going to find the place is if somebody rings us up and tells us where to look. So what we have to do is concentrate on *other* places where it might have happened. That means gardens, public parks, abandoned buildings and pieces of waste ground, all within the city boundaries. Agreed?'

The DCs nodded.

'When you joined the CID you probably thought your days

of pounding the pavements were over,' Rutter said. He smiled. 'Well, lads, I hate to break this to you, but you couldn't have been more wrong. By the time this investigation's over, your feet will have swelled to twice their normal size, and you'll think back to your days on the beat as a kind of golden age.' He paused for a moment. 'But when we catch our killer – and we *will* catch him – the buzz you'll get out of it will be like nothing you've ever known before.'

Beresford found Woodend sitting at the team's table in the Drum and Monkey. The chief inspector still had a half-full beer glass in front of him, but seemed to have no interest in draining it.

'Where are the others, sir?' Beresford asked.

'The others?' Woodend repeated, as if his mind had been somewhere else entirely. 'What others?'

'Inspector Rutter and Sergeant Paniatowski, sir.'

'The Inspector's gone back to work with the team "at the heart of the investigation".'

'Sorry?'

'He's in the HQ basement.'

'And the sergeant?'

'I . . . er . . . sent Monika home. She was lookin' tired, so I told her to go an' grab a couple of hours kip.'

Tired? Beresford thought.

The dynamic Sergeant Paniatowski? Tired?

At this early stage of the inquiry?

'So did you spend a profitable mornin' at Hawtrey and Pine's?' Woodend asked.

'I'm not sure I'd exactly say that it was profitable, sir,' Beresford admitted. 'But I did everything that you told me to do.'

'Includin' gettin' Bradley Pine's office sealed up until I have the time to take a look at it?'

'Yes. And I also went to listen to what the men working at Hawtrey-Pine Holdings had to say.'

'An' what *did* the men have to say?'

Beresford outlined what Harry Ramsbotham had told him about the break-up of Hawtrey's marriage, and Pine's injection of cash into the company. Then he recounted his conversation with the Three Stooges.

'So at least one of those fellers blames Bradley Pine for Alec Hawtrey's death, does he?' Woodend asked, when the constable had finished.

'Yes, sir, but I wouldn't pay too much attention to his views, because he's also halfway to thinking that there's a Roman Catholic conspiracy to take over the world,' Beresford pointed out.

'Still, if he thinks that what happened on the mountainside was Pine's fault, there's others who might think it as well,' Woodend mused.

'Others?'

'We know that whoever killed Pine had a burnin' hatred for him.'

'Yes?'

'An' if I was a widow who blamed him for my husband's death, I think that's just the kind of hatred that I might have.'

'You think that Mrs Thelma Hawtrey might have killed him?' Beresford asked.

'I think anybody an' everybody *could* have killed him,' Woodend replied. 'An' it would certainly be jumpin' the gun to assume that Mrs Hawtrey was our prime suspect. On the other hand, it's only human nature to blame other people for your own deep loss – an' who would Mrs Hawtrey be more likely to blame than Bradley Pine?'

'But when you think about the way that Pine was killed—' Beresford protested.

'It was a powerful blow that did for him, but the Doc said a woman could have found the strength to inflict it, if she'd been angry enough.'

'But the mutilation! Surely a woman wouldn't have had the stomach to do that?'

'Ever heard the sayin' "The female of the species is more deadly than the male"?' Woodend asked. 'Anyway, she didn't have to do it herself, did she? Maybe she's got a brother who did it for her. Or a cousin. Maybe she even hired an outside "hit-man". Though I must admit that if *I've* no idea about how to find a contract killer in Central Lancashire, I don't imagine that *she* does, either.'

'Are we going to question her, sir?' Beresford asked.

Woodend laughed. '*Now* who's the one who's eager to pin it on the poor woman?' he asked.

'I didn't mean . . . I never intended to suggest . . .' Beresford mumbled.

'We'll get round to talkin' to Mrs Hawtrey eventually,' Woodend said. 'But first we'll go an' look at where our Mr Pine worked an' played.'

Thirteen

Henry Marlowe stood at the top of the steps outside the main entrance to Police Headquarters. He was wearing his full dress uniform, which, it always seemed to him, succeeded in making him seem both noble and grave.

He looked down at the pack of journalists who had gathered at the foot of the steps. There were around a dozen of them with notebooks in their hands, and though a couple of these worked for local papers, most were from the nationals.

Which was excellent!

And what was even more gratifying was that there were a couple of camera crews in evidence.

Marlowe recollected how furious he'd been with Bradley Pine when Pine had snatched the nomination from right under his nose – and had to force himself not to smile at the memory.

Rather than the defeat he'd taken it to be then, it had all been for the best, he told himself. He could quite see that now.

Because he'd never have got press coverage like this if he'd won the nomination the first time around, whereas Bradley Pine's murder had focussed press attention on the campaign – and given it just about as good a launch pad as any prospective MP could ever hope for.

Marlowe held up his hands – palms outwards – to call for silence from the hacks.

'I find myself in a very difficult position,' he said. 'Whilst, on the one hand, I am both delighted and honoured to announce that I am standing as candidate for this constituency, I am, on the other, mortified that such an announcement should ever have been made necessary. The tragic and brutal murder of Bradley Pine has robbed this community of a talented, caring man who would have striven ceaselessly to improve the conditions of those who had voted for him, and the least I can do is to promise that I, too—'

'Have you resigned from your post?' asked a female voice from the middle of the press pack.

'—if elected, will put the needs of my constituents above all other considerations.'

'Have you resigned?' the woman repeated.

And now several of the other journalists were starting to ask the same question.

'Not, I have not resigned,' Marlowe said, giving into the inevitable. 'I have taken leave of absence, though, if I am elected to parliament, I will, of course, immediately—'

'Should you be wearing that uniform if you're on leave of absence?' the woman interrupted.

'Strictly speaking, I should perhaps have taken it off before I addressed you,' Marlowe conceded, 'but it seemed to me that you would wish to be briefed as soon as possible, and—'

'Given the seriousness of the crime, wouldn't you have served the community better by staying on in your post and leading the investigation yourself?' the woman asked.

The cameras, which had been directed at Marlowe up until this point, had now swung round and were pointed at the reporter.

Who *was* the bloody woman? Marlowe wondered.

She looked like one he'd had some dealings with before, a real chancer called Elizabeth Driver – but Driver had jet black hair, and this woman was a dazzling blonde.

'The senior officer I have left in charge of the case is perfectly capable of conducting an investigation without any guidance from me,' Marlowe said – though even as he was speaking the words he realized they didn't quite seem to be conveying the message he'd intended them to.

'So are you saying a chief constable isn't really necessary at all?' the woman asked, with a kind of naïve innocence.

It *was* Elizabeth Driver, Marlowe realized. Dark or blonde, the poisonous little bitch was back!

'I'm not sure I understand the question, Miss Driver,' he said, stalling for time.

The cameras swung back to Elizabeth Driver, as if they had decided to turn what should have been a coronation into nothing more than a vulgar tennis match.

'If a very important investigation like this one doesn't need a chief constable to guide it, then surely that's even truer of the less significant ones?' Elizabeth Driver amplified. 'In other words, Mr Marlowe, what's the *point* of having a chief constable at all?'

The cameras swung back to a visibly sweating Marlowe.

'My officers can conduct the investigation without my assistance because they are effective,' he said. 'And the reason they're effective is because that's what I *trained* them to be.'

'So if they don't catch the murderer in this case, it will actually be your fault?'

There was more to this politics business than at first met the eye, Marlowe thought. When you were a chief constable, everybody listened to what you had to say in respectful silence. When you became a politician, it seemed you were fair game for anyone who fancied taking a shot at you.

'This is a pointless discussion, Miss Driver, since the murderer *will* be caught,' he said.

'Can you guarantee that?' Elizabeth Driver asked.

'Any crime reporter worth his or *her* own salt surely knows that there's no such thing as a guarantee in a criminal investigation,' Marlowe said, in a tone which he hoped would be withering enough to finally shut the woman up.

'I'm sorry,' Elizabeth Driver said, looking deeply perplexed for the benefit of the camera. 'I thought that I'd just heard you say quite clearly that the murderer *will* be caught.'

'Well, of course, I sincerely believe that he will be,' Marlowe said, feeling as if he were drowning.

'So are you willing to stake your own reputation on the murderer being arrested?' Elizabeth Driver asked.

'Yes, I will stake my reputation on it,' Marlowe promised.

After all, he thought, what else *could* he have said?

Bradley Pine's office in Hawtrey-Pine Holdings had been so neat and efficient that it could have come straight from the Ideal Office Exhibition.

Woodend and Beresford had found no personal photographs there. Nor had there been any magazines – except those relating to the mattress trade. And the two policemen had failed entirely to discover any little notes that Pine might have written to himself about social engagements.

In short, there had been absolutely nothing of the man's personality about the room at all.

His home was providing no clues, either.

It was a modest detached residence in a street of modest detached residences. Pine could easily have afforded a much larger house, but since he seemed to make so little use of the space he already had, why would he have bothered?

The chief inspector and the constable tramped from room to room, looking for insights into the man who had inspired so much hatred that his murderer had not been content to merely end his life, but had violated his corpse as well.

The kitchen had all the pots, pans and electrical equipment necessary to produce a banquet, but the fridge contained no more than a pint of milk and a couple of bottles of white wine.

The living room had perfectly co-ordinated soft furnishings, but they gave off the distinct impression of having been chosen by an interior designer, rather than by the man who would have to live with them.

The bedroom was almost spartan in aspect, and the bedding had been tucked under the mattress with neat hospital corners.

As the two men returned to the hallway at the end of their search, they were both feeling vaguely let down.

Woodend picked up the mail which had been lying on the door mat when they arrived. There was an electricity bill, a couple of circulars, and an invitation to address a Rotary Club lunch, none of which told him anything about the late Bradley Pine.

But that did not necessarily mean that Pine *never* received personal letters, the chief inspector thought.

'When we get back to headquarters, remind me to get somebody to contact the Post Office,' he said.

'The Post Office?' Beresford repeated.

'Aye, I want any mail that Pine receives in the future to end up on my desk,' Woodend explained. He glanced up and down the neutral hallway again. 'So what do you make of all this, Constable?'

'I don't know, sir,' Beresford admitted. 'Mr Pine was either a very secretive man, or a very lonely one.'

'Or both,' Woodend said.

Perhaps it all sprung out of being an orphan. Perhaps the

main lesson that you learned there was never to get attached to other people – or even to personal possessions – because you knew that they could be taken away from you at any moment. Perhaps you came to believe that the only way to survive the experience was to avoid anything at all which could make you vulnerable.

But then what do I know? the chief inspector asked himself.

How could a man who had been brought up in the bosom of a close, loving family even begin to conceive of what it was like to grow up in an institution, as Bradley Pine had?

'Sooner or later, I'm goin' to have to visit this orphanage,' he told Beresford, 'but today I think we'll just settle for a visit to the Widow Hawtrey.'

When Monika Paniatowski had left the Drum and Monkey, she'd gone straight back to her flat.

Once inside the place which she sometimes saw as her refuge – and sometimes as her isolation cell – she made sure the door was locked securely behind her, and drew all the curtains. Then – and without even bothering to undress – she threw herself on to the bed.

She had been planning to go to sleep – partly because she was feeling exhausted, and partly because she hoped that sleep would offer her at least a temporary escape for all that haunted her. But the deep, forgetful oblivion that she craved for eluded her, and instead she found herself wrapped up in a disturbing and troublesome dream.

Fate had come calling on her.

He was tall and thin, and dressed in a monk's habit. He stood at the top of a long staircase which was surrounded by a swirling mist. And she stood at the bottom, looking up at him.

Fate crooked his finger, to indicate she should join him, and though she didn't want to, she knew that she had no choice in the matter.

She put her foot on the first step, and she was a small child again, fatherless, and travelling across war-torn Europe with her mother.

She advanced to the second step, which she found herself sharing with the stepfather who had abused her and the priest who had refused to listen to her cries for help.

Bob Rutter and his blind wife were waiting for her on the third step – and though she knew she should pass straight by them, she found herself stopping to give Bob a passionate kiss.

She pulled away, and advanced to the fourth step, but somehow Bob and Maria had got there before her. Maria was lying down, the wound in her head gushing bright red blood. Bob looked first at his dead wife with compassion, then at his ex-lover with contempt.

Monika rushed on to the next step, where poor DCI Baxter was waiting for her. But she didn't want him. She needed him – but she didn't want him.

'Look at me,' Fate boomed out from above her.

She raised her eyes reluctantly. She was close enough to see his face now – but there was no face to see, only a deep, black nothingness where a head should have been.

'I have been playing games with you,' Fate told her. 'You exist to be the butt of my sick jokes. You have no other purpose.'

'I know that,' she said. 'I think I've always known that.'

'Another step, Monika!' Fate ordered. 'Take another step!'

'I don't want to!'

'Take another step!'

She lifted her leg to mount the next stair, but it wasn't there. The whole staircase had suddenly disappeared, and she was falling . . . falling . . . falling . . .

When she awoke, she was bathed in sweat and her whole body was trembling. With shaky hands she reached for the packet of cigarettes on her bedside table and lit one up.

She thought about her dream. It was comforting – in a way – to believe that everything was predetermined, and that, however miserable you were, there was nothing you could do about it.

It was comforting – but was it true?

There was a part of her which still believed that we make our own choices – and that most of the choices she had made had been disastrously wrong.

Worse yet, she had a growing conviction that she had *known* they were wrong when she'd made them, and had chosen them precisely *because* they were wrong.

It was almost as if she wished to punish herself – as if

something inside her had decided she was unworthy of happiness.

She felt a gaping void in her life – and wondered if she would ever be able to find anything to fill it.

Fourteen

The brass plaque screwed into the gatepost had two fir trees etched on it, and the words 'The Firs' were engraved underneath. There was no number – though the house had obviously originally been designated one – but then neither was there a number on the gateposts of any of the other houses that looked out on to Lawrence Street, Bankside.

Numbers, the owners of these houses seemed to be saying by this sin of omission, were intended for much meaner dwellings than these – terraces clinging desperately to steep hillsides; semi-detacheds which were owned by bank clerks, junior school teachers and others of that ilk. In Bankside, where every house was double-fronted and detached, it would have been the height of vulgarity to give a home a number.

Woodend and Beresford walked up the drive, and when Woodend rang the bell, they heard an elaborate chime reverberate down the hallway on the other side of the front door.

The door was opened by a woman who was in her mid thirties. Had she lived in one of those houses which had numbers, she would probably have been wearing an apron at that time of day, but the owner of The Firs – and, from her manner, that was obviously what she was – was dressed in a smart suit.

'Can I help you?' she asked, in an accent which wasn't *quite* posh, but could have been with just a little more work.

She was a good looking woman as she was now, Woodend thought, his glance taking in her green eyes, pert nose and generous mouth. But when she was in her late teens and early twenties she must have been a *real* stunner – the sort of woman who turns every head in the street and causes drivers to crash into lamp posts.

He held out his warrant card for her to see.

'Mrs Hawtrey?' he asked.

'Yes.'

'We'd like to ask you a few questions, if you don't mind.'

'Is this about poor Bradley Pine?'

'That's right.'

The woman nodded. 'Of course, it would be, wouldn't it? I suppose that after what happened to him, I should have been expecting a call from you, but somehow the idea never did occur to me. Still, I'd be glad to help in any way I can. Won't you come inside?'

The lounge of The Firs was as large as the ground floor and back yard of a terraced house combined. The furnishings were opulent, the fabrics lush, and Beresford – who had had fewer opportunities than Woodend to see how the affluent lived – was most impressed.

Mrs Hawtrey directed the two policemen to a leather sofa, offered them a drink – which Woodend politely refused for both of them – and then sat down in an armchair opposite.

'Having offered you my help, I'm not sure there's much I can tell you that would be of any use to your investigation,' she said. 'In all honesty, I'd have to say that Bradley Pine was no more to me than a business partner.' She paused. 'Actually, it's not strictly accurate to say that he was even that.'

'No?' Woodend said, quizzically.

'No,' Mrs Hawtrey replied. 'I'm entitled to slightly more than half the profits of Hawtrey-Pine Holdings – and my very sharp accountant makes damn sure that I get them – but, other than that, I have virtually nothing to do with the business at all.'

'*Virtually* nothing?' Woodend repeated. 'That's not quite the same as saying *absolutely* nothing, is it?'

'No, I suppose it isn't. But any contact I *do* have with the company is largely of a ceremonial nature.' Mrs Hawtrey laughed lightly. 'I'm a bit like the Queen, in that way.'

'A bit like the Queen? You mean that it's your job to declare things open?' Woodend guessed.

'Exactly, Chief Inspector! The company had a new work-shop built last year – it needed it to meet increased demand for our mattresses – and I was asked to cut the ribbon at the grand opening. Which I dutifully did. Naturally, Bradley Pine, as the managing director, was there too.'

'But other than on occasions like that, you didn't see him at all?'

'No, I can't say that I did.'

'Not even socially?'

'I suppose it depends what you mean by *socially*. We have a number of friends and acquaintances in common, so we did sometimes run into each other at parties and weddings – and when that happened, we'd obviously exchange a few words.'

'What kind of words?'

'Superficial chit-chat, I suppose you'd call it. "How are you doing, Thelma?"; "I'm fine, Bradley. How are you? And, more to the point, where's my profits cheque, ha, ha, ha?" You know – the sort of things that people say to each other when they haven't really got much in common.'

'So, all in all, you wouldn't say that you regarded him as a friend?' Woodend asked.

'Not really, no. He was Alec's friend – had been even before they went into business together – and after Alec died, well . . .'

She let her answer trail off.

'So if Mr Pine had any enemies who'd be more than happy to see him dead, you wouldn't know about them?'

'I'm afraid not.'

Woodend leant forward slightly. 'Can I be frank with you, Mrs Hawtrey?' he asked.

'Of course.'

'It might be a little painful.'

'Go on,' Thelma Hawtrey said, though now there was a hint of caution in her voice.

'I was wonderin' if your husband's death changed your attitude to Mr Pine in any way.'

'What's my attitude to Bradley got to do with his murder?' Thelma Hawtrey asked sharply.

'Probably nothin' at all,' Woodend lied. 'But I'm tryin' to build up a picture of Bradley Pine in my mind, you see, an' it would help me to know how other people – all kinds of other people, includin' yourself – felt about him.'

Thelma Hawtrey considered the matter for some moments.

'If what you're asking me is if I blamed Bradley for Alec's death, then I suppose that, at first, I did,' she admitted.

'But not any more?'

Thelma Hawtrey shook her head. 'No, not any more, Chief Inspector. I've come to accept that Alec was up on that mountainside because that was where he wanted to be. And – by all the accounts I've been given of that terrible, terrible day – Bradley did do everything he possibly could have, in the circumstances, to save Alec's life.'

'So you've no hard feelings towards him at all?'

'Occasionally I do catch myself thinking that Bradley could have done more to try and persuade Alec not to go on the climb, but then I tell myself that I'm not being fair.'

'Do you really?' Woodend asked, sounding unconvinced.

Thelma Hawtrey gave him a look which would have turned a lesser man into a pile of smouldering cinders.

'Yes, I do,' she said emphatically. 'Because if Bradley's to blame, then I'm . . . I'm *doubly* to blame.'

'You mustn't let yourself get upset, Mrs Hawtrey,' Beresford said, sympathetically.

But the warning had come too late, and tears were already beginning to stream down Thelma Hawtrey's face.

'I . . . I could have talked him out of making the climb just as easily as Bradley Pine could,' she said, between sobs.

'Mrs Hawtrey . . .' Beresford said imploringly.

'I could have talked him out of it *more* easily. I . . . I . . . wasn't just his friend, as Bradley was, you see. I was his *wife*. And . . . and he was only doing it because of me.'

'Because of you?' Woodend asked.

'Alec was . . . he was older than me, and sometimes that bothered him a little. He went climbing to prove to me that he was still as strong and vigorous as when we married. But he didn't *have* to prove it. It didn't bother me that he'd become middle-aged. I loved him just the way he was.'

'Can we go now, sir?' Beresford asked urgently.

'Yes,' Woodend replied. 'I think we better had.'

'Well, apart from reducing poor Mrs Hawtrey to a flood of tears, we didn't achieve much in there, did we, sir?' Beresford asked – with just a hint of reproach in his voice – when he and Woodend were out on Lawrence Road again.

'So that's what you think, is it?' Woodend asked, inserting his key into the door lock of the Wolseley. 'That we didn't achieve much?'

'Do you think we *did*?' Beresford asked, shocked.

Woodend got into the car, and reached across to open the front passenger door.

'Mrs Hawtrey was remarkably frank an' open with us, wouldn't you say?' he asked, as Beresford climbed into the passenger seat.

'Yes, sir, I would,' the constable replied, closing his door. 'It must have taken real guts to admit that there are times when she blames herself for her husband's death.'

'That could be it. Or perhaps, by doin' that, she was just tryin' to shift the spotlight,' Woodend said.

'I'm sorry, sir?'

'Maybe she decided that her claim that she bore Bradley Pine no ill will for what had happened simply wouldn't stand up to much more examination, so she started cryin' as a way of switchin' the focus on to herself.'

'She did seem genuinely upset,' Beresford pointed out.

'So would I, if I thought the police were gettin' dangerously close to suspectin' me of murder,' Woodend countered.

'I think you're wrong, sir,' Beresford said.

'An' I'm convinced I'm right,' Woodend said firmly, turning the key in the ignition. 'I'm about to pull off, lad, an' when I do, I want you to turn your head quickly and take a look at Mrs Hawtrey's upstairs windows.'

'Why would I do that?' Beresford wondered.

'Because I'm tellin' you to.'

Woodend slid the Wolseley into gear, and pulled away from the kerb. Beresford turned quickly, as he'd been instructed.

'Well?' Woodend said, as they left The Firs behind them.

'I saw the bedroom curtains twitch,' Beresford admitted.

'Did you, now?' Woodend asked. 'So, far from lyin' on her bed wracked in sobs – as you might have expected her to be – the Widow Hawtrey was, in fact, watchin' to make sure that we were really leavin'.'

'I don't see that proves anything,' Beresford said stubbornly.

Woodend sighed. 'When you've been in this game as long as I have, lad, you develop an instinct for knowin' when the person you're questionin' is either lyin' or tryin' to hide somethin' from you. An' Mrs Hawtrey – for all her tears – was doin' both.'

Fifteen

Bob Rutter was the first member of the team to arrive at the Drum and Monkey for the early evening drink which had become a firmly established tradition during investigations, but Woodend and Beresford were not far behind him.

'Where's Monika?' Rutter asked, looking over Woodend's shoulder. 'Will she be coming later?'

'No,' the chief inspector replied. 'I don't think she will.'

Rutter looked troubled. 'Any reason for that?'

'No *particular* reason, no. She's . . . er . . . well, I suppose she's feelin' a bit off-colour.'

'She looked more than *a bit* off-colour earlier,' Rutter said. 'Do you have any idea why—'

'Leave it, lad,' Woodend interrupted – in a tone which made it clear that it was not so much a suggestion as an order.

'I'm sorry, I didn't mean to—'

'I said *leave it*!'

The chief inspector picked up his freshly-pulled pint and took a healthy swig, though he did not look as if he were enjoying it much.

'If you'd been tap-dancin' on the table when we walked in, I'd have assumed you'd found the spot where Bradley Pine was killed,' he said to Rutter. 'But since you weren't, I'm assumin' you haven't.'

'And you assume right,' Rutter agreed. 'Are *you* getting anywhere from your end, sir?'

'I think I've got a suspect,' Woodend told him, 'though Constable Beresford here is convinced that I'm way off the mark.'

'Thelma Hawtrey?' Rutter guessed.

'Thelma Hawtrey,' Woodend agreed.

He glanced down at his watch, then up at the television which was mounted high on the wall – and only normally switched on when a major football match was being played.

'The local news is just startin',' he called across to the land-lord. 'Would you mind if we watched it?'

'Not at all, Mr Woodend.'

The television warmed up just in time to catch the start of the interview that the chief constable had given to the press earlier in the day.

'You have to admit, he does look good in that dress uniform,' Rutter said grudgingly.

'A tailor's dummy would look good in it,' Woodend replied sourly. 'An', come to think of it, a tailor's dummy would probably make a much better chief constable.'

Marlowe launched himself confidently into his prepared statement, but seemed to be instantly nonplussed by the off-screen female voice demanding to know if he'd resigned.

'It's a grand thing, is a free press,' Woodend said.

Marlowe was doing his best to cut the woman off, but was meeting with little success, and after a few more words had been exchanged, the camera swung round on to her.

'Good God!' Rutter exclaimed. 'That's Elizabeth Driver!'

'I'm surprised that *you're* surprised,' Woodend told him. 'This kind of case is meat an' drink to our Liz.'

'*Yes, I will stake my reputation on it,*' Marlowe was saying, on screen.

Woodend shook his head.

'Silly, silly man,' he said, though he did not look entirely distressed at having heard Marlowe make such a gaffe.

The chief constable disappeared from the screen, and was replaced by a weather man promising a fine few days ahead.

'I wish I'd been there,' Woodend said. 'It was entertainin' enough on the telly, but it must have been real fun in the flesh.'

Beresford drained his pint and stood up. 'Would it be all right if I went now, sir?' he asked.

'Aye, get yourself home, lad,' Woodend told him. 'I'll see you first thing in the mornin'.'

The chief inspector watched the constable leave the bar, then turned to Rutter and said, 'Given that it's a well-known fact the quickest way to promotion is to stay up drinkin' with your boss until the early hours of the mornin', you're probably wonderin' why an ambitious bobby like young Beresford hasn't availed himself of the opportunity when it was offered to him.'

Rutter nodded, but said nothing.

'It puzzled me for a while, an' all,' Woodend continued. 'I was on the point of askin' him about it directly, but then somethin' inside me – a vague uneasy feelin' – made me pull back at the last minute. So instead, I made a few discreet inquiries among the neighbours, an' discovered that his mam was sufferin' from Alzheimer's disease. Well, then everythin' fell into place, didn't it? The reason he's so keen to get home is that though the neighbours are more than willin' to keep an eye on her when he's not there, he feels obliged to spend as much time with her as he possibly can.'

'Is that right?' Rutter asked abstractly, as if his mind were not really on the subject in hand.

'It is right,' Woodend confirmed. 'It's quite refreshin', in this day an' age, to come across a young man who's prepared to put his family obligations above his career, don't you think?'

'Hmm,' Rutter replied.

'You haven't heard a single word I've just said, have you, Bob?' Woodend asked.

'What was that, sir?'

'I thought not! What's botherin' you? Is it somethin' to do with the investigation?'

'Not really,' Rutter admitted. 'Did you notice that Elizabeth Driver has dyed her hair?'

'I couldn't very well have missed it. Although, strictly speakin', it's more of a case of her goin' back to her natural colour than of her dyin' it. If you remember, she was blonde the first time we crossed swords with her, when she was tryin' to bugger up our investigation in the Westbury Manor murder.'

'Don't you think she looks a bit like Monika now?' Rutter asked, and once again, it was clear he hadn't been listening.

'I can't say I noticed the resemblance myself,' Woodend confessed, 'but then *I* wasn't really lookin' for it.'

'I think she does,' Rutter mused. 'In fact, I think she looks a *lot* like Monika.'

It was already dark when Monika Paniatowski reached St Mary's Church, and she found herself wondering if she hadn't – perhaps unconsciously – been waiting for just this cover of darkness before she made her move.

95

'You can analyse yourself too much,' she thought. 'You can analyse yourself to the point of madness.'

She checked over her shoulder to see if anyone was watching her, then pushed the door open and entered the church.

Once inside, confronted by the vastness of the holy cavern, she was suddenly unsure what to do next.

Perhaps she should just stay where she was, at the back of the church, and wait for something – anything – to happen. But was anything *likely* to happen?

Perhaps she should go and sit down in one of the pews. But what would be the point of that? It wasn't as if she was there to *pray*!

'Hello,' said a soft, welcoming voice.

She turned. 'Hello, Fred,' she said.

'What can we do for you this time?' Father Taylor asked. 'Do you want to interrogate us about poor Mr Pine again?'

She hadn't been thinking about the investigation at all, and so the question knocked her completely off-balance.

'No, I . . . I . . .' she began uncertainly. 'I'm off-duty.'

'Ah, so it's not Sergeant Paniatowski I'm speaking to at the moment, but only Monika,' the priest said. 'Am I right?'

'Yes, I suppose you are.'

'And why is Monika here? Has she, perhaps, dropped in for no more than a nice friendly chat?'

'A friendly chat would be nice, Father Fred,' Paniatowski heard herself admitting.

'Here? Or would you be more comfortable in the vestry?'

'I think I'd be more comfortable in the vestry.'

'Then the vestry it shall be.'

They sat facing each other on two rickety chairs, in a room where the walls were draped with choirboys' cassocks which smelled vaguely of adolescent uncertainty.

'What's the secret of happiness?' Paniatowski asked.

Father Taylor smiled. 'I know just what you're expecting me to say,' he told her.

'Do you?'

'You're expecting me to say that the key to true happiness is the love of God.'

'And isn't it – at least as far as you're concerned?'

'Of course it is. In the long term. Looking at the big picture.

But we're only human, Monika, and even though we know that God loves us as we should try to love Him, we still have our own little crises to deal with. And as much as we know that they are of no real significance at all, they can still hurt – they can still cause us to behave badly.'

'Tell me about your crises,' Paniatowski said.

Father Taylor smiled again. 'Is this some kind of test that you're putting me through?' he asked.

'I don't honestly know,' Paniatowski admitted. 'Does it matter if it is?'

'Not really.' The priest cupped both his hands tightly around his left knee. 'I sometimes find it hard to love other people as I know God loves them,' he said. 'Unworthy as I am, in my own self, I still find myself sitting in judgement on them. And though God has forgiven them, I'm not sure that I'll ever be able to do the same. Do you understand that?'

Oh yes, she understood that all right. Understood that she would never forgive her stepfather and the priest who went drinking with him – and that Bob Rutter would never forgive *her*.

'But these feelings do eventually pass,' Father Taylor continued. 'Over time, I come to understand that I have no right to judge, and eventually I find myself seeing these fellow sinners of mine just a little as they must appear in the light of God's all-forgiving eyes.'

'Is there anything else you sometimes have a crisis about?' Paniatowski asked.

'I have just confessed to you the depths of my own unworthiness. Isn't that enough for you?'

'No, it isn't,' Paniatowski said. 'I don't know why it shouldn't be, but it just isn't.'

The priest released his grip on his left knee, and cupped his right one just as tightly.

'Very well,' he said, 'I'll tell you more. Though I believe that my role in life has been chosen for me by God, and though I am usually grateful beyond words that He has selected me, there are times when I'm angry about it, too – when I feel not so much picked *out* as picked *on*.'

'I . . . I don't think I've ever heard a priest talk like this before,' Paniatowski said.

97

'And perhaps you should not be hearing one talk like it now,' Father Taylor replied.

'*When* do you feel angry in that way?' Paniatowski asked, urgently.

'I really do think I've said enough.'

'Please! Tell me!'

The priest shrugged, helplessly.

'A young couple came to see me the other day,' he said. 'The wife had just given birth to a baby boy, and they wanted to arrange a christening. They brought their daughter with them – a beautiful little girl of four. She was holding on to her father's hand, and at one point, I saw her looking up at him. And what a look it was – so full of trust, so full of love. And I knew at that moment – though, at a deeper level I must *always* have known it – that I was doomed never to have a child look at *me* in quite that way.'

And neither will I, Paniatowski thought bitterly. I can never have children – this defective body of mine makes that impossible – so I won't experience it, either.

'There's another look I miss,' the priest said, guiltily. 'The look that a woman like you might give to a man like me, if we were entirely different people in an entirely different place.' He paused for a moment. 'You seem shocked by what I've just said, Monika.'

'No, I—'

'What did you think? That a priest was above such thoughts and yearnings? Did you imagine that the holy oil with which we are anointed was some kind of magic potion which took away our sex drives completely?'

'No, I—'

'It doesn't work like that. If sacrifice involves no pain, then it is no real sacrifice at all. And if we have no weaknesses of our own to battle against, how will we ever understand the struggles against weakness that must be endured by those whom God has put into our care?'

Paniatowski stood up.

'Are you leaving?' Father Taylor asked. 'Have I scandalized you – or merely bored you?'

'No, I'm . . . I haven't . . . it's not either of those things. I'm nervous. That's all. And when I'm nervous, I need to smoke. So that's what I'm doing. I'm going outside for a smoke.'

'You may smoke in here, if you wish, Monika. As you already know, Father Kenyon does.'

'No, I'll . . . I'd prefer to smoke in the open air.'

'And will you be coming back when you've finished your cigarette, Monika?'

'I'm not sure.'

Father Taylor shook his head. 'Which means "no",' he said. 'I think that's the right decision for you to make. I don't think you *should* come back tonight. But you will come back another time, won't you?'

'Yes . . . No . . . I think so, but I'm not making any promises.'

'It doesn't have to be me who you come and see,' Father Taylor said. 'Perhaps it *shouldn't* be me. Come and see Father Kenyon. Or see a priest in another parish, if you'd feel more at ease with that. But please don't stop now, having begun the journey back.'

'There is no journey back!' Paniatowski protested. 'As I told you earlier, I just dropped in for a friendly chat.'

'If you prefer to think of the steps you take as "friendly chats", then there can be no harm in that,' Father Taylor told her. 'But keep on having these chats, Monika, I beg you.'

'I don't need your religion,' Paniatowski said fiercely.

'You're wrong about that,' Father Taylor said, with absolute conviction. 'I see a lot of very unhappy people in my role as parish priest, Monika – but I have to tell you, in all honesty, that you're more in need of spiritual comfort than any of them.'

Sixteen

It was seven thirty-five in the morning, and Henry Marlowe sat in the hospitality suite of the BBC's Manchester studios, preparing himself for a radio interview. He was not alone. Bill Hawes, his constituency agent, was by his side, as he intended to be – especially after the fiasco on police headquarters' steps the previous afternoon – for every waking minute of every day until the election was over.

'Now remember, Henry, old chap, this is *national* radio you're going on,' Hawes cautioned.

'I know that,' Marlowe said, with some irritation.

'The Party bosses in London will be listening to your performance with keen interest,' Hawes pressed on, 'and how well you do may affect whether you're welcomed to Westminster as a cabinet minister in the making or as mere cannon fodder for the voting lobbies.'

'If I ever *do* arrive in Westminster,' Marlowe said bitterly. 'If I'm ever *elected.*'

'You'll be elected,' Hawes said.

His tone was confident and reassuring, but Marlowe took no comfort from that. He was perfectly well aware that Bill Hawes was a professional fixer – a political manipulator – and sounding confident was what he did, whether his candidate of the moment was an easy shoo-in for the seat or didn't have a cat in hell's chance of winning it.

'I don't want to be wrong-footed like I was yesterday,' Marlowe said.

'And you won't be,' Hawes promised. 'I've already thrashed out the ground rules with the man who'll be interviewing you, and he's given me his word that there'll be no mention of the fact that you've left your post in the middle of an important murder inquiry.'

'There shouldn't have been any mention of it at the press

100

conference, either,' Marlowe said, making it sound as if it had all been Hawes' fault.

'But even though you should skirt around the question of the murder investigation, you should still pay tribute to Bradley Pine as your predecessor,' Hawes advised.

'Should I?' Marlowe asked peevishly. 'Why?'

'Because it would seem mean-spirited of you not to.'

Marlowe sighed heavily. 'All right, I'll talk about what a hero Bradley was, and how he—'

'Not that, for Christ's sake!' Hawes said, in a panic. 'Whatever you do, don't talk about what happened on that bloody mountain!'

'But if I'm supposed to be paying tribute to him—'

'Find another way to do it. *Any* other way. Talk about his commitment to the Boy Scouts or old people's homes. Tell lies, if you have to – we can always find some way to gloss over them afterwards – but whatever else you do, don't so much as *mention* Alec Hawtrey's death.'

'Can I ask why?' Marlowe asked, with a show of petulance.

It was Hawes turn to sigh. 'I should have thought it was bloody obvious,' he said.

'Well, it isn't to me,' Marlowe counted. 'Alec Hawtrey was cremated, remember. Nobody can prove anything one way or the other now.'

'Nobody *has* to prove anything,' Hawes said, talking slowly and carefully, as if addressing a particularly slow learner. 'Even a hint of what happened could sink you. Besides, the people involved in the *cover-up* haven't been cremated, have they? They're still around, with their memories fully intact. And we know exactly who they are, don't we, Henry?'

Marlowe shuddered. 'Yes,' he agreed, 'We know who they are.'

When Joan Woodend had been in the early stages of recovering from her heart attack, she'd commented on the irony of the fact that she – who'd always scrupulously eaten her greens – should have been struck down with such an affliction, whilst Charlie – who had lived on a diet of cigarettes, beer and fried food for as long as she'd known him – should still be glowing with health.

101

Joan being Joan, of course, she hadn't actually used a fancy word like 'irony'.

What she'd said was that it was 'bloody funny, and she didn't mean funny ha-ha', that she was the one who was lying in the hospital bed.

And Woodend himself had been forced to agree with her.

What had happened to his wife had shaken the chief inspector to the core, but had made absolutely no difference at all to the way he led his own life, and at about the time that Henry Marlowe was being questioned on the radio by a suitably deferential interviewer, he himself was tucking into a subsidized fry-up in the Whitebridge police canteen.

The other two people at the table had chosen not to join him in playing Russian Roulette with their arteries. Beresford – who had cooked his mother's breakfast before he left home, and then sat there watching her, to make sure she ate it – had settled for a poached egg on toast. Paniatowski had said she only wanted an orange juice – and didn't seem to even have the stomach for that.

Woodend mopped his egg yolk with a piece of fried bread, and popped it into his mouth.

'Here's the plan for this mornin',' he told Beresford. 'Monika an' me will be piecin' together everythin' we can about Thelma Hawtrey's friends an' relations, an' what I want you to do, lad, is to approach the same question – but from a different angle.'

'What angle would that be, sir?' the constable asked.

'Take yourself off to Hawtrey an' Pine Holdings again. I want to know how Thelma behaved when she paid her occasional visits to the factory. Was she on more or less friendly terms with Pine, as she claims – or did she look at him like she wanted him dead?'

'I still think you're wrong about her, sir,' Beresford said.

'I know you do,' Woodend agreed. 'But I'm beginnin' to suspect that's probably because you fancy her.'

'Fancy her!' Beresford repeated, shocked.

'There's no shame in it,' Woodend told him. 'None of us are immune to the call of the flesh.'

'But she's an *old woman!*' Beresford said, clearly horrified.

102

'My guess is that she's somewhere in her mid-thirties,' Woodend pointed out.

'Yes,' Beresford agreed. 'That's what I said.'

Woodend cut up his remaining bacon rind into bite-sized pieces, speared one, and aimed it at his mouth.

'If *she's* old, what does that make me?' he asked.

'It's different for you, sir,' Beresford said.

'Is it? How?'

'You're a man.'

'Aye, an' apparently a very *ancient* one.'

'I didn't mean to suggest—' Beresford began.

'Go an' do your job, lad,' Woodend interrupted him. 'An' if they've carted me off to the mortuary by the time you get back, you can always hand your report in to Sergeant Paniatowski, can't you?'

Father Taylor entered the parishioner's side of the confessional, sat down heavily, and turned his head towards the grille.

'Bless me, Father, for I have sinned,' he said. 'It is three days since my last confession.'

'Which is not an excessive amount of time,' said Father Kenyon mildly, from the other side of the grille.

'I have been guilty of impure thoughts and impure feelings.'

'Go on.'

'A woman came to the church— '

'That would be Sergeant Paniatowski, would it?'

'Yes, it was her. I saw at once that she was a lost soul. I wanted to lead her back to the light.'

'That is why God has put us here on this earth. That is why we serve Him as His priests.'

'But somehow that no longer seems important to me. I want to *know* her – in all senses of the word – and what she chooses to believe – or chooses not to believe – doesn't matter to me.'

'You must *make* it matter to you,' Father Kenyon said sternly. 'It is your duty.'

'I know that, and I have been trying, Father. I can't tell you how much I've tried. But I have failed.'

'Then you must try even harder. You say you have sinned, and I agree with you. But do you repent those sins?'

103

'I . . . I want to.'

'We both know that is not good enough,' Father Kenyon said heavily.

'Yes,' Father Taylor agreed. 'We both know that.'

Seventeen

It wasn't so much that there was one law for the rich and another for the poor, Bob Rutter thought, as that the poor let things happen *to* them, whereas the rich *made* the things happen.

The origin of this socio-political flight of fancy of his was a small patch of land in one of the more affluent suburbs of Whitebridge, beside which he was now standing. Once, the land had housed a tumbledown cottage, surrounded by countryside. But as Whitebridge had expanded in response to the newly emerging middle class's hunger for quality double-fronted houses, the countryside had been gobbled up, until finally it was no more.

The developers had tried to buy the cottage, but when the cranky old man who lived in it had refused to sell, they'd had no choice but to build around it. True, they'd done the best they could, contriving to construct in such a way that it was only through their back windows that the nearest new residents would catch sight of the bucolic slum, but the cottage had still been generally regarded as something of a blot on the newly urbanized landscape.

Then the old man had died and left the cottage to a nephew, who immediately put it on the market. Several construction companies made a bid for it, and, in a less affluent part of town, one of them would undoubtedly have succeeded in buying it. But the residents here had no wish to see a new building replace the old one, and – since they were the sort of people who *made* things happen – they had clubbed together and put in a bid of their own.

And this was the result – a green area with trees, bushes and a few flower beds, which was too small to be called a park, but just about large enough to bear the name of 'gardens' without seeming too ridiculous.

The residents had been so proud of their initiative that they had put up a plaque to commemorate it.

Lower Bankside Gardens
Purchased by the Residents' Association
for the benefit of all

Whilst he approved of their decision to buy the land, Rutter found the plaque rather smug and self-congratulatory, and there was one small – and admittedly unworthy – part of him which was half-hoping that this was the spot on which Bradley Pine met his end.

But it was not to be. The grass was undisturbed, the spring flowers bloomed unbowed – and there was no dark staining of the earth to suggest that it was here that Pine's blood had drained away.

He had all but completed his search when he heard an angry voice say, 'This is private property, you know!'

Rutter turned. He was being addressed by an old man with a red face and a huge, white, walrus moustache.

'Can't you read?' the man demanded.

Rutter looked down at the plaque again. 'It says "for the benefit of all",' he pointed out.

'Yes, but that doesn't mean *you!*' the man said. 'It means the residents. This is an *exclusive* estate, you know.'

'So I believe,' Rutter replied. 'But, you see, sir, I'm a police officer, and we can go where we like – within reason, of course.'

'Got a warrant card?' the old man asked, still not quite willing to allow his outrage to go into retreat.

Rutter produced his card, and held it out.

'Inspector, eh?' the old man said. He held out his hand. 'I'm Binsley Morrisson.'

Rutter took the hand. 'Pleased to meet you, sir.'

'Sorry to have got the wrong idea,' Morrisson said. 'Should have been able to tell from the way that you're dressed that you weren't part of the usual riff-raff that drifts in here and acts like it owns the place.'

Morrisson looked around him, and seemed somewhat disappointed to discover that there were no shady characters around at that moment who could prove his point.

'I wanted to put a wall right around the entire estate, you know,' he continued.

'Did you indeed?'

'I most certainly did. But the Residents' Association wanted nothing at all to do with the idea. Came up with some damn silly excuse about it contravening the planning regulations.'

'As a matter of fact, it probably—' Rutter began.

'So I've been forced to take on the responsibility for the security of the area myself,' Morrisson said. He reached into his pocket, and pulled out a leather notebook. 'It's all in here, you know.'

'*What's* all in there?' Rutter wondered.

'My notes. Every time I see a suspicious character wandering around, I jot down his description. Used to take those descriptions straight to the local police station, but I could see the desk sergeant wasn't really interested. I'm sorry to have to say this about one of your lesser colleagues, Inspector, but the man seems to have no initiative at all.'

Rutter was finding it hard to keep his face straight.

'Maybe all these people you're worried about had a perfectly legitimate reason for being in the area,' he suggested.

'Like what?'

'Well, for example, they could have been tradesmen – plumbers or electricians.'

'Some of them did have bags that could have contained tools,' Morrisson admitted.

'Well, there you are then.'

'Burglars need tools, don't they? And crooks don't dress up in striped jerseys, and carry sacks on their backs labelled "Swag". They pretend to be perfectly ordinary chaps. I'd have thought, *as a policeman*, you'd have known that.'

'Burglary's not really one of my specialities,' said Rutter, who was now finding it almost impossible to keep his grin in check.

'And that's precisely the problem,' Morrisson said triumphantly, as if Rutter had proved his case for him. 'The police simply don't know what's going on. But I do, and when things do go seriously wrong – as they're bound to do – that sergeant down at the local station will suddenly be very grateful for all the details I've got jotted down in my notebook.'

107

'Do you confine yourself to descriptions of people, or do you notice cars as well?' Rutter asked idly.

'Well, of course I notice cars,' the old man said. 'Criminals are *allowed* to drive cars – more's the pity.'

Was it possible, Rutter wondered, was it just vaguely possible that . . . ?

'How often do you go out on patrol?' he asked.

'Never thought of what I do as going out on patrol,' Morrisson said. 'But you're damn right – that's exactly what I do.'

'How often?' Rutter asked patiently.

'I'm out for the greater part of the day. To tell you the truth, Inspector, my lady wife gets nervous if I'm in the house for too long at a time.'

'And do you patrol at night?'

'Usually. I like to do a final tour before I have my cup of Horlicks and retire for the night.'

'Were you out the night before last – in the fog?'

'I most certainly was. You probably wouldn't know this – not being a specialist in burglary – but criminals like the fog. They think it means they can move about without being spotted.' Morrisson puffed out his chest. 'But, of course, they haven't reckoned on me.'

'There can't have been many people, or cars for that matter, about on a night like that.'

'There weren't. Very few, in fact. But it only takes one bad apple, as the old saying goes.'

'I wonder if you happened to notice a green car, some time between nine and ten o'clock,' Rutter said.

'I saw a green *Ford Cortina*, if that's what you're asking about,' the old man said.

'At what time?'

'Couldn't say precisely. I'd guess it was some time between nine and ten o'clock.'

He's throwing my own estimate back at me, Rutter thought.

'Could it have been a little earlier – or a little later – than that, do you think?' he asked.

'Suppose so,' Morrisson admitted reluctantly.

'What are the chances that this green Cortina was being driven by one of your neighbours?'

'No chance at all.'

'How can you be so sure?'

'Make it my business to know what everybody who lives in this area drives. Nobody owns a Cortina.'

The right kind of car, spotted at roughly the right time! Bingo! Rutter thought.

'Cortinas are normally purchased by travelling salesmen and people of that ilk,' the old man continued, dismissively. 'No one from Bankside would be seen dead in one.'

But maybe Bradley Pine *had* been.

'Tell me more about it,' Rutter said.

'Not much more to tell. It was going slowly, but I expect that was because of the fog.'

'How many people were there in it?'

'Only the driver.'

'Could you describe him to me?'

'Afraid not. I only saw him from a distance, and it *was* foggy. He wasn't a midget, but he wasn't a giant, either, if that's any help.'

'Could the driver have been a woman?'

The old man sighed. 'I suppose so. In my time, ladies didn't drive, but anything's possible, these days.'

'You didn't happen to take down the registration, did you?' Rutter asked hopefully.

'Not all of it – fog, again – but I did manage the last part.' Morrisson opened his notebook and flicked through a few pages. 'Here it is. 732 B. Is that any help to you?'

It was a perfect match with Pine's car, Rutter thought, and whilst it was just possible that there was another green Cortina around with the same end-designation, it didn't seem at all likely.

'Could you tell me where the Cortina was coming from, and where it was going to?' he asked.

'It was coming from the centre of town,' the old man said, pointing vaguely in the direction of the railway station. 'And it was heading that way,' he continued, indicating the gently sloping hill which was all that separated Lower Bankside from *Upper* Bankside.

Eighteen

Beresford stood at the main gate of Hawtrey and Pine Holdings, trying to decide not only *who* he should ask if it was true that Mrs Hawtrey would have liked to see Bradley Pine dead, but also *how* he should phrase the question.

'Back again, lad?' asked a voice.

Beresford turned, and saw old Harry Ramsbotham standing there.

'That's right, I'm back,' he agreed.

The old man had a string bag in his hand which contained a packet of sugar and a bottle of milk, and now he held it up for Beresford's inspection, as if it were some sort of prize.

'I've just been doin' my shoppin',' he announced.

'Is that right?' Beresford asked.

'Most people aren't allowed to nip out without permission durin' the course of the workin' day,' Harry continued, 'but I've been doin' it for close on to fifty years now.'

'That is a long time,' Beresford said, and he was thinking, *How could* anybody *do* anything *for nearly* fifty *years?*

'It was old Mr Hawtrey who first said that it would be all right, an' nobody's told me anythin' different since. It's a bit of a tradition, you see, and even Mr Pine didn't want to go against tradition.'

'I can imagine he wouldn't,' said Beresford, who was starting to get some insight into what made the old man tick.

'Well, now I've been out an' got the makin's of it, I might as well offer you a brew,' Harry said.

'I'm not sure I can—' Beresford began.

'Come on!' the old man urged. 'You can't start work without a cup of tea inside you.'

Perhaps he was right, Beresford thought. And perhaps, over

the brew, he might learn something which would put his investigation into gear.

Beresford followed Harry down the steep concrete steps which led to the basement boiler room.

'I started workin' down here in 1915,' the old man said. 'Course, they didn't put me in charge of the whole thing right away – I was only a lad at the time – but my immediate boss died in 1924, an', right away, old Mr Hawtrey called me up to the office to see him.'

Some sort of response was obviously expected.

'Did he, indeed?' Beresford asked.

'*Called me up to his office,*' Harry repeated. 'An' there's not many workin' men from this factory who can say they've been in there.'

'I imagine not.'

'Well, Mr Hawtrey didn't ask me to sit down – I was in my workin' clothes, so that was perfectly understandable – but he did offer me a cigarette. Then, when we'd both lit up, he asked me if I thought I could handle the job of lookin' after the boilers on my own. I told him I thought I could, an' he said that were grand, an' that in future he'd be payin' me ten shillings a week more. Well, to be honest with you, I'd have taken the job for the same money I'd been earnin' before, but, of course, I didn't tell old Mr Hawtrey that.'

'Of course you didn't,' Beresford agreed.

They had reached the foot of the stairs, and were facing a large steel door, which was closed.

'It's locked, but I've got my own key to it,' Harry said complacently, reaching into his pocket.

The boilers were not half as large or impressive as Beresford – who was no great technical brain – had been expecting.

'They're all oil-fired these days,' Harry said, noticing the surprised expression on his face. 'It wasn't like that when I first started workin' here. Then, all the boilers ran off coke.'

'It must have been hard work, stoking them.'

'It was. You could lose pounds in sweat in this job. But still, I was sorry to see them old boilers go. I'd got to know them, an' all their little quirks, you see, whereas these new boilers have got no personality at all.'

He could almost have been talking about his last two bosses – Hawtrey and Pine – Beresford thought to himself.

Harry sighed, regretfully. 'Yes, I was sorry to see them boilers finally go, but I suppose we all have to move with the times, don't we? An' one thing you *do* have to say about these new boilers is that they do leave me a bit of space for myself.'

Harry had made good use of his space, Beresford thought. There were two battered armchairs, which stood on an off-cut of carpet in a flower pattern which had been fashionable just after the War. There was a kitchen table, on which had been placed a spirit stove, a kettle, teapot and two large enamel mugs. And there was a small black-and-white television, with a spider's web of wire which served as an aerial, resting on a packing case.

But it was the far wall which was most surprising. Shelves ran along it at waist height, and on those shelves were bits of junk which seemed to be vaguely connected with mattress manufacturing. Above the shelves, reaching almost to the ceiling, Harry had pasted a montage of newspaper clippings, publicity handouts and catalogue covers.

'I call it my museum,' Harry said proudly, seeing it had caught Beresford's attention. 'The Museum of the Mattress. When I've made us a brew, I'll show it to you.'

The old man pumped the spirit stove on the table, lit it, and then perched the kettle on top.

'Do you see much of Mrs Hawtrey these days?' Beresford asked, trying to sound casual.

'Not a lot.' Harry replied. 'She was always here, of course, when she worked in the typin' pool, but she's hardly set foot in the place since she married the boss – an' that must have been a good fifteen years ago now.'

The kettle came to the boil, and Harry Ramsbotham poured the hot water into the teapot.

'Still, she must have been a few times,' Beresford said. 'Like when she opened the new workshop.'

'That's right, she was here for that,' Harry agreed. 'Well, I suppose we might as well take a look at my museum while the tea's brewin'.'

Reluctantly, Beresford rose to his feet and allowed himself to be led over to the shelves.

112

Harry picked a wad of cotton-packing, which must once have been white, but had now gone brown with age.

'This was the flock we used for stuffin' the mattresses when I first joined the company,' he said. 'We bought it in big bales, from one of the mills. Of course, that mill, like most of the others, has closed down now.'

'Very interesting,' Beresford said.

Harry replaced the wadding reverentially on the shelf, and picked up a coil of metal.

'And this is one of the first springs we used. Looks a bit clumsy now, doesn't it? But it was very advanced for its time.'

'When Mrs Hawtrey opened the new workshop, how did she and Mr Pine seem to be getting on?' Beresford asked.

'That's Mr Hawtrey and the *first* Mrs Hawtrey on their weddin' day,' Harry said, pointing to a photograph in the middle of one of the faded newspaper articles that he'd pasted to the wall. 'An' that's old Mr Hawtrey – Mr Alec's father – standin' next to them.'

The two men in the picture were wearing morning suits, and the bride was dressed in an elaborate lace and silk gown. They stood as stiff as tailor's dummies, and though they were all probably very happy on this special day, the smile the photographer had demanded from them made them look almost manic.

His mother and father had been married at around the same time, Beresford thought, and though these people were dressed in a far grander style than his parents had been, he was still reminded of the wedding photographs which sat on the sideboard at home. Looking at his mother now – with that dead expression in her eyes – it was almost impossible to believe that she had once been young and vital, had probably danced with gay abandon and treated life as if it were a joy to experience.

'Have I lost you, lad?' Harry asked.

'What?' Beresford said, startled.

'This is an article about the house that the Hawtreys moved into just after they married. Caused quite a stir at the time, it did. To be honest with you, most people didn't care for it at all.'

Beresford could quite see why it hadn't been exactly popular. Whitebridge folk tended to be quite conventional when it came to matters of design – and there was nothing at all conventional about this house. For a start, it was three storeys high, rather than the normal two. Then there was the fact that there was a veranda running along the front. (Why, people must have asked when they saw it, would anybody want a veranda in *Lancashire*?) And as if all that were not enough to cause outrage, there was a terrace running the entire length of the first floor, supported by eight thick pillars.

'They had an architect design it for them, but most of the ideas about how it should look came from Mrs Hawtrey,' Harry said.

'How did they feel when they learned that most people didn't like it?' Beresford asked.

'I don't know how Mrs Hawtrey felt, but Mr Hawtrey didn't really care. It was enough for him that it was what his wife wanted – an' he'd have done anythin' for her in them days.'

'Where is it?' Beresford asked, allowing his natural curiosity to divert him from the line of questioning he had been intending to persue. 'I know most places in Whitebridge, but I don't think I've ever seen it.'

'Ee, lad, it's long gone. The council slapped a compulsory purchase order on it, an' pulled it down. It stood in the way of redevelopment, you see, an' people's dreams don't matter to the planners. The one good thing about the whole sorry business was that the first Mrs Hawtrey wasn't here to see it bein' pulled down, because it would have broken her heart. But then, I suppose, her heart had *already* been broken, because she'd got divorced an' moved away by then.'

'That's certainly all very interesting,' Beresford said, 'but what I was wondering was—'

'Here's an article on Mr an' Mrs Hawtreys first holiday abroad. It wouldn't be exactly what you'd call news these days, would it?'

'No, it—'

'But back then, you see, most folk had been no further than Blackpool, so it had somethin' of a novelty about it.'

The picture in this article showed the Hawtreys standing on a beach, with camels in the background. They had their children with them, a boy of about thirteen and a girl a couple of years younger. The girl looked happy enough, but the boy had the worried look of someone with a lot on his mind.

'An' over here's an article on Mr Hawtrey's funeral,' Harry said, pointing out a page of newspaper which – being more recent – had yellowed less than most of the others. 'That's the *second* Mrs Hawtrey by the grave.'

'She's standing quite close to Mr Pine, but she's not really looking at him, is she?' Beresford asked.

'You don't have much interest in my museum, do you, lad?' Harry asked, in a tone which was mid-way between anger and sadness.

'Yes, I do,' Beresford protested. 'Honestly, I do!'

'I may be gettin' old, but I'm still a long way from senile – an' I can see what you're after,' Harry said.

'I promise you, I'm not—'

'My old dad never taught me much, but one thing he always said is that you should hold your employer in respect,' Harry said. '"It's the wages they pay you that puts food on the table an' keeps a roof over your head," he told me.'

'All I want to know is how Mrs Hawtrey and Mr Pine got on after Mr Hawtrey's death,' Beresford protested.

'An' do you know what else my old dad said?'

'No.'

'He said, "It doesn't matter what your boss does in his private life – it's not your place to judge him, an' it's not your place to criticize him." There's not many people still hold them views these days, but I do.'

'Mr Pine's dead,' Beresford pointed out.

'So he is, but that still doesn't give me licence to tear his good name to shreds. Anyway, I thought it was Mrs Hawtrey you were more interested in.'

'Yes, it is, but—'

'Now that Mr Pine *is* dead, she's the only boss I've got. That may have slipped your attention, but it certainly hasn't slipped mine.'

'I didn't mean to offend you, Harry,' Beresford said, remorsefully. 'I honestly didn't.'

'Didn't you?' the old man countered. 'Well, you succeeded, whether or not. I think you should go now – an' I'd rather you didn't come again.'

Nineteen

The public service bus did not actually pass *through* Upper
Bankside – the residents would not have wanted their living
space polluted by the intrusion of mass transportation – but it
did skirt the area, and there was a bus stop just beyond the
end of Lawrence Road, at which a number of women in cheap
coats and thick stockings were just alighting.

Woodend, sitting behind the wheel of his Wolseley, turned
to Paniatowski, who was in the passenger seat.

'Of course, what the women who reside around here – I
beg your pardon, what the *ladies* who reside around here –
would really like to have would be *live-in* servants,' he said.
'An' there'd certainly be plenty of space to accommodate them
in those big double-fronted houses. But since the War, you
can't get anybody to do that kind of job, however much you're
willin' to pay, so they've just had to settle for a daily visit
from the charwomen.'

'You can't be sure that Thelma Hawtrey has one though,
can you?' Paniatowski pointed out, as the women crossed the
street and began to walk down Lawrence Road.

'I'd be most surprised if she didn't,' Woodend replied. 'It'd
be seen as lettin' the side down to actually do any of your
own cleanin' yourself. Besides, I've had a look at the finger-
nails on the woman, an' you don't keep your nails lookin' like
that if you do any bloody work.'

He eased the car into gear, and began to drive slowly down
Lawrence Road. The ragged column of charwomen was already
beginning to thin out, as some of its number peeled off and made
their way up the driveways to one or other of the big houses.

'We won't know which of them "does" for Mrs Hawtrey
until she reaches the house, so you'll have to move a bit
sharpish and catch her up before she reaches the front door,'
Woodend said.

'What if she doesn't want to come with us?' Paniatowski asked. 'I mean, it's not as if we're arresting her, is it?'

'True,' Woodend agreed. 'So you'll just have to use your powers of persuasion, won't you?'

'And if she says she can't be late for work?'

'Tell her she's nothing to worry about, because we'll ring Mrs Hawtrey up, an' explain that she's helpin' us with our inquiries.'

'And will we really do that?'

'Really do what?'

'Ring up Mrs Hawtrey?'

'I don't see why we shouldn't.'

'Don't you?' Paniatowski asked. 'Suppose we *do* ring her up and tell her what's going on. What do you think is the first thing that Mrs Hawtrey will do when the charwoman does eventually arrive on her doorstep?'

'I imagine she'll ask her exactly what the police wanted to question her about.'

'And the charwoman will tell her that what we've been asking questions about is *her*.'

'Yes, she will.'

'And doesn't that bother you?'

'Not a lot.'

'You're not worried that when Mrs Hawtrey learns we're taking such a close interest in her, she might get rattled?'

'On the contrary,' Woodend said. 'Getting rattled is exactly what I *want* her to do.'

The nearest café to Upper Bankside – and it was not *that* near, because Banksiders would never demean themselves by entering such an establishment – was called The Cosy Corner. It had formica-topped tables, a linoleum floor, and a large metal urn which gurgled constantly and occasionally let loose a jet of steam. It was just the sort of place you might expect to find a woman in the heavy brown coat and knitted woollen hat, but the woman in question certainly didn't seem very happy to be there at that particular moment.

'I'd normally like nothin' better than to be sittin' in a nice café, sippin' a nice hot cup of tea,' she explained to Woodend and Paniatowski, 'but I do have a job to do, you know – an' I am paid by the *hour*.'

Woodend reached into his pocket, pulled out a ten shilling note, and laid it on the table.

'That should more than cover the time you'll lose, shouldn't it, Mrs Chubb?' he asked.

'I suppose so,' the woman agreed. 'But there's other things to be taken into consideration as well, aren't there?'

'Such as?'

'I don't want to get anybody in trouble.'

'Why should you even think that you would?'

'Well, you're the police, aren't you?'

'So we are,' Woodend agreed. 'But the questions we want to ask you are very innocent ones, an' if you feel uncomfortable about answerin' any of them, you don't have to. All right?'

'All right,' Mrs Chubb agreed, though she still sounded dubious about the whole idea.

'How long have you been working for Mrs Hawtrey?'

'Must be a good ten years now.'

'Which means that you were working for her long before her husband was killed?'

'Yes, I was.'

'How did she take his death?' Woodend wondered.

'How would you expect her to take it? She was absolutely devastated, as anybody in her place would be.'

'But I expect her family were very supportive of her in her time of need,' Paniatowski said.

'Her family?' Mrs Chubb repeated.

'Yes.'

'She hasn't got no family.'

'None?' Woodend asked.

'None at all.'

'That's very unusual, isn't it?'

'I suppose it is, if you don't happen to know the circumstances.'

'An' what *are* the circumstances, in her case?'

'Accordin' to what Mrs Hawtrey told me once, her family were big landowners somewhere down south, an' when her mum an' dad were killed in a tragic motorin' accident, the rest of the family – all the uncles an' aunts an' cousins – got together an' grabbed the land for themselves. Well, she couldn't stand to be anywhere near them after that happened, could she? So she came up north to start a new life for herself.'

'You don't sound as if you entirely believe the story,' Monika Paniatowski said.

'Well, I do and I don't, if you see what I mean,' Mrs Chubb replied. 'I believe her mum an' dad were killed, an' that the relatives grabbed what they could – because that's what *some* relatives do. My Auntie Betty had this lovely grandfather clock, which she'd definitely promised to me, but she'd no sooner passed on than my cousin, Vera—'

'What part *don't* you believe?' Paniatowski interrupted.

'The bit about them bein' big landowners.'

'And *why* don't you believe it?'

'Because I've worked for a lot of posh folk in my time, an' I could tell that Mrs Hawtrey hadn't been posh for that long.'

'So she didn't have any relatives to give her the support she needed,' Paniatowski said. 'Which means, I suppose, that she just had to rely on her friends instead.'

'Didn't have many of them, neither.'

'And why was that?'

'Lots of reasons,' Mrs Chubb said evasively.

'Tell me a few of them,' Paniatowski suggested.

'Well, like I may have hinted earlier, she wasn't quite posh enough for some of her neighbours.'

'What else?'

'I did hear that most of Mr Hawtrey's old friends wouldn't have anythin' to do with him after he married her. They're *Catholic*, you see,' Mrs Chubb said, mouthing the word 'Catholic' with much the same reverential dread as some women mouthed the word 'cancer'. 'They don't believe in divorce, you know. They're old-fashioned in that way.'

'So the neighbouring ladies didn't have much to do with her, and neither did her husband's old friends, but did she have any male friends of her own?' Paniatowski asked.

'That Mr Pine, the one who got himself murdered—' Mrs Chubb stopped suddenly. 'Hang on, is that what this is all about?'

'Don't go worryin' your head over that,' Woodend told her. 'Just carry on with what you were sayin'.'

'That Mr Pine came round to the house a few times in the first couple of weeks after Mr Hawtrey's funeral, but you could tell he wasn't really welcome, an' in the end, the visits stopped.'

'How could you tell he wasn't really welcome in the house?' Woodend wondered.

'Well, Mrs Hawtrey was very cold an' distant with him. Not that you can altogether blame her – he was with her husband when he died, you see, an' maybe he could have done more to save him.'

'Where did you get that idea from, Mrs Chubb?' Paniatowski asked. 'Did it come from Mrs Hawtrey?'

'What idea are you talkin' about?'

'The idea that maybe Mr Pine could have done more to save Mr Hawtrey?'

'No, I can't say I really got it from her,' Mrs Chubb said, slightly unconvincingly. 'It was more just what I was thinking myself.'

'You didn't really answer the question about Mrs Hawtrey's male friends,' Paniatowski pointed out. '*Does* she have any?'

'Not really,' Mrs Chubb replied – just a little too quickly.

'Lyin' to the police is a serious matter, you know,' Woodend said, in his gravest and most official voice.

'I'm not lyin'!' Mrs Chubb protested.

'Of course you're not. I know that. But maybe you're not quite telling us the *whole* truth?' Paniatowski suggested, gently.

'I don't actually *know* anythin',' Mrs Chubb told her, reluctantly.

'But you have *guessed* something?'

Mrs Chubb shrugged. 'I notice things.'

'Like what?'

'When I leave that house of an afternoon, it's in a perfect condition. Everythin's neat an' tidy, an' you could eat your dinner right out of the toilet bowl, if you were so inclined.'

'I'm sure you could.'

'So if anythin's changed between me leavin' the house one day an' comin' back the next, I notice it.'

'Would you care to give us an example?'

'There's always brown ale in the fridge, even though Mrs Hawtrey doesn't much like the taste of it herself – an' sometimes, I'll find empty bottles in the rubbish bin.'

'So she's had a visitor who drinks brown ale, and you think that must mean that's he's a man?' Woodend asked.

'Of course it's a man!' Mrs Chubb said scornfully. 'It's a man's drink, isn't it?' She turned to Paniatowski. 'How many women do you know who drink brown ale?'

'None that I can think of,' Paniatowski admitted.

'Well, exactly!' Mrs Chubb said triumphantly. 'And that's not all he drinks. He doesn't say no to a glass or two of wine, either.'

'How do you know that?'

'Mrs Hawtrey likes the odd tipple herself – not that there's anythin' wrong with that – and most mornin's I'll find a wine glass sittin' on the coffee table with her lipstick all around the rim.'

'Go on,' Woodend encouraged.

'But some nights, there's been *two* glasses used – an' she's washed up the second one.'

'How can you tell?' Woodend wondered.

Mrs Chubb turned to Paniatowski again.

'Men!' she said, with mild contempt.

'Men!' Paniatowski agreed.

'There's an art to washin' up, which is unknown to *all* men an' *some* women,' Mrs Chubb told Woodend, 'and Mrs Hawtrey is one of them women who doesn't know how to do it properly. How can I tell! What a question to even have to ask me!'

'What a question,' Paniatowski echoed obediently.

'I can tell because the glasses that she *does* wash up are always left streaky,' Mrs Chubb told Woodend.

'Anythin' else?' the chief inspector asked.

'He smokes.'

'How do you know? Doesn't *she* smoke?'

'Of course she does. *Everybody* smokes! But she smokes filter-tipped, and his are untipped. Mrs Hawtrey puts *his* fag ends in the bin, but when I'm emptyin' it out, I can't help noticin' them.'

I bet there's not much you can't help noticin', you nosy old bat, Woodend thought.

'Is that it?' he asked.

'That's it,' Mrs Chubb agreed.

'Are you sure?'

The charwoman fidgeted in her seat. 'Well, there is one more thing,' she admitted, 'but it's a bit personal, if you see what I mean, an' I don't like to talk about it.'

'You can say anythin' at all – however personal – to us,' Woodend assured her. 'We're a bit like doctors, in that way.'

'Or priests,' Paniatowski added.

'Well, Mrs Hawtrey doesn't really do anythin' at all around the house,' Mrs Chubb said. 'Even the simplest little job – one that she could finish in a minute, while she's waitin' for the kettle to boil – she leaves for me to do in the mornin'.' She paused. 'Not that I'm complain' in any way, shape or form,' she added hastily. 'If she did it all herself, she wouldn't need me.'

'Understood,' Woodend said.

'But every now an' then, she does strip down the bed. She doesn't actually put the new sheets on – that would be too much to ask of her – but she takes the dirty sheets an' puts them in the washin' machine, so they're already half-way through their cycle by the time I arrive. An' why do you think she does that?'

'Because she doesn't want you to see that the sheets are stained?' Paniatowski guessed. 'Because she doesn't want you to know that she hasn't spent the night alone.'

Mrs Chubb jutted out her chin in a prim and righteous manner. 'What people do in their own homes is their own business,' she said. 'But I still think they could have some standards.'

Twenty

Rutter spread the map of the Whitebridge area across the table in the public bar of the Drum and Monkey.

'The green Ford Cortina was spotted here,' he said, indicating a point in Lower Bankside. 'It's unfortunate that my witness can't say for sure exactly what time he saw it – and doesn't know who was driving it – but in my mind there's no doubt at all that it was Pine's car.'

'Nor in mine, either,' Woodend agreed.

'Now, the car was coming from the centre of town, which is here, and the body was found here, on the dual carriageway,' Rutter continued, pointing to two spots on the map. 'Does the fact that it was ever in Bankside make any sense to either of you?'

'No, it doesn't,' Paniatowski said. 'If it was the killer behind the wheel, and he was taking Pine's body to be dumped, why would he go that way? The quickest route out to the dual carriageway from the centre of town is in completely the opposite direction.'

'And if Pine himself was driving the car, what was he doing going towards Upper Bankside?' Rutter wondered. 'We know from what the charwoman said that his relations with Mrs Hawtrey have been distinctly chilly since her husband's death, so why would he even be thinking of calling on her?'

'No reason at all,' Woodend said. 'But I can think of somebody else who might have had a very good reason for payin' her a visit.'

'Her lover?' Paniatowski asked.

'That's right,' Woodend said. 'Her wine-drinking, untipped-cigarette-smoking, bed-staining lover.'

He paused, to take a drag on his own untipped cigarette.

'I can see two possible ways that this whole thing could have developed,' he continued. 'The first is that Thelma

Hawtrey makes the decision to take a lover simply because she's lonely, or because she's missin' the sex. But later, when the affair's been goin' on for some time, she suddenly realizes that she can use this lover of hers to kill Bradley Pine.'

'And the other way it could have developed is that the *only* reason she takes a lover in the first place is *so* she'll have someone to kill Pine,' Monika Paniatowski said.

'That's right. She has no relatives she can turn to – they're either dead, or she's lost contact with them years ago. She has no male friends to speak of, either. An' even if she had, it'd be stretchin' friendship a bit too far to ask that friend to kill for her. So she has to find some other way to recruit her accomplice. An' where would be a better place for recruitin' him than in bed! I don't imagine that findin' a man willin' to sleep with her would have been much of a problem, because she *is* a good-lookin' woman.'

'And once she's got him into bed?' Paniatowski asked.

'She'll have played the poor bugger like a violin for months – maybe even years. An' just when he's so hopelessly in love with her that he can't bear to live without her – when he's prepared to do anythin' at all to keep her – she tells him exactly what her price for stayin' with him is.'

'That would explain why she's been keeping him a secret from everyone else all this time,' Paniatowski said. 'She will have seen that we couldn't possibly suspect the man of murder if we didn't even know he existed!'

'I'm still more than a little bit troubled about the *nature* of the attack,' Bob Rutter said.

'In what way?'

'Dr Shastri said there'd been a lot of anger – as well as a lot of force – behind the fatal blow.'

'So?'

'Why would the lover have been angry with Pine?'

'He wasn't angry with Pine,' Woodend said. 'He was angry with Mrs Hawtrey, for talking him into carryin' out the murder. Or maybe he was angry with himself – for agreein' to it. Whichever was the case, it was Bradley Pine who bore the brunt of the anger.'

'Perhaps,' Rutter conceded. 'But even allowing for that, I still don't see why he would have driven the Cortina – presumably with Pine's body in the back – up to Mrs Hawtrey's house. Surely, once he'd done the deed, he'd have wanted to dump the corpse as soon as possible.'

'You'd think so, wouldn't you?' Woodend said. 'But remember that the body wasn't just dumped – it was muti-lated as well.'

A look of pure horror came to Rutter's face. 'And you think that she . . . that she . . . ?'

'I think she wanted to do that part of the business herself. I think that once he'd killed Pine, her lover went to her house to pick her up, and they *both* drove out to the dual carriageway, where Mrs Hawtrey first smashed Pine's mouth in, and then slit his stomach open.'

'If that's true, she's not just a murderer – she's a complete bloody monster!' Rutter said.

'If that's true, she certainly is,' Woodend agreed. 'An' once we've got a warrant from a friendly magistrate to search her house, we just might have the evidence to *prove* she is.'

Woodend stood in the centre of the large living room of the house in Lawrence Road. He had hardly moved at all for several minutes. Thelma Hawtrey, in contrast, seemed unable to keep still, and was continually pacing from one end of the room to the other, then back again.

'This is bloody outrageous!' she said angrily, as she passed by Woodend for fifteenth or sixteenth time. 'You have absolutely no right to invade my house in this manner.'

'We've got every right,' Woodend replied evenly. 'An' since you've seen the search warrant for yourself, you *know* we've got every right.'

There was the sound of banging overhead.

'They're in my bedroom now,' Thelma Hawtrey said bitterly. 'They're destroying my home, and I still have no idea what you're looking for.'

'If it'll make it any easier for you to bear, I'll *tell* you what we're lookin' for,' Woodend said. 'We're lookin' for evidence.'

'Evidence!' Mrs Hawtrey repeated. 'Evidence of *what*?'

'Any kind of evidence. But it would be especially nice if we could find somethin' that would not only reveal your lover's identity to us, but also give us an indication of where we might find him.'

'My lover?' Thelma Hawtrey said. 'You want to find the identity of my *lover*?'

'You don't really think that the trick to soundin' innocent is simply to repeat everythin' I say, do you?' Woodend asked. 'Because I'll tell you right now, it doesn't work.'

'Is that really what you said? That you're looking for my lover?'

'In fact, Mrs Hawtrey, the more you try that particular trick, the less effective it becomes.'

'Even if I did have a lover, why would you want to find him?' Thelma Hawtrey asked.

'Oh, that's an easy one to answer. We want to find him because we think he helped you murder Bradley Pine.'

Thelma Hawtrey laughed, hysterically. 'That really is too funny for words, you know,' she said.

'Well, I certainly hope you'll still be findin' it amusin' when you're both standin' in the dock,' Woodend countered.

Rutter had started by searching the area around the part of the driveway which was closest to the house, and was gradually working his way towards the point at which it let out on to the road outside. He had chosen this particular task himself, not because he expected to find anything out there – he was sure that he wouldn't, since Pine had almost certainly been killed elsewhere – but because rummaging through other people's homes had always been one of the aspects of police work that he most disliked.

His aversion to it came, he supposed, from his childhood. His father had run a small greengrocer's shop in London, and the family had lived above it. His mother had loathed the business, and loathed the area in which it was located, and her solution had been to pretend that none of it existed.

The flat had provided her with an escape from the real world. She had treated it almost as if it were sacred – a kind of holy hot air balloon, which allowed her to hover above, and remain totally untouched by, all the distasteful things which were going on at street level. It gradually became her life, and she would rather have lost an arm or a leg than give up even one tiny corner of it.

Thus, though Rutter could – and did – force himself to execute search warrants, he often felt, when he left the premises, as if he had been raping his mother's dream, and so generally avoided it whenever he could.

He had reached the big double gates. Large rhododendron bushes grew on either side of them, giving this part of the garden a rather funereal air – and him something of the creeps.

He was on the point of widening his search – perhaps following the progress of the walls round the small estate – when a sudden burst of sunshine hit the bushes, and he saw that, from under the foliage, something was glinting at him.

It could be anything – the silver foil wrapper of a discarded chocolate bar; a bottle which some thoughtless drunk had thrown over the wall on his ambling way back home; a coin or cheap brooch dropped by a hapless magpie and never retrieved – but he supposed that now that he was there, it was probably worth investigating it more fully.

He crouched down in front of the bush, pushed one of the branches to one side with his hand – and saw the watch. He picked it up carefully in his handkerchief, straightened up again, and moved away from the shadow of the bushes so he could examine it in better light.

He could tell immediately that it was a very expensive timepiece – far better than he could ever have afforded on a detective inspector's salary. There was a little dirt on it, but it bore none of the signs of deterioration which it would have acquired if it had been lying there a long time. Besides, it was still working perfectly. In fact, the only damage which seemed to have been done to it was that the leather strap was broken.

Rutter turned the watch over, hoping to find an inscription on the back of it, and was disappointed to discover that there wasn't one.

He took another step back, and considered how the watch might have got there.

It could, he supposed, have fallen off a man's wrist when he was opening the gates. But would it then have flown far enough to have landed where he'd discovered it? And even if it had, surely the owner would have noticed the loss of such an expensive watch before too long, and immediately gone searching in the places he might have dropped it.

Rutter wrapped the handkerchief around the watch and

slipped it into his pocket. Then he knelt down again, in order to see if the rhododendron bush had any more treasures it might be willing to yield up.

'You've been here for over an hour,' Mrs Hawtrey said. 'If there *was* anything to find, don't you think you'd have found it by now?'

'This is a big house,' Woodend reminded her. 'There's lots of places in it where you could have hidden things.'

'But I *have* nothing to hide, for God's sake!' Mrs Hawtrey protested. 'My life's an open book.'

'Oh, I sincerely doubt that,' Woodend told her. 'I doubt, to be honest with you, that anybody's is.'

A door to the hallway opened, and Bob Rutter entered the living room. 'Could I have a word, sir?' he asked.

'Certainly,' Woodend said. 'What's on your mind?'

'Not here,' Rutter cautioned. 'I think it would be much better if we talked outside.'

'Whatever you say,' Woodend replied, following him to the door.

It was five minutes before Woodend returned to the living room, and when he did he was holding his hands palm upwards, and carrying a handkerchief in them.

'What's that?' Thelma Hawtrey asked. 'The Holy Grail?'

'No,' Woodend said. 'But for my money, it comes pretty damn close to it.' He carefully unwrapped the package, and held it out for the woman to see. 'Does this look familiar to you?'

'Oh, my God, it's Brad's watch!' Mrs Hawtrey gasped.

'Do you know, I rather thought it might be,' Woodend said.

'Where did you . . . where was it . . .'

'Where was it found? Near the gates. Just about where the struggle must have taken place.'

'The struggle? What struggle? I have absolutely no idea what you're talking about.'

'I've told you before that just repeatin' my words won't do you any good,' Woodend said.

'But I really *don't* have any idea,' Mrs Hawtrey protested.

'Oh, I think you do,' Woodend said confidently. He cleared his throat, as he always did on such occasions. 'Thelma

Hawtrey, I am arrestin' you for the murder of Bradley Pine,' he continued. 'You do not have to say anythin' but anythin' you *do* say may be taken down an' used in evidence against you.'

Twenty-One

There were three interview rooms in Whitebridge Police Headquarters. They were all rather depressing – and deliberately so – but Interview Room C, which had the smallest window and the least natural light, was the dreariest of the trio. And Interview Room C was the one in which Woodend had chosen to conduct his interrogation of Thelma Hawtrey.

Woodend looked across the table, at the woman who he had already charged with murder.

She looked very calm, he thought. No, that wasn't it at all. She didn't just *look* very calm – she *was* very calm.

'You may as well make a clean breast of it right from the start, you know, Thelma,' he said.

'I've done nothing wrong, and I've nothing to come clean about,' Thelma Hawtrey said firmly. 'And I would prefer it, Chief Inspector Woodend, if you would address me as either Mrs Hawtrey or Madam.'

Woodend sighed. 'Look, Mrs Hawtrey, you know we found Bradley Pine's watch in your garden, don't you?

'I know you *say* that you did. But I've no proof you didn't put it there yourselves.'

'Now why should we have done that?'

'I should have thought that was obvious.'

'Not to me, it isn't.'

'Then I'll explain it to you. I've seen Henry Marlowe on the television. He's desperate for *someone* to be arrested for Bradley's murder, and you've decided that I'm the perfect candidate. But before you could arrest me, you needed some kind of proof, and *that's* why you planted the watch.'

'Your argument might sound a bit more convincin' if it had been only the watch that we found,' Woodend said. 'But it wasn't. We also retrieved a button that matches the ones on the jacket that Bradley Pine was wearing when his body was discovered.'

'You could have planted that, too.'

'An' what about the bloodstains, Mrs Hawtrey?' Woodend asked, exasperatedly. 'Because you do know that we found bloodstains on the ground, don't you?'

'None of which has anything to do with me.'

'Up until now, we've been assumin' that Pine was already dead by the time he reached your house, and that he was only taken there so that you could accompany him on his last journey to the lay-by,' Woodend said.

Thelma Hawtrey smiled. 'You almost make it sound like a funeral cortege,' she said.

'But he wasn't dead at that point, was he?' Woodend asked, ignoring the interruption. 'He was killed in *your* garden, by *your* lover, who'd been waitin' for him in the bushes. How'd you get him to come to your house on a night when he must have had lots of other things to do, and there was thick fog which made goin' anywhere a bit of an effort? Exactly what tale did you spin him, Mrs Hawtrey?'

'I didn't spin him any tale, as you put it, and, *as far as I know*, he didn't come to the house.'

'Maybe you didn't know anythin' about it, after all,' Woodend conceded. 'Maybe it was all your lover's idea, an' he kept you completely in the dark about the murder until after the deed itself was actually done.'

He paused, to give Thelma Hawtrey time to speak, but it was clear that she wasn't going to.

'If that is the case,' he continued, 'then the worst thing that you can possibly do, from your own viewpoint, is to take the fall for him. So why not tell us his name, then we can go an' pick him up? I promise you, Mrs Hawtrey, that the moment he's confessed, all charges against you will be dropped, an' we'll have you back in your own home within half an hour.'

'There is no lover, and though you have charged me with Bradley Pine's murder, you'll never make the charges stick.'

'Won't I? What makes you think that?'

'I still have faith in British justice. I still believe that the guilty will be punished, and the innocent will go free. And I'll go free, Mr Woodend – because I didn't do it!'

'What about all the evidence which seems to say different?' Woodend asked quietly.

'Look, maybe I was being unfair to you to even suggest that you planted the watch,' Thelma Hawtrey said. 'Perhaps you've behaved properly throughout this whole sorry business, and you really did find the watch in my garden, after all. And maybe Bradley Pine was killed there, too. I honestly don't know. But it still had nothing to do with me.'

What had happened to bring about the change in her, Woodend wondered. While they'd been searching her house, she'd seemed as nervous as a kitten. Now, in the intimidating atmosphere of the interview room – and after she'd actually been *charged* – she seemed perfectly in control of herself.

Woodend reached into his pocket and pulled out a packet of Capstan Full Strength.

'Would you care for a cigarette, Mrs Hawtrey?' he asked, offering them across the table.

Thelma Hawtrey shook her head. 'No, thank you.'

'Go on,' Woodend urged. 'I'm only offerin' you a smoke, you know. It's not all part of some kind of clever trick to get you to lower your guard, I can promise you that.'

'I never thought it was a trick,' Thelma Hawtrey said – still calm, still very much in control. 'But it just so happens that I don't smoke untipped cigarettes.'

'No, you don't, do you?' Woodend agreed quietly. 'There were half a dozen opened packets of cigarettes lyin' around your house at various points, but not a single one of them was untipped. So where did all the untipped butt ends come from?'

'What untipped butt ends?'

'The ones that kept appearin' in your rubbish bin.'

Thelma Hawtrey's left eye suddenly began to twitch.

That question had shaken her, Woodend thought. Finally, he'd been able to come up with a question that had bloody shaken her!

'Who . . . who was it who told you about the untipped cigarette ends?' she asked.

'If it's true – an' I believe it is – then the source doesn't really matter, does it?'

'It was that awful Chubb woman, wasn't it?' Thelma Hawtrey demanded. 'The nosy bitch!'

'Aye, it was her,' Woodend admitted. 'An' we got a lot more

132

information from her, as well – the brown ale that got drunk, when you never touched the stuff yourself; the one wine glass you washed up, while you left the other for Mrs Chubb to deal with; the bed sheets that you stripped off personally, so she wouldn't find out what you'd been doin' between them . . . Need I go on?'

Thelma Hawtrey was looking more than rattled – she looked as if she'd gone into shock. With what obviously took her a huge effort, she managed to fold her arms across her chest.

'Well, *do* I need to go on?' Woodend asked.

'I'd like to talk to my solicitor now,' Thelma Hawtrey said.

'You can certainly do that if you want to,' Woodend agreed, 'but once we put things on a formal footin', that's how they have to stay, an' I think you might be better off just tellin' me—'

'My solicitor,' Thelma Hawtrey said. 'I demand to speak to my solicitor.'

'She's asked for Foxy Rowton,' Woodend told the rest of the team as they sat over steaming cups of industrial-strength tea in the police canteen.

Paniatowski consulted the background notes she'd started making the moment that Thelma Hawtrey had been arrested.

'Rowton?' she said. 'But he's not the solicitor that she normally uses to handle her affairs.'

'No, he isn't,' Woodend agreed. 'But maybe somebody's told her that he's the feller you go to when you're in such deep shit that it's starting to spill over the top of your wellingtons.'

'What I don't understand is why she didn't ask for him when you first charged her,' Rutter said.

'I think I've got an answer to that,' Woodend told him. 'When we brought her in, she was confident that she could beat the murder charge. An' maybe she was right about that. If her lover did everythin' – killed Pine, took his body to the lay-by an' carried out the mutilation – then there'd be no *physical* evidence to tie her to the killin' at all.'

'And so what if the murder was committed in her garden?' Paniatowski added. 'When we find a body, we don't automatically arrest anybody who happens to be living near the scene of the crime, do we?'

'So what was it that panicked her?' Rutter asked.

'It was when I talked about the untipped cigarette ends that

133

Mrs Chubb had seen in the waste bin,' Woodend said.

'Why should that have done it?'

'Because, although she already knew that we thought she had a lover who'd helped her to carry out the murder, she didn't think we'd ever be able to trace him. But when I mentioned the cigarette ends, she began to get some idea of the extent of the resources we've got at our disposal. From that, it was a short step to convincin' herself that if we really wanted to find him, we would. An' maybe she thinks he's the weak link in the chain. Maybe she thinks that the second we slap the cuffs on him, he'll tell us everythin' we want to know.'

'You could be right,' Rutter said.

A uniformed constable entered the canteen, and walked straight over to their table.

'Excuse me, sir,' he said to Woodend.

'Yes?'

'Mrs Hawtrey and her solicitor would like to see you now.'

Woodend nodded. 'Well, that's it then,' he told his team. 'It's all over bar the shoutin'.'

Foxy Rowton had a thin, pointy face and restless, searching eyes, but his nickname came not so much from his looks as from the manner in which he conducted his business. Half the serious criminals in Whitebridge had his telephone number either memorized or tattooed on their arms, and there were any number of men who, thanks to his efforts, were still walking free when – if justice had been allowed to run its course – they would have been banged up long ago.

Rowton was sitting in the interview room, next to his client, with his hand resting reassuringly on her arm. He gave the briefest of nods when Woodend entered the room.

'Please sit down, Chief Inspector,' he said, as if this whole encounter was taking place on his *own* territory.

Woodend sat, without comment. After all, why not let Rowton have his moment at centre stage when, in the few moments, he'd become no more than a minor character in the drama which was being played out.

'My client wishes to make a short statement, then is prepared to answer any questions you may care to put to her,' Rowton said. 'Is that acceptable to you, Chief Inspector?'

'Aye, as long as she *does* eventually answer my questions.'

'She will.'

'Then I'm all ears.'

'I was not expecting Bradley Pine to come to my house that night,' Thelma Hawtrey said, almost as if she were reading – badly – from a prepared script. 'But though I was not expecting him, I would not have been at all surprised if he had turned up unannounced. He often did that – especially late at night.'

'Hang on!' Woodend said. 'You told me you'd hardly seen him at all since your husband's funeral – an' even then it had been mostly by chance.'

'First the statement, then the questions, if you don't mind,' Foxy Rowton said, rebukingly.

'Oh, all right! Just get on with it!' Woodend replied.

'That is precisely what my client was attempting to do when you interrupted her,' Rowton said. He turned to that client now. 'Do please carry on, Mrs Hawtrey, whenever you feel ready.'

'I heard a few cars that night, but not as many as usual, probably because of the fog,' Thelma Hawtrey continued. 'Two of them even stopped quite close to my house, but since no one rang my door bell, I assumed they were either neighbours themselves, or were visiting neighbours. I was drinking wine as I watched the television, and without really noticing I was doing it, I finished a whole bottle. I suddenly realized I was quite drunk, and decided to go to bed. When I got out of my chair to turn the television off, the nine o'clock news was just starting.'

Woodend waited for her to say more, but she had plainly reached the end of her tale.

'Is that it?' he asked.

'What more do you want?' Rowton asked. 'What more *can* Mrs Hawtrey tell you than what actually happened?'

'Well, she could give me the name of her lover, for a start.'

Rowton looked pained. 'Is that really absolutely necessary, Chief Inspector?' he asked.

'You bet it bloody-well is!'

Rowton nodded to his client. 'Go ahead.'

'For the past three years, since shortly after my husband's death, I have been having an affair with Bradley Pine,' Thelma Hawtrey said.

'What!' Woodend exploded.

135

'That was clear enough, surely,' Rowton said.

'You were havin' an affair – an' nobody else knew about it?' Woodend asked, incredulously.

'We were very discreet,' Thelma Hawtrey said.

'But why, for God's sake? You were both free as birds. You could have done what you liked.'

'This is Whitebridge, where we are ruled not by a monarch and her government, but by the tyranny of public opinion,' Foxy Rowton said.

'An' what's that supposed to mean, exactly?' Woodend asked.

'It means that in some circles, though not perhaps the ones that you move in, Chief Inspector, there is a very keen sense of what is appropriate behaviour and what isn't.'

'I haven't had much of a social life since my husband's death,' Thelma Hawtrey said, 'but if it had become generally known that I'd started an affair so soon after his funeral, I would have had no social life at all.'

'But it's now three years since your husband died,' Woodend said. 'Surely there was no need to keep it a secret any longer.'

'Not from my side, no,' Thelma Hawtrey agreed. 'But there was from Bradley's. The electors of Whitebridge would not look favourably on a candidate who had a mistress.'

'Then why didn't you get wed?'

'We could have done that, I suppose. Bradley wanted to. But I have no wish to be married again to anyone – and certainly not to Bradley.'

'No?'

'No!'

'Why not?'

'Mainly because I didn't love him. In fact, I'm not sure that I even *liked* him that much.'

'Then why . . . ?'

'But he was a stallion in the bedroom, and – in some strange way – that helped to ease the grief I was feeling for Alec.'

'This is bollocks!' Woodend said. 'You think that you can keep your real lover hidden away from me by confessin' to an affair you never had. Well, I'm not buyin' it!'

'Mrs Hawtrey and Mr Pine were not always as discreet everywhere else as they had to be in places where they were both well known,' Foxy Rowton said.

'Meanin' what?'

'We found excuses for us both to be away from Whitebridge at the same time,' Thelma Hawtrey said. 'Bradley would say he had to attend a mattress conference somewhere, and I would come up with some other convenient reason to explain my absence. Then we'd spend a few days in a hotel together, as man and wife. London was one of the places we went to. Brighton was another.'

'An' I suppose you're about to tell me you can prove that, are you?' Woodend asked sceptically.

'Yes, she is,' Foxy Rowton said. 'The last time they went away together was only three weeks ago, just before the start of the election campaign.'

Mrs Hawtrey smiled. 'Bradley said he needed a break before the campaign started to hot up,' she said.

'They stayed in the Grand Hotel in Great Yarmouth for the weekend,' Rowton continued. 'You'll find Mr Pine's name down in the register, and I'm sure that if you show Mrs Hawtrey's photograph to the hotel staff, they'll be more than willing to identify her as the woman they knew as *Mrs* Pine.'

Woodend had a sinking feeling in the pit of his stomach. Both Thelma Hawtrey and her solicitor sounded so sure of what they were saying that it simply had to be true.

'So the only way Mrs Hawtrey could have got her lover to kill Mr Pine was if she'd persuaded Mr Pine to hit himself over the back of the head, and then drive himself out to the lay-by, which – considering he was already dead – would have been no mean feat,' Rowton said.

'You're a very funny man,' Woodend told the solicitor. 'You should be on the stage.'

Rowton looked suitably modest. 'I bet you say that to all the solicitors who manage to run rings round you,' he said.

Twenty-Two

Holy Trinity Catholic Orphanage for Boys had been established in a large country house which stood shivering at the foot of the Pennine Hills. Its design had been grand in concept but crude in execution, and the result was a heavy sandstone structure which squatted instead of soared, and had probably once been a Victorian wool-millionaire's misguided idea of gracious living.

The director's office, to which Woodend was shown, was panelled in dark oak and filled with heavy furniture which had been out of style long before the Second World War. There were photographs of groups of boys on the walls, and a display case holding sporting trophies and thus proclaiming to the whole world that even orphans can sometimes win prizes.

The director himself, Father Swales, was in his late sixties. His face was heavily lined, and his gnarled hands gave evidence of advanced arthritis, but his pale eyes suggested kindness as well as authority, and his welcoming smile was that of a man who was far from giving up on life.

'You wanted to ask about Bradley Pine,' he said.

'That's right,' Woodend agreed.

The director shook his head sadly. 'Poor Bradley. To have come so far and yet have died in such a violent manner.'

'You remember him well, do you?'

'Oh yes, even after twenty-five long years, I remember him. But I must admit, it is far from clear to me how my memories of him will help you to catch his murderer.'

'I'm not sure, either,' Woodend admitted.

But apart from the line of inquiry he was now following, what other options were open to him?

There was no disputing that Thelma Hawtrey's revelations had been a blow, and that they'd unravelled what he'd thought was a cast-iron case as if it were no more than a ball of string. So now he was like a gambler, who puts his last pound on the outsider in the last race of the day – or a centre-forward who hopes against hope that his misplaced shot will magically rebound into the goal-mouth in the few remaining seconds of the game.

'I like to build up a picture of the victim in my head,' he explained to the director. 'It helps me to see the world as he might have seen it – and sometimes, it leads me to his killer.'

The director nodded. 'Very well, if you think it might help you, I will do my best to paint a picture for you of the boy I knew,' he promised. 'Bradley was eleven when he came to us, and had already known more despair, at that tender age, than most of us will experience in a lifetime.'

'You're sayin' he'd had a rough childhood?'

'He had a *vile* childhood. His own mother died when he was just a baby. His father married again, and he and his new wife had another child – a little girl. It could have been a shining bright new start for all of them.'

'But it wasn't?'

'His father and his stepmother had skills by which they could have earned a very decent living – he was a motor mechanic, she was a ladies' hairdresser – but they were hopeless alcoholics, and so neither of them held a job down for very long. Bradley and his little half-sister were both badly neglected by them, and sometimes – when the drink took one of the parents the wrong way – they were actually physically abused.'

Woodend remembered what Monika Paniatowski told him about cigarette-burn scars on Bradley Pine's arms.

'How did he come to be an orphan?' he asked.

'Bradley's parents died in a car crash – doubtless they were both drunk at the time – and since he had no other relatives able or willing to take care of him, he was sent here.'

'An' how did he settle in?'

'Remarkably well. The orphanage is, by its very nature, a highly structured society, and structure was something that had been sadly lacking in Bradley's previous life. He embraced the order he found here. His locker was the tidiest and best set-out that I think I have ever seen.'

'An' that was a habit which stayed with him,' Woodend

said, thinking of the arrangement of both Pine's office and his home.

'He also developed a remarkable self-discipline,' the director continued. 'Once he had decided there was something he wished to achieve, he would work towards that goal with a slow, single-minded determination. He exhibited absolutely none of the impatience that most children – and indeed, a great many adults – would have shown in his situation.'

'In other words, he was a bit cold an' ruthless,' Woodend suggested.

'I suppose you could apply that term, if you feeling unchar-itable,' the director said, with a hint of mild rebuke in his voice, 'but I would much prefer to describe him in the way I just have. At any rate, I was not at all surprised to learn that he had risen to be a partner in the company we placed him in as a fifteen-year-old boy. Of all the orphans who have passed through this institution, he was the one of whom I expected the most.'

'What can you tell me about his friends?' Woodend asked.

'He didn't have any,' the director replied, without a second's hesitation. 'And that was not because the other boys wouldn't accept him, but because he wouldn't accept them.'

'Why was that?'

'I suspect it was because he thought he didn't *need* them.'

'Everybody needs somebody.'

'Indeed they do, and in his case, the person he seemed to need was his sister, who had been placed in St Claire's Orphanage, in the care of Sister Martha and her nuns.' The director paused for a moment. 'I think that little girl was the only person in the whole world who Bradley ever really cared about.'

'What was the age difference between them?'

'Round about four years. I suspect Bradley had to be both mother and father to her, almost from the moment she was born. And it was perhaps because of that – and perhaps because of what they had had to endure together – that they had devel-oped an amazing bond with each other.'

'An amazin' bond,' Woodend repeated, musingly. 'How would you know that? Did he tell you?'

The director laughed. 'As if he would have confided in me! As if he would have confided in *anybody*! No, Chief Inspector, he didn't tell me – I observed it for myself.'

'So you allowed Bradley Pine an' his sister to see one another sometimes, did you?'

'Not at first. Sister Martha and I discussed the matter when the children arrived at our respective orphanages, and we came to the conclusion that to allow them to meet would have a disturbing effect on both of them. We even feared that, in order to be together, they might contemplate running away. It wouldn't be the first time something like that had happened with orphans who'd been separated.'

'So what eventually made you change your mind?'

'Bradley did. Not so much from what he said, as by the way he behaved – by his general approach to life. I soon came to understand that he would never do anything which might upset his sister, and that he was far too much of a realist to ever think that running away would be a solution to their problems. He was prepared to wait, you see – he was *always* prepared to wait.'

'How do you mean? Prepared to wait.'

'He never complained about the amount of time we allowed them to spend together when he was still living here, nor about the number of occasions on which he was permitted to visit her once he had left the orphanage himself. But the second she was old enough to leave St Claire's, he found her a job which ensured that they would see each other every day.'

'An' where was this job?' Woodend asked.

'In Whitebridge, of course,' the director replied, sounding slightly surprised that Woodend even needed to ask the question. 'He found her a position in the typing pool of the company he himself was working for.'

Woodend, Rutter and Paniatowski were sitting around their usual table in the Drum and Monkey. It had been obvious – from the moment he had entered the pub – that the chief inspector had something of significance to tell his team, and once the drinks had arrived, he launched straight into it.

'The story that Thelma Hawtrey told her charlady about her life before she came to Whitebridge had some truth in it, but not a lot,' Woodend said. 'Her parents were killed in a car crash, but they weren't big landowners – not by any stretch of the imagination. What they actually were was a pair of drunks who'd never amounted to anythin'.'

'You can't blame her for lying about that,' Rutter said. 'It isn't something anybody would find it easy to admit to.'

'Agreed,' Woodend said. 'But the other thing she forgot to mention to Mrs Chubb is that Bradley Pine was her half-brother.'

'You're sure about that?' Rutter asked.

'I'm sure. The only reason she came to Whitebridge at all was that her brother made all the arrangements.'

'Then she was lying when she said that Pine was her lover!' Rutter exclaimed.

'Was she?' Woodend asked.

'Of course. If she was his sister—'

'She changed the bed-sheets after he'd visited her,' Monika Paniatowski interrupted. 'And when they went away together, they booked into hotels as husband and wife.'

'I asked her why they didn't get married, an' she said it was because she didn't want to,' Woodend continued. 'But now we know the truth, don't we? They didn't get married because they *couldn't.*'

'But that's monstrous!' Rutter said.

'They've loved each other from the time they were little kids,' Woodend said. 'I don't know when they started to crave for each other sexually, but whenever it was, they held back until they'd both left the orphanage. An' I think that's all down to Pine's determination. The director told me he always knew what he wanted, but would wait patiently until the time was right to get it. That's what he was doin' in that case – waiting patiently until the time was right.'

'How can you be so sure they didn't have a sexual relationship while they were still in the orphanages?' Paniatowski asked.

'Their meetings were always supervised. If there'd been any hint of physical attraction passin' between them, Thelma would never have been allowed to come to Whitebridge when she'd just turned fourteen.'

'So when do you think their affair *did* begin?' Rutter asked.

'My guess would be that it began the second she started workin' in the typin' pool.'

'And did it carry on, even after she'd begun seeing Alec Hawtrey?'

'Oh yes! In fact, I think she only made her play for Hawtrey because Pine told her to.'

'That doesn't make sense,' Rutter protested. 'If he loved her, as you say he did—'

'He wanted to get on in life. He wanted them *both* to get on in life. He hadn't earned enough money from his patent to buy his own factory, but he could just about scrape together a sufficient amount to buy his way into Hawtrey's Mattresses – if Alec Hawtrey was willing to let him. And once Hawtrey had made the settlement on his first wife – a settlement made necessary by his affair with Thelma – he didn't have a lot of choice *but* to take on a partner in the long term.'

'I still don't get it,' Rutter said. 'I can just about see Pine encouraging Thelma to split up Hawtrey's first marriage, but why would he then agree to letting her become the second Mrs Hawtrey?'

'To make sure that when Alec Hawtrey *did* take on a partner, that partner was Bradley. It was like havin' a spy right in the middle of the enemy camp. Besides, why would he object? He couldn't marry Thelma himself, could he? And if she was married to a good friend, who eventually became his partner, he'd have all the excuse in the world for bein' in her company.'

'But knowing he had to share her—'

'Maybe he didn't,' Woodend argued. 'Maybe she stopped sleepin' with Alec the moment they were married. Maybe that's why Alec went mountain climbin' – because he thought that might excite her, an' make her want him back in her bed again. But even if Pine did have to share her, it's possible it didn't bother him overmuch. Not everybody places as much of a premium on sexual fidelity as . . . as . . .'

Oh shit! he thought, as he felt his words dry up in his mouth.

Caught up in making his case, as he had been, he'd inadvertently wandered back in Rutter's emotional minefield again – for though he hadn't actually been going to say, '. . . as Maria did,' he was sure that Bob was perfectly capable of burning those words on to his own brain himself.

'Besides, even if he had to share her body with Alec Hawtrey, he had her heart all to himself, and that was probably all that mattered to him,' Paniatowski said, coming to the rescue.

'Exactly,' Woodend agreed gratefully.

'I don't really understand why we're still discussing Pine's relationship with his sister,' Rutter said, eager to move away from the subject as soon as possible. 'After all, that's not going to help us to find our murderer, now is it?'

'Not *that* murderer, no,' Woodend agreed.

'What other murderer *is* there?' Rutter wondered.

'Think about it,' Woodend said. 'In carryin' on as they always had, Pine an' Thelma were playin' a very dangerous game. An' what would have happened if Alec Hawtrey found out about it?'

'At the very least, they'd have become social pariahs,' Monika Paniatowski said, embracing Woodend's line of argument. 'There's absolutely no doubt in my mind that Alec Hawtrey would have divorced Thelma, and Bradley Pine would have lost any chance of pursuing his political ambitions.'

'The business partnership would have broken up – there's no doubt about that, either – and the business itself would probably have collapsed,' Woodend continued. 'An', very possibly, both Thelma Hawtrey an' Bradley Pine would have gone to prison.'

'But why should Alec Hawtrey have started to suspect what was going on?' Rutter asked. 'They'd been getting away with it for years.'

'An' maybe they thought that their luck couldn't hold for very much longer,' Woodend suggested. 'Or perhaps Alec Hawtrey was *already* startin' to get suspicious.'

'So they killed him?'

'It's a possibility.'

'It's pure speculation!' Rutter protested.

'Speculation is what we do, lad,' Woodend said patiently. 'It's how we work. We're presented with numerous strands of life, an' the way we narrow them down to leads which are worth followin' is by *speculation*.'

'Even so—'

'Say we're right – Monika an' me. Say Thelma an' Pine *had* decided they had to get rid of Alec Hawtrey. What better way would there be to go about it than by stagin' an accident on a mountainside?'

Twenty-Three

It hadn't taken Beresford long to prepare his mother's evening meal, for though she had once been a wonderful cook herself, she would now very rarely eat anything other than baked beans on toast.

Watching her eat it – since even this simple task could sometimes be something of a challenge for her – he found himself wondering what he would do when the increasing demands of his job eventually made it impossible for him to look after her any more.

'You don't have to sit there like a stuffed owl, you know, Colin,' Mrs Beresford said. 'I'm sure there are any number of things that you'd rather be getting on with.'

Beresford smiled, sadly.

There were times when his mother seemed so lucid – so aware of the world around her. On such occasions it was almost possible to believe that her Alzheimer's had been no more than a bad dream from which he was just waking up. But if that were really the case – and sometimes he found himself questioning what *was* real and what *wasn't* – the period of wakefulness did not last long, and soon he was back in his nightmare again.

'You never talk to me much about your work, these days,' his mother said, between mouthfuls of baked beans. 'Why is that?'

'I didn't think you'd be interested,' he said weakly.

'Didn't you? Well, I can assure you that I am. So why don't you tell me about it now?'

'There's this murder case that we're investigating at the moment,' Beresford said, feeling his mental floodgates burst open, and the words come spilling out. 'My boss, Chief Inspector Woodend, has been letting me carry out a lot of inquiries on my own. I think that's because he's impressed with the work I did on the Judith Maitland case.'

'That's nice,' his mother said, encouragingly.

'It is,' Beresford agreed. 'In fact, it's a lot more than just nice. He's giving me a chance that no other chief inspector on the Force would even think of giving me. The thing is, I'm not sure he's right to have so much faith in me. There are times when I think that any success I had with the Maitland case may have been no more than a fluke.'

'Oh dear! That must be very worrying for you, son,' his mother commiserated.

'Very worrying,' Beresford agreed. 'You see, Mum, I don't want to tell him just how unsure of myself I am, in case he stops trusting me to do the job. On the other hand, I'm terrified that I might miss a vital clue, and let him and the rest of the team down.'

'It is a problem,' his mother agreed.

'I suppose I could ask Sergeant Paniatowski what to do,' Beresford continued. 'She's not *that* much older than me, so she probably remembers what it was like to have doubts about herself. Of course, there's always the danger that if I do that, she'll go straight to Mr Woodend and tell *him* exactly what I've told *her*. So what do you think I should do, Mum?'

His mother pushed her plate of beans to one side.

'Didn't you . . .' she began. 'Didn't you . . . I'm sorry, I've forgotten your name for the minute.'

'Colin,' Beresford said dully. 'My name's Colin.'

'That's right,' his mother agreed. 'Didn't you used to be a policeman, Colin?'

It was easier to walk through the church door this time, Monika Paniatowski thought. It was getting easier every time she did it.

But why should it ever have been *hard*? She was no longer the frightened little girl she'd been the last time she had attended church on a regular basis. She was a grown woman – a detective sergeant in the Central Lancs Constabulary. It had been nothing but an act of cowardice on her part to ever allow her past to intimidate her as she had.

Father Taylor was standing near the main door, almost as if he had been waiting for her to arrive.

'Now that's what I call a quick response,' he said. 'Not only has it only been missing for a little over half an hour, but I haven't even got around to reporting it gone yet.'

'What's missing?' Paniatowski asked, mystified. 'What haven't you reported?'

'My bicycle. I left it outside the church, and when I went back – no more than five minutes later – it wasn't there any more.'

'Was it chained up?'

'No.'

'You should have a chain, you know.'

'I do, but I never bother to use it.'

'Did you see anybody suspicious hanging around at the time you parked the bicycle?'

Father Taylor laughed. 'Monika, Monika, Monika . . .' he said, shaking his head.

'What's so funny,' Paniatowski demanded.

'It was just a *joke*, dear Monika. I thought you'd have seen that long before now.'

'So you didn't have your bicycle stolen after all?'

'Yes, I did. Or, at least, it's gone missing. But the point of the joke was in my pretending to think that a detective sergeant – with much more important things on her mind – would even be *interested* in a stolen bicycle.'

Paniatowski smiled weakly. 'I get it now,' she admitted. 'But if your bicycle has been stolen—'

'Monika, Monika, Monika,' the priest repeated, shaking his head again. 'My bike doesn't *matter*.'

'Of course it does. There are laws—'

'If it's only been borrowed, it will be returned. If it's been stolen, then perhaps whoever took it needed it more than I do.'

'Still, you do need the use of your bike, if you're to visit your parishioners and—'

'If I don't get it back, Father Kenyon will probably give me a little money from the parish funds to buy another one. And he doesn't, well, I've been blessed with strong legs, and I can always walk.' Father Taylor's face grew more serious. 'You must learn not to focus your attention on the small matters whilst the larger matters are still left unresolved. You must not use the *little* picture as a way of escaping having to deal with the *big* one.'

147

'Is that what I was doing?'

'Yes, I truly think it was.'

'And what big picture am I attempting to escape from?'

'The state of your spiritual health, of course.'

'I didn't come here to talk about that.'

'Then why *did* you come here?'

A good question, Paniatowski thought. *Why* did *I come here?*

'I had a little free time on my hands, and I thought the walk up the hill might be good exercise,' she said aloud.

'Of course! That would explain everything,' Father Taylor agreed. 'Can I ask you another question?'

'If you want to.'

'If I were to suggest that we walked over to the confessional together, would you turn me down?'

'Not at all.'

'You wouldn't?'

'No. I'd be perfectly willing to walk over to it with you. It's going *into* it that I'd object to.'

'Then let's go somewhere else,' Father Taylor suggested. 'I know a little spot, not far from here. I can't say it has a pretty view to look at, or a brilliant band to listen to. I can't even claim it serves the best food in town – because it doesn't have a kitchen.'

'You're talking about the vestry, aren't you?' Paniatowski asked, with a smile slowly creeping across her mouth.

Father Taylor laughed again. 'Yes, you're quite right, Detective Sergeant, I'm talking about the vestry,' he admitted. 'Are you willing to accept my less-than-dazzling invitation?'

Paniatowski shrugged. 'Why not?' she said.

There was still what Woodend would have called, 'a good two hours suppin' time' left in the day, but Bob Rutter had had enough of pouring beer down his throat, and told his boss that he'd decided to have an early night.

The moment he'd reached his car, he began to think that he'd made a mistake. True, he hadn't wanted to spend any more time in the pub, but there was nothing else that he particularly wanted to do either.

For an hour or two, he drove around, thinking about the past and fretting about the future.

He was so lonely, and there was a part of him that wanted to ask Monika if they might pick up again where they had left off. But he understood – deep within himself – that he could never do that. However much he missed her – and he did – however much he wished he could take her in his arms again – and he ached to do just that – he knew that the shadow of his wronged, dead wife would always be hanging over them like a poisonous cloud.

So what was he to do? What was he to *bloody* do?

Still unable to bring himself to move into the house he had once shared with Maria, he had taken a room in a moderately priced boarding house on the edge of town, and it was to there that he finally decided to head.

It was already after eleven when he pulled up in the street outside, and most of the houses were in darkness. He hoped that once he was in bed himself, he would eventually drop off to sleep.

He was slipping his key into the lock when he heard a voice just behind him say, 'Bob!'

He turned around, and saw a blonde woman standing by the gate.

'Monika?' he asked.

Then he realized that it was not Monika at all, and when he spoke again, his voice had hardened.

'You've got a nerve,' he told the woman.

'I know I have,' Elizabeth Driver replied.

'How did you know where to find me?' he asked.

Elizabeth Driver laughed, but it was a nervous laugh rather than an amused one.

'I'm a reporter,' she said. 'It's all a part of my job to know where to find people.'

'You haven't been following me, have you?' he demanded angrily.

Elizabeth Driver shook her head. 'No, I haven't been following you, I promise you that.'

'Then how did you know I was going to turn up here at just this time. Until ten or fifteen minutes ago, I didn't even know it myself.'

'I had no idea when you'd arrive. But I knew you had to come eventually, and I've been waiting.'

'For how long?'

Elizabeth Driver shrugged. 'A couple of hours. Maybe more. I don't really know.'

'*Why* have you been waiting?'

'Because I needed to talk to you, and I knew if I approached you anywhere else, you'd probably refuse to speak to me.'

'I should refuse to speak to you now,' Rutter said.

'I know you should. But please don't!'

Rutter sighed heavily. 'Say what you've got to say – and then get the hell out of here.'

'I wanted to say how sorry I am for ever telling Maria about your affair with Sergeant Paniatowski,' Elizabeth Driver said.

'Why should you want to do that now?' Rutter demanded angrily. 'Is it because she's dead?'

'No, it's not at all because she's dead, though that only makes it even worse than it would have been otherwise. I should never have told her at all – even if she'd been going to live to a hundred.'

'Then why did you?'

'Because I thought there'd be a story in it. Because, at the time I did it, I thought that getting stories was the only thing that really mattered in life. But I don't think that now.'

'Why are you telling me all this?' Rutter asked.

'Because I want your forgiveness.'

'I don't know if I *can* forgive you.'

'Thank you.'

'For what? Did you hear what I said?'

'You said you don't know if you can forgive me – but that's not the same as saying you know you *can't*, is it, Bob?'

'No,' Rutter agreed. 'It's not the same.'

'Think about it,' Elizabeth Driver told. 'Search your soul, to see if you can find a little charity somewhere in it for me. If you can, it will be a great weight off my shoulders.'

'And if I can't?'

'If you can't,' Elizabeth Driver said, 'I suppose that's no more than I deserve.'

Then she turned on her heel, and walked quickly away up the street.

Henry Marlowe had been drinking steadily since late afternoon, and now he was unquestionably – demonstrably – drunk.

'Bloody Woodend!' he growled.

'It was your decision to assign him to the case,' Bill Hawes, his political agent, pointed out.

'I know it was my bloody decision, but what choice did I have? I needed a quick result, and Woodend, of all the officers serving under me, was the man most likely to get me one. But I never thought – not for a second – that he'd arrest Thelma Hawtrey.'

'I fail to see why you're getting so het up about it,' Dawes said. 'So what if he arrested her? He let her go again, didn't he?'

'Yes, he let her go.'

'Well, then?'

'But you don't know the bastard like I do. Once he's got a scent in his nose, he won't let go until he's sunk his teeth into something.'

'But is there anything there for him to sink his teeth into? Is Thelma Hawtrey aware of what happened up that mountainside?'

'How the bloody hell am I expected to know that?'

'I thought perhaps you might have asked her.'

'I might have *asked* her,' Marlowe repeated bitterly. 'Oh, absolutely! I could just have gone up to her, and said casually, "Do you know what your boyfriend did to your husband on that mountainside?" That would have been a brilliant stroke, wouldn't it?'

'The only reason I raised that particular point is because, if he *didn't* tell her, then the secret died with Bradley Pine, and you're in the clear.'

'Died with him?' Marlowe repeated, slurring his words. 'How could it have *died with him*, when all those top bobbies up in Cumberland know about it?'

'They'll say nothing, because they're almost as guilty as you are.'

Marlowe shuddered. 'Guilty?' he repeated. 'Am I guilty?'

'What else would you call it?' Hawes asked practically. 'But, as I said, it's as much in their interest to keep it quiet as it is in yours.'

'And then there's that other bugger, who knows *exactly* what happened,' Marlowe said.

'Jeremy Tully? The company's accountant? But he's in Australia now, isn't he?'

151

'It doesn't matter where he is,' Marlowe moaned. 'If Woodend decides he wants to find him, that's just what he'll bloody-well do.'

Twenty-Four

Had Bradley Pine still been alive, the letter would have been delivered to his home address, but since he was now occupying a refrigerated drawer in the police morgue, it was diverted instead to Whitebridge Police Headquarters, where it was waiting on Woodend's desk when he got into work the next morning.

It was postmarked 'Western Australia', and contained a single sheet of paper. Even before he started to read it, Woodend could tell from the wild handwriting that the sender had been very agitated.

> I know you are no worse a man than most of us, Bradley. The Devil tempts us all. He tempted Jesus Christ on a mountainside, just as he tempted you. But Our Lord resisted – and you did not. Before I went away, I begged you to confess your sins, but you would not listen. And now, I beg you again to confess. There will be no rest for either of us until you do.
>
> What if you die, Bradley? What if you have a fatal accident before you cleanse your soul? Confess! For the love of God, confess.
>
> Jeremy

Woodend lit up a Capstan Full Strength, and took a deep and thoughtful drag of it.

'Speculation' was what Bob Rutter had called the theory that he'd been propounding in the Drum and Monkey the previous night. Well, this was more than speculation – this was proof positive!

But so what?

'Stop thinking about it, Charlie!' he said aloud. 'It's nothin' but a waste of time.'

153

A *complete* waste of time, in fact!

A *bloody* waste of time!

Because if Bradley Pine *had* killed Alec Hawtrey, then any chance of bringing him to justice had ended with his own murder. And if Thelma Hawtrey had assisted Pine – or at least, strongly encouraged him to go ahead – there was absolutely no way of proving it now.

Woodend took another drag on his cigarette. 'Focus on the matter in hand,' he ordered himself. 'Focus on Pine's death!'

And then, completely ignoring his own sound advice, he picked up the phone and asked to be connected to Superintendent Springer of the Cumberland Constabulary.

It was ten minutes before Springer could be tracked down, but when he finally came on to the line he seemed more than delighted to be talking to an old colleague from his days in Scotland Yard.

'It's really quite absurd that we don't see much more of each other, Charlie,' he said.

'It is,' Woodend agreed.

'How far is your patch from mine, would you think?' Springer asked. 'Sixty miles, more or less?'

'Somethin' like that.'

'So it's two hours at the most – even in bad traffic. There's no reason at all why we shouldn't get together. You and Joan should come up for dinner. Soon! And rather than drive back to Whitebridge, you could spend the night with us. The house is plenty big enough for you to bring your Annie, too, if she's available – though if she's anything like my kids, she won't want to be spending her time with old farts like us.'

Woodend chuckled. 'She probably wouldn't, but she couldn't even if she wanted to, because they're keepin' her very busy in that nursin' school in Manchester – or so she'd have me believe.'

'But you an' the missus could certainly come up?'

'I'll have to check with Joan first, but I'm sure she'd enjoy it as much as I would,' Woodend said.

He meant it. A lot of the bobbies who he'd worked with in the Yard had got right up his nose most of the time, but Ron Springer never had. He was a bloody good bobby, and a thoroughly decent feller.

154

'Anyway, that probably isn't why you're calling me now, is it?' Springer asked.

'No, it isn't,' Woodend agreed. 'I'm ringin' you about a feller called Alec Hawtrey, who was killed in a mountaineerin' accident on your territory about three years ago.'

There was a pause at the other end of the line, then Springer said, 'Why would you be asking about that, Charlie, after all this time?'

'Any reason why I shouldn't?' Woodend countered.

'I suppose not. But that's all over and done with, isn't it?'

'Well, yes, in a way, I suppose it is,' Woodend agreed. 'But, as it happens, I'm investigating the murder of a man called Bradley Pine, who was standin' as Conservative—'

'I read the newspapers, Charlie,' Springer interrupted. 'I know all about that.'

'An' Pine, in case you haven't made the connection, was the *same* Bradley Pine who was with Alec Hawtrey when he died.'

'And did everything he possibly could to keep him alive. But Hawtrey was in his fifties, and had a broken leg.'

'You seem to be remarkably well informed about the incident,' Woodend said.

'I was there,' Springer told him.

'Why was that?'

'Policing up here's not at all like it is down there in Lancashire. We have to get involved in all kinds of things that you lot never even have to bother your heads about.'

'Which means what, exactly?'

'One of our jobs is to provide tactical support to the mountain rescue teams, and, during the particular incident you're asking about, I was the one who happened to be co-ordinating it.'

'An' did you notice anythin' out of the ordinary?'

'What do you mean – out of the ordinary?'

'I wouldn't have thought the phrase was too difficult to understand,' Woodend said, wondering exactly what was going on at the other end of the line. 'I mean strange! Unusual! Not quite the norm!'

There was another pause from Springer.

'Listen, Charlie,' he said finally, 'I've known you for a long time, and chancing your arm because you think you've finally got Henry Marlowe out of the way is just the sort of thing I'd expect you to do.'

'Pardon?' Woodend said.

'But he may *lose* the election, you know, in which case, he'll be back with you as chief constable.'

'So what?'

'And even if he wins, he might still have some considerable influence – even at a distance – over how the Central Lancs Force is run. So if I was you, I wouldn't even think of crossing him.'

'I've no idea what you're talking about,' Woodend confessed.

'Pull the other leg, Charlie – it's got bells on,' Springer said.

'You really *have* lost me,' Woodend protested.

'Three years ago, there was a climbing accident in the mountains involving two experienced climbers and a novice,' Springer said, as flatly as if he were reading it off a piece of paper. 'The novice broke his leg, probably through his lack of experience. The other two climbers did all they could to save him, but it was a losing battle from the start, and, weakened as he was by his injuries, he died of exposure. That's not only all you *need* to know – it's all there *is* to know.'

'Then why is this phone in my hand almost frostin' over?' Woodend wondered.

'Now *you're* the one who's not making any sense at all, Charlie,' Springer said.

'You say you've known me for a long time. Well, I've known you for a long time, an' all,' Woodend said. 'Three or four minutes ago, you sounded just like my old mate Ron. Then I mentioned Bradley Pine and Alec Hawtrey, an' suddenly you turn as cold as a Siberian blizzard. What's it all about?'

'It's not about anything,' Springer said. 'If I seem a little strange to you, it's probably because, at the moment, I'm under a lot of pressure at work.'

'Fair enough,' Woodend said, though he didn't sound entirely convinced. 'But to get back to that other matter—'

'What other matter?'

'Me an' Joan comin' up there, havin' dinner with you, an' maybe stayin' the night. By the middle of next week, the case I'm workin' on will either be solved or completely in the doldrums, so I can't see any reason why we shouldn't at least pencil in Friday or Saturday—'

156

'Listen, about that,' Springer interrupted.

'Yes?'

'I'll . . . err . . . have to talk to Mary, and see when we can fit it in,' Springer said. 'We'll definitely do it, but I can't promise it will be all that *soon*, because, as I've just explained, I've got a lot of work on.'

'I see,' Woodend said thoughtfully, 'So maybe we'll wait until things have eased off a bit for you.'

'Yes, I think that would be the best idea.'

'But in the meantime, if anythin' does occur to you about what happened to Alec Hawtrey on that—'

'Leave it, Charlie!' Springer urged. 'Alec Hawtrey's dead and buried. Let him rest in peace, for God's sake!'

And then he hung up.

Rutter and Paniatowski were in Woodend's office, studying a detailed street map of Whitebridge.

'If the boss and I are right, then the only reason that the killer drove the car back into Whitebridge is because he needed to get back here himself,' Rutter said. 'An if we work on that assumption, then it's only reasonable to also assume that he doesn't live more than a mile away from Greenfields. Would you agree with that?'

'Probably,' Paniatowski replied. 'Chances are that, however careful he'd been, there was probably some blood on him – and the longer he was out on the streets, the more chance there was of someone spotting that.'

Being in such close proximity to Bob Rutter again was a bit like forcing yourself to walk into the church after a long absence, she thought – you were probably never going to be entirely comfortable with it, but it got a little easier every time you did it.

'So let's see just what falls within that one-mile area, shall we,' Rutter suggested.

He picked up a compass, set it to scale, and drew a circle on the map, with the spot where the Cortina had been found at the centre of it.

To the south of the centre were the old cotton mills, the *raison d'être* for Greenfields ever having been built. To the east was the city centre, and the beginnings of the access road out to the dual carriageway. Council estates lay to the west,

157

and private housing estates to the north. St Mary's Church – the last place that Pine had been seen alive – was well outside the circle, but Bankside – where he met his death – was neatly dissected by it.

Rutter and Paniatowski gazed down at the line for a moment, then Rutter said, 'Maybe we've been overlooking the obvious solution.'

'That the killer could have been one of Thelma Hawtrey's neighbours?' Paniatowski asked.

'Exactly. A neighbour wouldn't have known exactly when Pine was planning to visit Thelma, but that wouldn't have mattered – because he could have seen him arrive through his front window.'

'But if that had been the case, he wouldn't have had time to set his ambush in the shrubbery.'

'If he was a neighbour, there'd have been no need for an ambush.'

'No?'

'No! Just put yourself in Pine's position for a minute. He's very careful about when he visits Thelma, because he doesn't want to be seen to be doing it. But with the cover provided by the fog, he probably thinks he'll be safe enough that night. Then, just as he's parking, he sees somebody coming out of one of the other houses. What's he going to do now? Is he going to walk straight up to Thelma's door, even though he knows that he's been spotted?'

'No, he isn't,' Paniatowski said. 'He's going to wait until the neighbour draws level with him, and then produce some kind of story which will explain why he's there.'

'Like what?'

'He'll probably claim that he's got lost in the fog.'

'Exactly. So he's standing there – worried, but not the least suspicious – as the neighbour approaches him. Now all that neighbour has to do is to get him to turn his back for a second, and the job's done.'

'So the neighbour says something like, "I thought I saw somebody moving around outside Mrs Hawtrey's front door"?'

'Yes. And Pine turns to look. He's already standing in the gateway, so when the blow is struck he falls straight into the rhododendron bushes.'

'And if the killer *was* a neighbour, he might also have been a friend of Alec Hawtrey's,' Paniatowski said, with growing enthusiasm. 'Living where he was, he could have worked out what was going on between Pine and Thelma, and been outraged that Thelma was dishonouring his friend's memory.'

'But would he have been outraged enough to *kill* Pine?' Rutter wondered. 'Enough to *mutilate* his body?'

They had been building up a bubble of excitement between them, but these last few words from Rutter quite punctured it.

'It's hard to imagine anyone hating Pine enough to do that,' Paniatowski agreed.

'If I could have got my hands on the bloody bastard who killed Maria . . .' Rutter said.

An awkward silence followed, as it always did when Maria's name accidentally came up.

Then Paniatowski said, 'Would you have killed Maria's murderer for what he did to her – or for what he'd done to you?'

'You can be cruel,' Rutter told her.

Had she *meant* to be cruel, Paniatowski wondered.

Had *she* been punishing *him* for what *he'd* done to *her*?

And if that was the case, did she have any right to do it?

'I'm not being cruel,' she said, pushing self-analysis to one side. 'I'm just doing my job.'

'Are you?'

'Yes.'

'Is that *really* what you're doing? And if it is, would you like to explain *how*?'

'The boss says we have to try to get into the heads of murderers, and if we need to use our own experiences to do that – however painful they might be – we just need to bite on the bullet and go ahead.'

'You're right,' Rutter said, somewhat pacified, 'and I apologize for taking it the wrong way.'

'And I apologize for pushing you like that,' Paniatowski said. 'You don't have to answer the question if you don't want to.'

'But I *do* want to, because you're spot on when you say that it might help,' Rutter told her. He thought for a moment. 'If I'm honest,' he continued, slightly shakily, 'I think I'd have to say I would have killed him for my own benefit, because

159

however much pain I could have caused Maria's murderer, it wouldn't have helped her at all.'

'So we think this murderer did it for himself, and not to avenge someone else?' Paniatowski said.

'That's what we think.'

'And because he was so full of hatred, he wanted to humiliate Pine even in death?'

'Yes.'

'Then what I still don't understand is why the murderer put Pine in the back of the car,' Paniatowski said.

'You've lost me,' Rutter admitted.

'If he was so keen to rob Pine of his dignity, why not cram him in the boot? Putting him on the back seat instead seems . . . I don't know . . . to be almost *cherishing* him.'

'And even with the thick fog, placing him on the back seat increased the risk tremendously,' Rutter said. 'It would have been *much* safer for him to hide the body away in the boot.'

There was a discreet cough behind them, and they turned to see Sergeant Dix standing there in the open doorway.

'What can I do for you, Sergeant?' Rutter asked.

'I just thought you'd like to know that me an' the lads are about to set off for Upper Bankside, sir,' Dix told him. 'Will you be coming with us?'

'Yes I will,' Rutter replied. 'Just give me a minute to finish off here, will you?'

Dix nodded and left.

'I think we might have hit on something important with this question of why the killer didn't put the body in the boot,' Paniatowski said. 'Do you want to bounce it around some more, later?'

Rutter smiled. 'That's a good idea. Bouncing ideas off each other was what we used to do in the good old days, wasn't it?

Paniatowski returned his smile. 'Yes, it was. That's exactly what we did in the good old days.'

'And there's no reason we can't get back into the habit.'

'None at all.' Paniatowski took a deep breath. 'We could perhaps discuss it over lunch,' she suggested.

Rutter shook his head. 'That's not on, I'm afraid. I've already got a lunch appointment booked.'

'With the boss?'

'No.'

'Then who with?'

'That's really none of your business, is it?' Rutter asked, an angry note suddenly present in his voice.

'I didn't mean to pry,' Paniatowski replied, surprised by the unexpected vehemence.

'I don't have to justify my movements to you,' Rutter said. 'You're not my wife, you know!'

'Thank you for taking the trouble to remind me, but I was already quite well aware of that,' Monika answered quietly.

Rutter slapped his forehead – hard – with the palm of his hand. 'Oh God, Monika, I didn't mean . . . I wasn't trying to say . . .'

'I know,' Paniatowski said.

'We'll meet up sometime this afternoon,' Rutter promised. 'There's . . . there's a lot to talk about, and I do think we're making progress.'

Then he stood up and strode quickly out of the office.

When Henry Marlowe put down the telephone, the look on his face was one of almost blind panic.

'That was the Cumberland Police on the line,' he told Bill Hawes. 'They've just had a phone call from Woodend. He wanted to know all about Alec Hawtrey's accident.'

'Who did he talk to?'

'Superintendent Springer.'

'And what does this superintendent know about it?'

'Everything! He was there on the mountainside at the time. It couldn't have been done without him.'

'"I am in blood stepp'd in so far, should I wade no more, returning were as tedious as go o'er,"' Bill Hawes said.

'What in God's name are you talking about, Bill?' Henry Marlowe demanded.

'It's a quote.'

'A quote!'

'From Shakespeare's *Macbeth,* or, as actors prefer to call it, the Scottish Play.'

'Oh, well that's a very bloody useful thing to know, isn't it, now?' Marlowe said.

'It is, as a matter of fact,' Hawes told him. 'It reminds us, in case we need reminding, that there's no going back – that once we've done something wrong, we have to *keep on* doing wrong in order not to be found out.'

'So what's the point?'

'The point is that once you'd told me this Superintendent Springer was involved in the incident, I ceased to be in the least bit concerned. Not only will he not shop you, Henry, he'll continue to tell lies – perhaps even bigger ones than he's told already – in order to protect you. He has no choice. He can't protect himself, if he doesn't first protect you.'

'I hope to God you're right,' Marlowe said.

So do I, Hawes thought. Because the last thing I need at this stage in the election is to have to come up with a *third* candidate.

Twenty-Five

The weather was still not quite warm enough for Dr Shastri to have abandoned the trademark sheepskin jacket which she wore over her sari, but, as she climbed down from her Land Rover, Woodend saw that her small delicate feet were now clad only in elegant thong sandals.

Actually, the chief inspector thought, 'climbing down' was not the right way to describe the motions she'd just gone through. Other people – ordinary people – climbed down from their Land Rovers. Dr Shastri seemed to float, and though she was not, in fact, bathed in a cloud of swirling rose petals as she descended, it almost *seemed* as though she were.

The doctor saw him standing there next to his Wolseley, and favoured him with a wide smile.

'Ah, my dear Chief Inspector!' she said. 'How thoughtful of you to drive all the way over here with the sole purpose of providing me with an escort from my vehicle to my place of business.'

Woodend grinned. 'Your place of business! Sometimes, you know, you talk just like my bank manager.'

'Yes, I suppose I do,' the doctor agreed. 'And is there not good reason for it, considering that, in many ways, the resemblance between the bank manager and the police surgeon is quite remarkable?'

'How do you figure that out?'

'I should have thought it was obvious. Both of us deal with customers who would never come to see us if they weren't already dead men.'

'True.'

'And though the bank manager may use only cutting words, whereas I use a very sharp scalpel, we are both intent on draining whatever is left of those poor customers' blood.'

'You really should go on the stage,' Woodend said, and –

unlike when he'd used almost the same words to Foxy Rowton, the solicitor – he meant it as a compliment.

'You seem very eager to move me into another line of work,' Dr Shastri said. 'But ask yourself this, my dear Chief Inspector – if I were gone, seduced by the glamour of a life in the lime-light, who would then be here to perform those miracles that you demand of me on almost a daily basis? And it *is* another miracle that you have come here to request, is it not?'

'Not quite a miracle,' Woodend said.

'No?' Dr Shastri asked sceptically.

'It's more like a small favour.'

'Now I am becoming most concerned,' Dr Shastri told him. 'To ask me for a favour is one thing, but if you go out of your way to soften your request by calling it a *small* favour, I can only assume it is, in reality, the size of an elephant. Am I not right?'

'Perhaps,' Woodend agreed. 'But not a *full-sized* elephant. At most, it's a cute little baby.'

'My concern is mounting by the minute,' Dr Shastri told him. 'But let us see this beast of yours anyway.'

'Do you happen, by any chance, to know the Cumberland police surgeon?' Woodend asked.

'We have met.'

'An' would you say that you're on good terms with him?'

'Of course I'm on good terms with him. All doctors are on the best of possible terms with each other – just as all policemen are on the best of possible with their own colleagues.'

Woodend thought of his own relationship with Henry Marlowe, and grimaced.

'Does that mean that he'd send you a copy of an autopsy report, if you asked for it?' he asked.

'I should think so. What is the name of this deceased person you have suddenly developed a morbid interest in?'

'He's a feller called Alec Hawtrey,' Woodend said.

The woman who answered the door of the house directly opposite Thelma Hawtrey's was called Mrs Comstock. She was somewhere in her mid-fifties, and had enough rings on her fingers to open a jewellery store.

'It's absolutely appalling that there was a murder just beyond my gate,' she said to Rutter, with tears in her eyes.

164

'Yes, it's always a shock when something terrible like that happens so close to home,' Rutter replied, sympathetically.

'I don't know how I shall bear it,' Mrs Comstock continued. 'All my friends will be laughing at me.'

'Laughing at you?'

'I can almost *hear* them telling one another that perhaps their houses didn't cost quite as much as ours did, but at least the streets in front of them aren't running with blood.'

'I can't begin to describe how deeply, deeply, sorry I feel for you,' Rutter said.

'We always thought we were above that kind of thing,' Mrs Comstock said, not even noticing the sarcasm. She sniffed. 'Of course, Mr Pine wasn't actually a resident,' she continued, brightening a little, 'so in a way, it doesn't really reflect on us at all, does it?'

'Did you see anything?' Rutter asked.

'When?'

'On the night of the murder.'

'No, we didn't. We only got back from our holiday – from our *vacation*, I should say – yesterday afternoon. We went on a cruise, in the Caribbean, you know. Very expensive, but absolutely delightful.'

'Do you have any holiday snaps that you could show me?' Rutter asked, and then, before the bloody woman could reply that she had, he quickly added, 'No, you won't have, will you? They won't be back from the chemist's yet.'

'Our *photographs* of the excursion are being developed in a professional laboratory, to the highest possible standards,' Mrs Comstock said, missing the point yet again.

'Well, much as I'd love to stay and chat some more, Mrs Comstock, I do have a murderer to catch,' Rutter said, before turning and starting to walk back down the drive.

'We used to go to Spain for our vacations, you know,' Mrs Comstock called after him. 'But we had to stop that, because every Tom, Dick and Harry goes there now.'

'My chief inspector went to Spain himself, last year,' Rutter said, over his shoulder.

'Well, that just goes to prove my point, doesn't it?' Mrs Comstock asked, stepping back into her expensive hallway and closing her polished oak door behind her.

Rutter walked down the driveway, then paused at the gate to look up and down the street.

This was not a promising area to trawl for eye-witnesses, he thought. The distance between the houses – the separation of one property from the next – was far too great for that. But when you really *needed* to find someone who'd seen what happened, you just had to hope – against the odds – that someone actually had.

Twenty-Six

'We've stumbled across somethin' very big here, Monika,' Woodend said gravely to his sergeant, 'somethin that goes far beyond the boundaries of a single murder. What we've got here is a conspiracy – an' I've absolutely no idea why it should have happened.'

Paniatowski nodded, but said nothing.

'I can understand why Bradley Pine killed Alec Hawtrey,' Woodend continued. 'He did it in order to protect the life he'd built up for himself and his relationship with Thelma. But what I simply can't get my head around is why Ron Springer – who used to be a bloody good bobby – should have allowed himself to be involved in the cover-up.'

'Hang on, aren't you getting a little ahead of yourself, here, sir?' Paniatowski asked. 'You can't say for certain that Pine *did* kill Hawtrey.'

'Can't I?' Woodend asked. 'Not even after Jeremy Tully's letter? What was that about, if it wasn't about murder?'

'Fair point,' Paniatowski conceded. 'But I'm still a long way from being convinced that whatever happened on that mountainside in Cumberland – even if it *was* murder – has anything to do with us.'

'We're *police officers*,' Woodend said.

'Yes, we are,' Paniatowski agreed. 'And our job at the moment is to catch Bradley Pine's murderer.'

'So if I was a surgeon who'd cut somebody to remove his appendix an' found he'd got stomach cancer, I should ignore the cancer an' just finish the job I'd originally set out to do, should I?'

'It's not the same thing,' Paniatowski said.

'It's exactly the same thing,' Woodend insisted. 'If we're in the process of investigatin' one crime, an' see another bein' committed, we don't just turn the other way.'

167

'But the crime you're talking about isn't being committed *now*. It happened nearly three years ago. The trail's cold.'

'You might be right that the murder trail's cold,' Woodend countered, 'but the trail leadin' to the cover-up is anythin' but. That stays hot for as long as the cover-up exists. I want to follow it, Monika. I *have to* follow it. And I'm not sure I can do it without your help.'

'But it didn't even happen on our patch,' Paniatowski protested. 'Following that trail would be just like advancing into enemy territory under heavy fire. And if anything went wrong, we could take a real fall for this, Charlie.'

'So you're sayin' you don't want anythin' to do with it?' Woodend asked disappointedly. Then he shrugged. 'Well, I can't entirely blame you for that, lass,' he continued, 'an' I want you to know that I won't hold it against you in the future.'

'I'm not saying I don't *want* anything to do with it,' Paniatowski told him. 'I'm saying I shouldn't *have* anything to do with it.' She paused for a second. 'But if you're going to stick your head above the parapet, I don't suppose I have any choice but to stick mine up next to it.'

'I appreciate it, Monika,' Woodend said. 'You're a good friend an' a good colleague.'

'I'm a bloody fool, is what I am,' Paniatowski replied. 'So what do you want me to do? March straight into Cumberland Police Headquarters and demand to know the truth?'

'No,' Woodend said. 'If I thought that would work, I'd do it myself rather than sendin' you. What you need to do instead, Monika, is to approach the whole matter from a completely different angle.'

'And what angle might that be?'

'Superintendent Springer assured me that there was absolutely nothin' abnormal about Alec Hawtrey's death – that, in fact, it was absolutely typical of the sort of thing that could happen to folk if they didn't take sufficient care on that mountainside.'

'So?'

'So I'd like you to go up there yourself – an' find out if the mountain rescue team agrees with him.'

The house next door to Mrs Comstock's was called 'Xanadu',

though there was nothing of the 'stately pleasure-dome' about its very conventional frontage.

The man who answered Rutter's knock on the door was in his late sixties. He had a shiny bald head and a large nose, under which rested a trim military moustache. He was dressed in a blue blazer with a badge on its pocket which depicted crossed rifles. He had stout brogues on his feet, and a silken cravat expertly knotted around his neck.

In some ways, he immediately reminded Rutter of Mr Morrisson – the vigilante with the notebook who patrolled Lower Bankside – but whereas Morrisson *hoped* other people would take him seriously, this man had the definite air of someone who clearly *expected* it.

The man ran his eyes quickly up and down Rutter, almost as if he were standing on parade, then said, 'Got the look of a policeman about you. Is that what you are?'

'That's right, sir,' Rutter began, reaching into his jacket for his warrant card. 'I'm a detective inspector in the—'

'Don't bother fetching out your papers, as if I was some sort of office-wallah,' the other man said dismissively. 'You say you're a policeman, and I believe you. What's your name?'

'Rutter.'

'It's a pleasure to meet you, Inspector Rutter. My name's Thompson. Lieutenant Colonel Thompson, to be strictly accurate, though I suppose you may as well forget the rank now I've left the Army. I've been expecting you since you took away that awful woman from across the road. I suppose you did *have to* let her go again, did you?'

Rutter smiled, despite himself. 'Yes, I'm afraid we did, sir. It turns out she hadn't done anything wrong.'

'Poppycock!' Colonel Thompson said.

'Poppycock?'

'Bound to have done *something* wrong – we all have – but if she didn't kill that Pine chap, you were probably quite correct to release her.'

'You said, a moment ago, that you'd been expecting me, sir,' Rutter said. 'Why was that?'

'Because I saw both the murderer and his victim.'

'Where?'

'Where do you think? Over there. Right in front of the awful Thelma's house.'

Was Thompson the sort of witness that bobbies conducting an investigation would give their eye teeth for, Rutter wondered. Or was he simply a nutter? At the moment, he was putting his money on the man being a nutter.

'If you *did* see them over there, why didn't you report it immediately?' he asked.

'Didn't know *what* I'd seen at the time, did I? Until I read in the morning paper that Pine had been croaked almost on my own doorstep, I thought that I'd been witnessing no more than the tail-end of a drunken party.'

'Go on,' Rutter said cautiously.

'I was out in the garden the other night, when I saw a green Cortina parked in front of Thelma Hawtrey's house.'

'What were you doing out in the garden?' Rutter wondered.

'Can't a man stand around on his own property when he wants to?' Thompson asked.

'There was a thick fog that night. It wouldn't have been very pleasant to be outside.'

Thompson snorted. 'Don't know the meaning of unpleasant weather till you've served in India.'

'Even so . . .'

'You're not going to let go of this until I give you an explanation you're happy with, are you?' Colonel Thompson asked.

'No. I'm afraid I'm not.'

'All right, I suppose I'd better come clean. My dear lady wife's quite a sweet old thing in her own way, but she does have some very strange ideas.'

'Like what?'

'Doesn't like me smoking in the house. Says it makes the place smell. Can you believe it?'

'It is a little unusual,' Rutter admitted.

'But be that as it may, one of the first things you're taught as a young officer is that you should never become involved in a battle that you know you can't possibly win, and if there was ever a perfect example of that dictum, this is it. So if the memsahib wishes to enforce a policy of no smoking in quarters, that's the way it has to be.'

'Quite,' Rutter said.

'And it's not such a high price to pay, considering that the woman's allowed herself to be dragged halfway around the world and back over the last thirty or so years,' Colonel Thompson said.

'So you came out into the garden for the purpose of having a smoke?!' Rutter said.

'Took you long enough to get there, didn't it?' Colonel Thompson said. 'Lucky you weren't facing wild tribesmen, or you'd have been dead by now. Anyway, the point is, I *did* come out into the garden, and that's when I noticed the car parked on the street in front of the Hawtrey residence.'

'Was there anybody in it?'

'I'll tell this in my own way, if you don't mind,' Colonel Thompson said sharply.

'Go ahead,' Rutter agreed.

'There was nobody there at first. Then a chap appeared out of the driveway. Can't give you much of a description, I'm afraid. In the fog, he was little more than a black shape. At any rate, he opened the boot of the car and—'

'You're sure he opened the boot?'

'Of course I'm sure. Wouldn't have said it if I hadn't been. He opened the boot, then he disappeared up the driveway again. And at that point, I must admit, I wandered off to the other side of the garden.'

'So you didn't see any more?'

'If you can stop interrupting for a moment, I'll tell you what I saw and what I didn't see.'

'Sorry,' Rutter said.

'By the time I returned to my original vantage point, the man had reappeared from the driveway, and this time he was holding another man up. I assumed the second man was drunk, but from what I've read in the papers, the other man was probably Pine – and he was dead.'

'That's more than likely,' Rutter agreed.

'The murderer . . . we are agreed that it was probably the murderer, are we?'

'We're agreed.'

'The murderer opened the back door of the car, and bundled Pine into it. He had a certain amount of difficulty doing it, but no more than he'd have had if Pine been dead drunk instead of simply dead.'

'Can I ask a question now?' Rutter said.

'Yes, *now* you may,' the Colonel conceded.

'Did it, at any point, look as if he might be thinking of putting Pine in the boot?'

'No, it didn't – though the boot was still open.'

'So what happened next?'

'Once he'd crammed Pine into the car, he slammed the door closed. It made quite a noise in the still night air, and I remember thinking that I hoped the poor drunk was well tucked inside the car, because if his arm had been hanging out, the force would have broken it.'

'What did the murderer do next?' Rutter asked. 'Did he get into the driver's seat?'

'No, he didn't. The boot was still open, remember.' Colonel Thompson paused for a moment. 'That wasn't some kind of test you were putting me to, was it?' he continued.

'A test?'

'To try and establish whether or not I'm gaga?'

'Of course not,' Rutter replied, hoping that he wasn't blushing.

'The killer went round to the back of the car, and closed the boot. And this time, he was much more careful about it. I thought at the time it was because he was showing some belated consideration for the residents.'

'But you don't think that now?'

'Chap who's just smashed another chap's head in isn't going to worry about causing offence to the local rate-payers, now is he?'

'So why *did* he close the boot so carefully?'

'I haven't the foggiest idea.' Colonel Thompson chuckled. 'That was rather good, wasn't it? It was foggy, and I haven't the foggiest idea.'

'Very droll,' Rutter agreed. 'I'll be sending a man round to take down your statement later, sir. That should be no problem, should it?'

'No problem at all,' Colonel Thompson agreed. 'I'll do my duty, as I always have.'

Twenty-Seven

Dr Shastri entered Woodend's office without knocking. For once there was nothing in her movements to suggest the gentle gliding of a butterfly. In fact, she came much closer to resembling an enraged wasp.

'In case you wish to keep a record of it for posterity, I should inform you that your little deception was effective for exactly one hour, thirty-five minutes and twenty-eight seconds, Chief Inspector,' she said.

'I beg your pardon?' Woodend replied.

'That is precisely how long it took me to discover I have been wasting my time. For a moment, it seemed to me just like a return to the bad old days, and I was very angry indeed.'

'The bad old days?' Woodend repeated, completely mystified. 'What bad old days?'

'The bad old days when I first came to this country of yours.'

'You're not makin' a lot of sense, lass.'

'Then I will explain further. Many of the English people with whom I worked at that time thought it might be most amusing to hold me up to ridicule. And so they talked in my presence about diseases I had never heard of – which is hardly surprising, since they had just invented them – and they sent me off on countless pointless errands. Nor did it stop there. They hid medical records from me, and sent me friends of theirs who claimed to be suffering terrible symptoms, but were only really *pretending* to be ill.'

'Why did they do that?'

'Because they considered it great sport to confuse the poor, unsophisticated Indian doctor – to make a complete monkey out of her, in fact. And it seemed to me that you were doing exactly the same thing yourself.'

'Come off it, Doc,' Woodend protested. 'First of all, if one

173

of us is unsophisticated, it certainly isn't you. An' secondly – an' more importantly – I've got too much respect for you to try an' make you look a fool.'

Dr Shastri nodded. 'Yes, that is the conclusion I had already almost reached myself, and I am pleased to have you confirm it,' she said. 'So I am no longer angry. You are far too nice a man to ever deliberately insult me, so if it is not an insult it must be an example of your strange English sense of humour, which you expected me to share. Very well, then, I must learn to develop this strange sense of humour, too, and when the opportunity arises, I will play a similar joke on you.'

'I still don't have the slightest idea of what you're talkin' about, Doc,' Woodend confessed.

'Of course you don't,' Dr Shastri replied, smiling knowingly. 'Would you care to hear what is in the autopsy report?'

She might *say* she wasn't angry any more, Woodend thought, but anger was still there, bubbling just below the surface.

'Yes, I'd like to hear what it,' he told her. 'An' I must say, you've got hold of it very quickly.'

'Indeed I have. But then, you always knew that I would, didn't you, Chief Inspector?'

'Did I? How?'

'Very good,' Dr Shastri said. 'Very nicely played. You kept your face perfectly straight, and you *almost* convince me that you had no idea what I was talking about. But to return to the report – Mr Alec Hawtrey broke his leg when he was climbing. He sustained no other injuries, but the broken leg alone was enough to make him less resilient than his companions in the face of the blizzard, and he died of exposure.'

'You still haven't told me how you managed to get hold of the report so quickly?' Woodend pointed out.

'I called my colleague in Cumberland, and reminded him of the jolly times we had spent together at medical conferences, playing "Pass the Vital Organ" and "Pin the Appendix on the Cadaver",' Dr Shastri said, regaining some of her normal good humour. 'Once I had him eating out of my hand, I asked him if he wouldn't mind sending me the autopsy report. He said that wasn't necessary, because we already had a copy of it.'

'What?'

'He did not perform the autopsy himself, you see. He was

intending to perform it, but then a Police Superintendent, by the name of Springer, informed him that it would instead be carried out by another medical examiner from outside the county.'

'Isn't that unusual?' Woodend asked.

'Very unusual indeed. But Superintendent Springer told him that the decision had been taken at the *highest levels* of the police authority, so he saw no point in arguing.'

'An' who *was* this medical examiner from outside the county, who actually did the job?'

Dr Shastri smiled again. 'So you continue with your little joke right through to the bitter end,' she said. 'I must make a note of that, so that when you become the victim of my revenge-joke on you, I can sustain it with equal ferocity.'

'I honestly don't know who he was,' Woodend said.

'If it pleases you so much, I can see no harm in going along with your game,' Dr Shastri said. She put her hand to her fore-head, as if thinking very hard. 'Who *could* it be?' she continued. 'If the death occurred in Cumberland, why would we have a copy of the autopsy report here in Whitebridge?'

'Because the medical examiner who carried out the autopsy was from Whitebridge himself?' Woodend asked, finally grasping the point.

'Exactly! It was my predecessor who actually performed the autopsy – Dr Pierson.'

Doc Pierson! Woodend repeated to himself.

The last case that he and Pierson had worked on together had been the murder at Dugdale's Farm. And Pierson really *had* made a monkey out of *him*, because in order to conceal a whole stinking level of municipal corruption, he had delib-erately distorted the medical evidence – and almost allowed the killer to escape.

The doctor was still serving time in HM Prison Saltney for that particular betrayal of his Hippocratic oath. But who could say how many more times before then he had fudged the evidence, in order to protect some rich or powerful member of the Whitebridge élite?

And given that Bradley Pine had been both rich *and* powerful, was the autopsy report really worth the paper it was printed on?

*   *   *

Constable Colin Beresford did not feel entirely comfortable about entering a Catholic church, and there was ample reason for this. When he had to fill in any forms which asked about his religion, he always wrote down 'Church of England', but his church-going was largely confined to christenings, weddings and funerals, and if he thought about God at all, it was only to wonder why He had chosen to inflict a mind-decaying disease on a woman who was still in her early sixties.

Still, once he was actually inside St Mary's, he could not help but be fascinated by what he saw. The place might not be holier than any of the churches he was used to, but it was certainly much more elaborate.

Looking around at the statues and paintings, smelling the incense which lingered in the air from the last service, he got the distinct impression that this was a religion which took itself very seriously indeed.

The priest's appearance came as something of a surprise, too. All the vicars who Beresford had come across had been old men – in their fifties, at least – but this man couldn't be more than thirty.

'Can I help you?' the priest asked.

'I'm looking for someone,' Beresford said.

The priest smiled. 'And is that someone God?' he asked. 'Because if He is who you're looking for, you've come to the right place.'

'No, I'm ... I'm looking for a police officer,' Beresford said, starting to feel a little confused.

'Then might I suggest you would be likely to be more successful if you began your search at a police station?'

'This officer – this *female* officer – is working on a case at the moment, and I thought she might be here.'

'You're talking about Monika, aren't you?'

'Yes, that's right. Sergeant Paniatowski.'

'She's not here,' Father Taylor said. 'Nor, as far as I know, is she expected in the near future. But if you'd care to leave a message with me, I'll deliver it to her the next time I see her.'

'No, that's all right,' Beresford said. 'I should be seeing her myself before too long.'

'Is what's troubling you something that only Monika can help you with?' the priest asked, with a concerned and sympathetic look on his face. 'Or might I, possibly, be of some assistance?'

'No, I'm very sorry, but it really does have to be Sergeant Paniatowski,' Beresford said.

'There's no need to apologize,' Father Taylor said softly. 'We all have the right to choose our own guides.'

'You're very understanding, Father,' Beresford said.

'I try to be,' the priest replied.

Once outside again, Beresford cleared his head of the slightly intimidating atmosphere of the Catholic Church by greedily sucking in the contaminated air of a Northern industrial town.

The priest had asked him why he had been looking for Sergeant Paniatowski. Well, the answer to that was simple enough.

He was a lost soul – though in an investigative, rather than a religious, sense.

He was a man out of his depth, wondering if he could keep treading water until he learned how to swim, or whether it might not be better to be hauled on to the shore and content himself, henceforth, with wearing a uniform.

Sergeant Paniatowski would advise him. Sergeant Paniatowski was the only person he could think of who would be *able* to advise him – which was why he had spent the best part of two hours aimlessly scouring Whitebridge for her, instead of simply waiting until they met up in the pub later.

He fully realized that this urge to talk to her immediately was nothing more than a sign of his own desperation, but there was nothing he could do about that. He was *so* desperate, in fact, that he'd almost poured out his troubles to the priest – and now he was beginning to wonder why he hadn't.

It was true that Father Taylor was not a bobby himself – and so would have had an imperfect grasp of the sorts of problems bobbies had to face – but he had appeared to be a kind man, an understanding man. And though Beresford was sure they had never met before, he'd seemed strangely familiar.

Though the Dirty Duck was rather a come-down for a woman used to living off a more-than-generous expense account, Elizabeth Driver was glad that she had chosen it as the place to have her lunch with Bob Rutter. She could see, just by looking at him from across the table, that he was far more at home there than he would have been at one of Whitebridge's more expensive restaurants – and it was very important that he *did* feel at home.

'I can't tell you how gratified I am that you said you'd meet me today,' she told him. 'I'm *especially* grateful because I know I don't deserve it – because we *both* know I don't deserve it.'

'There was a time when I'd have agreed with you,' Rutter replied. 'But not any more.'

'So what's changed?'

'My life has changed. And because of that, the way I look at everything else has changed, too.'

'Do you want to tell me about it?' Elizabeth Driver asked, only just resisting the temptation to reach across the table and place her hand softly on top of his.

'The one thing in life that everybody needs is forgiveness,' Rutter told her. 'I wanted my wife to forgive me, but now I'll never know whether she would have or not.'

'I'm certain she would have,' Elizabeth Driver said. 'I'm convinced she would eventually have come to see that what happened was all Monika Paniatowski's fault.'

'It wasn't all Monika's fault!' Rutter said, with a hint of rising anger in his voice.

'No, of course it wasn't,' Elizabeth Driver said hastily. 'I phrased it badly. What I meant to say was that the affair would never have happened if Monika hadn't been around – that you'd never have strayed from your marriage vows with any woman but her.'

'I think that's true,' Rutter said.

'I'm sure it is,' Elizabeth Driver said, reassuringly.

'Everybody makes mistakes, and everybody needs forgiveness,' Rutter said, returning to his earlier theme. 'That's why I'm trying as hard as I possibly can to forgive you.'

'And is it working?'

'I think I'm almost there.'

'You're so kind,' Elizabeth Driver said, in a voice she hoped sounded both deeply touched and deeply sincere.

Rutter shook his head vehemently. 'I'm not kind at all. I'm doing it for purely selfish reasons. If I can't learn to forgive you, then how will I ever learn to forgive myself?'

'I've been wondering how *I* could make amends,' Elizabeth Driver said. 'And I think I may have found a way.'

'How?'

'Through using the only real talent I have. I want to write a book on you and Maria.'

'What kind of book?'

'An inspirational book. One which shows how bravely you both coped with her blindness.'

'Until I betrayed her,' Rutter said.

'I wouldn't go into that.'

'You'd have to!' Rutter said fiercely. 'It wouldn't be an honest book if you didn't.'

'I'm not sure that's necessarily—'

'And if it wasn't an honest book, then it wouldn't be worth writing at all.'

'I can quite see that,' Elizabeth Driver lied. 'But have you thought about what it might do to your reputation if that part of the story appeared in print?'

'I don't care about my reputation.'

Elizabeth Driver pursed her brow thoughtfully. 'I suppose I could always protect you by changing the names,' she suggested.

'I don't want the names changing. Maria has the right to be admired under her own name – and I deserve to be vilified under mine.'

'And what about Monika?'

'Monika's name *would* have to be changed,' Rutter admitted. 'And she couldn't appear as she is – real flesh and blood. She'd have to be no more than a shadow.'

'That shouldn't be too much of a problem,' Elizabeth Driver said. She paused for a second. 'You sound as if you're almost ready to give me permission to go ahead with the project.'

'I *am* almost ready.'

'Though I must say, the way you've outlined what you want, it won't be quite the same book as I'd thought of writing. You make your agreement to it seem almost like a penance.'

'It's not *almost like* a penance at all,' Rutter told her. 'It *is* a bloody penance.'

Twenty-Eight

The Last Drop Inn was a squat stone building, with thick walls to repel the drifting snow, and ceiling heights designed with the much shorter men of earlier generations in mind. A large open fire burned brightly in the grate of the bar parlour, and its flames were reflected in the copper pots which hung on the walls.

It had already been a thriving pub when John Hancock had been the first man to sign a document containing what he and his fellow delegates considered to be self-evident truths. It had served pints of fine and frothy Lake District ale to passengers on the London mail coach on the very day that Louis XVI of France had lost his head. And when Victoria had ascended to the throne of England in 1837, its regular drinkers had shaken their heads and wondered just how a young, inexperienced girl like her could ever be expected to act like a monarch.

Monika Paniatowski quite liked the place herself, and knew that Woodend would have absolutely loved it.

She was sitting at a table with Brian Steele, leader of the mountain rescue team, and his nephew Craig. Brian struck her as a man who made decisions quickly, and probably didn't appreciate being questioned on them. Craig had an appealing innocence which reminded her a little of Constable Beresford's.

'To be honest with you, Sergeant, I don't see how what happened on the mountain over three years ago can have anything to do with a murder that's only a few days old,' Brian Steele was saying.

'Neither do I,' Paniatowski replied. 'But my boss wanted the questions asked, and I wasn't going to turn down the chance of spending the day up here among your lovely lakes.'

Craig Steele positively beamed with pleasure. 'I'm glad you like them, Monika.'

'That's *Sergeant Paniatowski* to you,' his uncle told him.

'I don't mind being called Monika, honestly I don't,' Paniatowski said, being deliberately girlish.

'Please yourself, then,' Brian said, taking slight umbrage at his ruling being overturned.

'Tell me about the rescue,' Paniatowski suggested.

'It was one of the worst blizzards I can ever recall experiencing, and I've been part of one mountain rescue team or another for nearly twenty-five years now,' Brian Steele said.

'Was it actually forecast that it would be such bad weather?' Paniatowski asked.

'Now why would you want to know that?' Brian Steele wondered, with the slightly suspicious tone to his voice that all men of action seemed to have when confronted with people who write up reports of their conversations with them in warm offices.

I want to know because, if I were planning any funny business on the mountainside, I might decide that bad weather would provide me with the perfect cover for it, Paniatowski thought.

But aloud, she said, 'I'm just trying to build up a general picture of how things were.'

'The blizzard came out of nowhere,' Brian said. 'It took *everybody* by surprise.'

'Especially those three poor buggers who were stuck up the mountain,' Craig added.

'Watch your language when there's a lady present,' his uncle warned him. 'Now, where was I? Oh yes, Pine, Hawtrey and Tulworth were staying at the Bluebell Hotel and—'

'Tully,' Craig interrupted. 'His name was Tully.'

'Pine, Hawtrey and *Tully* were staying at the Bluebell Hotel,' Brian said, flashing a look of annoyance at his nephew. 'Before they set out that morning, they left all the details of their planned expedition at the reception desk, just as they were supposed to do, so when they hadn't returned by nightfall, the hotel naturally phoned us.'

'We knew roughly where they were, but there was no way we could get to them in those conditions,' Craig Steele said.

'What the boy means is that we have one golden rule that we always operate under,' Brian explained. 'We're more than willing to put our own lives at risk in order to carry out a rescue, but that's not the same thing at all as being prepared to *throw* our lives away.'

'Getting *yourself* killed doesn't help the people who you're trying to save one little bit,' Craig added.

'Anyway, we got ready to go, and waited for the weather to lift,' Brian said. 'But it didn't lift the next day, nor the day after that. It wasn't until the fourth morning that it started to improve, and by then, the three of them had been stranded on the mountain for at least eighty hours.'

'It was when it *did* finally did start to lift that your feller actually turned up,' Craig said.

'Our feller? You mean Superintendent Springer by that, do you?' Paniatowski asked.

'No, not him,' Brian said dismissively. 'Ron Springer may have worked down in London once upon a time, but over the years he's got all that out of his system, and now he's one of ours.'

'Then who—'

'The feller that I'm talkin' about was a Lancashire bobby. What was his name, Craig?'

'Marlowe, I think,' Craig Steele replied.

'Marlowe?' Paniatowski repeated. '*Henry* Marlowe?'

'That's him,' Brian agreed. 'You sound as if it's news to you that he was ever here.'

'It is,' Paniatowski replied, thoughtfully. 'But please don't let me interrupt you.'

'It's not the first time that some bigwig or other has turned up at the scene of one of our rescues,' Craig said. 'They think it's glamorous, you see – a bit like putting a Stetson on and pretending you're a cowboy.'

'And we tolerate them poncing about like that because we have no choice in the matter,' Brian said.

'No choice?' Paniatowski repeated.

'You have to understand that we're a voluntary organization, and it's people like your Mr Marlowe who help to raise the funds we need to keep our operation going.'

'Of course, it doesn't take them long to realize that there's very little glamour in what we do – and a lot of hard slog,' Craig said. 'And it's usually at that point that they start saying that while they'd love to come along on the final stages of the rescue, they think they've pulled a muscle.'

Brian laughed. 'That's exactly what they say,' he agreed. 'Not that we'd have *let* them come along with us, anyway. It's a dangerous job we do, and there's no room for passengers.'

'You did let that Marlowe feller come along,' Craig pointed out.

'That was the exception to the rule,' Brian said, giving his nephew another warning glance. 'And there were two very good reasons for making it an exception. The first one was that he'd done some mountain climbing himself, and when he was talking to me, he managed to convince me that not only would he not be a hindrance in the rescue, but he might actually be some help.'

'And what was the second?' Paniatowski asked.

Brian looked a little sheepish. 'Superintendent Springer wanted us to let him come with us. He said that Mr Marlowe was considering entering politics, and it would sort of give him a leg up if he could be associated with the rescue.'

'I've never met a feller quite as keen to get himself in the limelight as Marlowe was that day,' Craig said. 'He'd hardly arrived at the rescue centre before he was asking my permission to use the radio telephone.'

'*I'd* put Craig in charge of that,' Brian said. 'It's a very responsible job, but I thought he could handle it.'

'So, since we didn't need the channel open for anything else, I said it would be all right,' Craig told Paniatowski. 'He made more than one call, and from the bits of the conversation that I happened to overhear, I'm almost sure he was talking to the newspapers.'

'Let's get back to the main point of the story, shall we?' Brian said. 'Springer asked me if we'd take Marlowe along, and I said yes. If anybody else had asked me, I'd have turned him down, but since Ron Springer's been a good friend to our unit, I decided to oblige him. But I want to make it perfectly plain to you that I'd *never* have agreed – however much pressure Springer had put on me – if I hadn't thought Marlowe was up to it.'

'Understood,' Paniatowski said.

'It was the helicopter that spotted them,' Brian continued. 'But there was no way it could have landed where they were, and even using a winch would have been difficult, so it was decided that we'd do the job from the ground. When we finally reached the three fellers, we could see straight away that while the others were in a pretty bad way, Hawtrey was beyond any kind of help we could give him.'

'He'd had a fall off the rock and broken his leg, hadn't he?' Paniatowski asked.

'That's right. And Pine had fashioned some rough splints for it, from the frame to his rucksack.'

'Had Hawtrey sustained any other injuries?'

'Wouldn't they be in the autopsy report?' Brian asked, with a hint of suspicion again.

'I suppose they would be, but I was just wondering if you'd noticed anything yourselves.'

'He'd injured his arm,' Craig volunteered. 'It was quite a nasty wound as well.'

'Did you see it yourself?' Paniatowski asked.

'Not personally, no.'

'Then how do you know it was nasty?'

'I could tell from the amount of blood there was on his trousers and his boots.'

'But that could have come from anywhere,' Paniatowski pointed out. 'How can you be so sure the wound was in his arm?'

'Because that's where he was bloodiest of all. The blood on his boots and trousers was just spattered, but on his arm – where it had soaked through the sleeve of his jacket – it was a thick stain.'

Paniatowski lit a cigarette, to give herself time to think.

'If he was still wearing his jacket, how was it possible that some of the blood had spattered on other parts of his body?' she asked, once she'd inhaled.

'It probably happened when they stripped off his jacket in an attempt to staunch the wound,' Craig replied.

'This is getting *less* like an interview, and *more* like an interrogation,' Brian said.

Paniatowski laughed. 'Sorry! I do tend to get carried away, don't I? I'll be asking you if you've paid your television licence fee next!'

Craig joined in her laughter, but Brian just said, 'I have paid it. I can show you, if you like.'

'What sort of state were Pine and Tully in when you found them?' Paniatowski asked.

184

'Pine had frostbite in one hand, but otherwise he didn't seem too bad,' Brian said. 'And he was certainly glad to see his mate.'

Bradley Pine, lying on the ground, looks up at Marlowe.
'Henry!' he gasps. 'Thank God you're here.'
'It was the least I could do for a friend,' Marlowe replies.
'If you'll just step aside, Mr Marlowe, I'd like to examine Mr Pine now,' Brian says, crisply and businesslike.
'No!' Pine says, raising an arm weakly into the air, as if that will ward off a fit mountain rescuer. 'No!'
'You have to be examined, Mr Pine,' Brian says firmly.
'Henry will do it.'
'I'm the one with the qualifications.'
'Henry . . . will . . . do it.'

'It's sometimes better to give way in these matters,' Brian Steele told Paniatowski. 'I was right, wasn't I, in assuming that, as a serving police officer, Marlowe would have kept himself up to date with the latest First Aid techniques?'

'Undoubtedly,' Paniatowski replied, with as straight a face as she could muster.

'And when a patient is as distressed as Pine obviously was, you can often do more harm than good by forcing the issue.'

'What state was Tully in?' Paniatowski asked.

'Tully was a mess,' Brian replied. 'Not physically – he was in better shape than Pine, in that respect – but mentally.'

Tully's eyes are wide and wild and filled with pain. He looks as if he were watching his own ghost walk before him. He doesn't even seem to realize that anybody else is there.
'We're the mountain rescue team. We're here to help you,' Brian Steele informs him.
'Asperges me,' Tully intones. 'Domine, hyssopo, et mundabor: lavabis me, et super nivem dealbabor.'
'You're not making any sense, man,' Brian tells him.
'Ab homine iniquo, et doloso erue me,' Tully says, and it is clear that it is not his rescuer he is speaking to.
'Pull yourself together!' Brian says sharply. 'When you've been through an ordeal like yours, you've got to pull yourself

185

together as soon as possible. You've got to come back to the real world.'

'Munda cor meum ac labia mea, omnipotens Deus, qui labia Isaiæ Prophetæ calculo mundasti ignito,' Tully replies.

'Most of what he said was in a foreign language,' Brian Steele told Paniatowski. 'German or French, or something like that.'

'It was Latin,' Craig corrected him.

His uncle looked at him sharply, as if annoyed that Craig knew something that he didn't.

'Who told you that?' he demanded.

'Tommy O'Donnell,' Craig said. He turned to Paniatowski. 'Tommy was another member of the team,' he explained.

'And how would somebody like *Tommy O'Donnell* know whether it was Latin or just gobbledegook?' Brian asked scornfully.

'He's a Catholic,' Craig said.

'Oh, is he?' Brian said. 'Well, that would explain it, I suppose. Is this Tully feller a Catholic, an' all?' he asked Paniatowski.

'I believe he is.'

Brian sniffed. 'Well, there you are, then. People are entitled to follow any faith they choose, even if it is Papist.'

'Did he say anything that *wasn't* in Latin?' Paniatowski asked.

'Not that I heard. But then I didn't have much opportunity to hear it, did I? Because that's when your Mr Marlowe decided to stick his oar into the proceedings again.'

'I thought he was taking care of Bradley Pine.'

'He had been. But he seemed to lose any interest in Pine, and from then on, all he cared about was Tully.'

Marlowe has stuck close to Tully all the way down from the mountainside, and now, when the ambulances arrive at the rescue centre, he announces that he will travel in the same ambulance as the man.

'You'll be in the way of the paramedics,' Brian Steele says.

'I'll be assisting *the paramedics,' Marlowe tells him.*

'Have they agreed to it?'

'They will. And anyway, what happens between them and me is no concern of yours. Your part of the rescue operation is over.'

186

'I don't want people falling down and kissing my feet for what I do for them, but I don't like being spoken to like that, either,' Brian Steele said. 'If the bugger hadn't been a policeman, I'd have dropped him where he was standing.'

'I wish you had,' Paniatowski said.

'Pardon?'

'I wish you had . . . had pointed out to him how ungrateful he was being,' Paniatowski quickly corrected herself. 'But there's one thing I still don't understand about this whole affair.'

'And what might that be?'

'I don't understand why I've never heard anything about any of this before today. Surely, if Mr Marlowe had rung the papers, as Craig says he did, his part in the rescue would have been splashed all over them.'

'So it would,' Craig agreed, 'if he hadn't had second thoughts about the whole thing on the way back to town.'

The ambulance carrying Jeremy Tully arrives at the hospital ahead of the one carrying Bradley Pine, and Marlowe is the first person to climb out of it. He sees the half a dozen news photographers who are gathered around the door which leads into the main hospital building, and visibly blanches.

The paramedics are already in the process of lifting Tully's stretcher out of the vehicle when Marlowe swings round to face them again.

'Wait!' he says.

'What do you mean?' one of the paramedics asks.

'Isn't plain English good enough for you?' Marlowe demands. 'I want you to wait until I tell you it's all right to bloody-well unload him.'

'Now just a minute—' the paramedic begins.

'And if you don't do exactly what I say, I'll personally ensure that the local police make your life a bloody misery from now on,' Marlowe hisses.

The mountain rescue Land Rover and Superintendent Springer's car pull up behind the ambulance. Craig Steele gets out of the one, and Springer out of the other. They reach the ambulance at roughly the same time.

'What's the delay?' Springer asks.

'Get rid of them,' Marlowe says, gesturing towards the pressmen.

187

Superintendent Springer looks puzzled. 'But I thought you told me that you wanted them to—'

'I want them out of here!'

Springer walks over to the reporters, and explains that his colleague has decided that it would be best for the injured men if they weren't bothered by reporters at this point. He apologizes for the inconvenience, and promises them he'll find a way to make it up to them in the near future.

The journalists readily agree – this is, after all, nothing more than a common or garden mountain rescue, and now Springer's in their debt, he'll throw them something really juicy next time.

Marlowe waits until the reporters are well clear of the area, and only then does he allow the paramedics to get on with their job.

'So why do you think there was a sudden about-face on Mr Marlowe's part?' Paniatowski asked.

'Who knows?' Craig Steele replied. 'I was right there, and I certainly don't. Maybe it was something that Mr Pine had said to him. Or maybe it was what Mr Tully wanted.'

'I thought you said Tully was speaking in *Latin*!' said his uncle, still smarting over the earlier revelation of his ignorance.

'Perhaps he'd switched back to English,' Craig suggested. 'Or perhaps Mr Marlowe knows Latin.'

Mr Marlowe doesn't know his arse from his elbow most of the time, Paniatowski thought, but she kept it to herself.

'What happened after that?' she asked.

'We wouldn't know,' Brian Steele told her. 'Our job was done. And unlike your Mr Marlowe, we didn't want to get in the way of other professionals who were trying to do theirs.'

'So we all went straight to the pub and got absolutely legless,' his nephew said.

'So we stood down from duty,' Brian Steele corrected him.

'But I do know that Mr Marlowe didn't leave immediately, because I saw him in town the next day,' Craig said.

Twenty-Nine

'They may well be livin' in the so-called "Permissive Society" down in London, an' possibly they are in Manchester an' all,' Woodend said, gazing into his pint of bitter as if he suspected that the answer to all the mysteries of the world were contained in a single glass, 'but the idea of "doin' your own thing" is still an alien concept to Whitebridge.'

Bob Rutter grinned. 'And what do you think the reason for that is, sir?' he asked.

'It's because the glue that's always held industrial towns like this one together is *conformity*. The mills dictated the pattern of life, you see, lad. Everybody started work at the same time, everybody left work at the same time – and everybody went on holiday at the same time, usually to the same place, while all the mills were closed down for maintenance. An' even though the mills have gone, we're still livin' in their shadow.'

'I don't see that should necessarily stop the *middle* class from "doing their own thing",' Rutter said.

'That's where you're wrong, lad. They don't have to conform to the same things as the workers, but they still *do* have to conform. There's as much a proper way to dress – an' a proper way to behave – up at that Golf an' Country Club as there is down in the cobbled streets. There's rules which are not written down, but everybody still knows. An' if you want a good example of what happens when you break the rules, you've only got to look at the case of Alec Hawtrey.'

'Yes, I can imagine he was somewhat shunned by some of his old Catholic friends, because they didn't recognize that his second marriage was—' Bob Rutter began.

'From what I've heard up at the Golf Club, he was shunned by nearly every bugger – because if you can't fit in with one part of the Establishment, you'll find yourself unwelcome in *any* part of it.'

189

'Poor devil,' Rutter said.

'Poor devil, indeed,' Woodend agreed. 'Alec Hawtrey seems to have sacrificed a great deal by givin' into the temptations of the—' He stopped abruptly, and made great show of checking his watch. 'I wonder where the devil young Monika's got to?' he continued. 'She should have been back from her trip to the Lakes by now.'

'He sacrificed a great deal by giving into the temptations of the *flesh*,' Rutter completed. 'Isn't that what you were about to say?'

'Aye, I was,' Woodend admitted. 'However careful I try to be, I always seem to be puttin' my foot right in it on that particular question, don't I? I'm really very sorry, lad.'

'There's no need to apologize. We can't make what's happened go away by just ignoring it.'

'Monika said pretty much the same thing to me. An' you may well both have a point. On the other hand, there isn't much to be gained by constantly draggin' it into the spotlight, is there?'

'As a matter of fact, there is,' Rutter said. 'It's only by frankly and openly confessing our sins that we can ever hope to put them behind us. That's why I'm seriously considering Elizabeth's idea of—'

He stopped himself speaking mid-sentence, just as the chief inspector had done earlier.

'What was that?' Woodend asked.

'Nothing.'

'Which Elizabeth are we talkin' about? Do I know her?'

'Let's change the subject,' Rutter suggested forcefully. 'What do you make of what the old colonel told me this afternoon?'

'Well, he pretty much confirmed what we already suspected, didn't he?' Woodend said. 'That the killer was actin' on his own.'

'True. But Colonel Thompson also confirmed that the killer made no effort to put the body in the boot, and I still haven't been able to work out why that should have been.'

'It was a foggy night, an' there weren't many people about on the streets,' Woodend pointed out. 'Maybe the killer thought puttin' him on the back seat would be safe enough.'

'There weren't *many* people about, but there were *some* – which meant there was still an element of risk,' Rutter countered. 'Say he'd been pulled up at a traffic light, and a passing pedestrian had just happened to look into the car. Say there'd been an accident somewhere on his route, and the traffic patrol sent to deal with it had flagged him down.'

'There'd only have been a slight possibility of either of those things actually happenin'.'

'Agreed. But why run any risk at all, when he didn't have to?'

'You're right, of course,' Woodend agreed. 'An' since, accordin' to your pal the colonel, he *had* opened the boot, his initial thought *must have been* to put Pine in there.'

'And then there's the difference between the ways he closed the door and closed the boot,' Rutter said. 'Colonel Thompson says that he *slammed* the back door, but he shut the boot very gently.'

'Almost as if he didn't want to damage whatever – or *whoever* – was inside it,' Woodend mused. 'Perhaps he *did* have an accomplice after all, an' the accomplice was hidin' in the boot.'

The bar door swung open, and Monika Paniatowski walked in. Even from a distance, both men could see that her face was flushed with excitement, and as she strode across the room it looked as if she could hardly wait to tell Woodend and Rutter what it was that she'd discovered.

'Did you know that Mr Marlowe was in the rescue party that brought Pine, Hawtrey and Tully down from the mountainside?' she asked, the moment she'd reached the table.

Woodend frowned. 'No, I certainly bloody didn't! An' perhaps more to the point, *why* didn't I know?'

'Because Marlowe didn't want to advertise the fact that he'd been there at all. Nor would I, if I'd helped to cover up a murder!'

'So you're comin' round to the idea that what Tully wrote in his letter was no more than the simple truth?'

'The evidence certainly seems to be pointing that way.'

Paniatowski quickly filled Woodend and Rutter in on her conversation with the mountain rescue men, including the details of the blood spatters on the trousers and boots, and the patch of blood on the sleeve of Hawtrey's jacket.

'Maybe all the blood *did* come from a wound in his arm,' Woodend suggested.

191

'The sleeve of his jacket wasn't torn!' Paniatowski countered. 'If it had have been, I'm sure either Brian or Craig Steele would have mentioned it. If it had have been, they'd have seen the wound on the arm for themselves, instead of just being *told* about it.'

'I still don't see why the sleeve *had* to be torn,' Woodend said.

'Neither do I,' Rutter agreed. 'As a kid, I was always falling down and grazing my knee without actually tearing my pants.'

'But this wasn't just a graze,' Paniatowski pointed out. 'Hawtrey must have lost at least a pint of blood.'

'Good point,' Woodend conceded. 'But if that's the case, why didn't these Steele fellers – who are experienced mountain rescuers – reach the same conclusion that you did?'

'Because they'd got plenty of other things to think about at the time,' Paniatowski argued. 'Hawtrey was dead. There was nothing more they could do for him, and they were well aware of it. So they paid him virtually no attention at all. Besides, conditions were still hazardous, even though the blizzard had lifted somewhat, and their main concern was to get the living – Pine and Tully – back to safety. But the *really* big difference is that they weren't looking for signs of foul play – why should they have been? – but I *was*!'

'So are you sayin' that you don't think Alec Hawtrey *was* wounded in the arm?'

'No, I'm not saying that at all. The patch of blood on the sleeve of his jacket would seem to indicate that he was almost definitely wounded there, possibly during the struggle.'

'Well, then?'

'But what I *am* putting forward is the idea that there was another wound – a *fatal* one – on some other part of his body. What I *don't* know is how Marlowe managed to persuade the local medical examiner to ignore the wounds.'

'He didn't have to,' Woodend said. 'It was good old Doc Pierson, our completely discredited police doctor, who carried out the autopsy.'

'Well, that explains everything!' Paniatowski told him.

'No, it doesn't,' Woodend contradicted her. 'We know Doc Pierson was willin' to bend the rules on other occasions – that's why he's in gaol now. But Marlowe had nothin' to gain by helpin' to cover up a murder. In fact, he had one hell of a lot to lose.'

'Maybe Bradley Pine told him there hadn't *been* a murder at all,' Paniatowski suggested.

'An' why would he have believed him, when, accordin' to you, there was clear evidence of foul play somewhere on Hawtrey's body?'

'Perhaps Pine managed to persuade the chief constable that he and Hawtrey had got into a fight over Thelma, and he'd killed Hawtrey accidentally.'

'Even if Marlowe had believed that – which would be stretchin' even *his* credulity to the absolute limit – he'd still be running one hell of a risk assistin' in a cover-up,' Woodend said dubiously. 'An', knowin' him as I do, I can't honestly see our Mr Marlowe sticking his neck out for *anybody*.'

'Perhaps he had no choice in the matter,' Paniatowski said. 'Perhaps Marlowe's got a guilty secret, and Pine knew all about it.'

'Now that is a possibility,' Woodend said.

It was more than a possibility, and it didn't even have to be a *big* secret that Pine had got hold of. Given that Marlowe was already planning to stand for parliament at the time, even a sordid *little* secret – for example, a liking for wearing women's underwear – would have been enough to sink his political ambitions.

'But we've still got a big problem, even if we're finally thinkin' along the right lines,' Woodend said, frowning deeply. 'Marlowe's never goin' to admit to his involvement, however much we try to pressure him. An' we can't have another autopsy carried out on Hawtrey, because – very conveniently for everybody involved in the cover-up, an' very *inconveniently* for us – the bugger was cremated.' He gazed down into the pint glass again, and when he raised his head he was looking considerably more cheerful. 'Still, we've got at least a couple of strings left to our bow, haven't we?' he asked the other two.

'And what strings might they be?' Rutter wondered.

'The first one is Jeremy Tully. He knows exactly what happened on that mountainside – because he was there.'

'And now he's in Australia,' Paniatowski said.

'Which is a long, long way, but that still doesn't mean he's beyond our reach,' Woodend told her. 'I've been on the phone to the Australian police this afternoon, an' they've promised to interview him as soon as possible.'

'Is the other string Doc Pierson?' Rutter asked.

'The other string's Doc Pierson,' Woodend agreed. 'I've made an appointment to visit him in Saltney Prison tomorrow mornin'.'

'Why should *he* be willing to tell you what you want to know?' Paniatowski asked.

'No reason at all, that I can think of,' Woodend conceded. 'So I'll just have to charm him into it, won't I? An' – let's be honest about this – I'm well-known for my charm.'

'Practically world-famous,' Rutter said, deadpan.

A waiter arrived with a vodka for Paniatowski, and the sergeant drained it in one gulp.

'I think I'll have an early night,' she said, placing the empty glass on the table.

'That's not like you at all,' Woodend told her.

And it wasn't. Normally Monika would rather do anything than go back to her lonely flat.

'I've done a lot of driving today, and it's rather taken it out of me,' Paniatowski explained.

And *that* wasn't like her, either, Woodend thought. She loved driving. It never seemed to tire her.

'I'd better be going, too,' Rutter said, standing up. 'I'm due to meet someone in half an hour.'

'About the case?' Woodend asked.

Rutter hesitated. 'No, it's a personal matter,' he said finally.

Woodend looked first at Rutter, then at Paniatowski, then back at Rutter again.

What the bloody hell was going on with these two, he wondered.

Thirty

Whoever had last been using the two chairs in the vestry had placed them much closer together than they had been previously, and though both Father Taylor and Paniatowski could have repositioned one of them before sitting down, neither of them chose to.

'This is becoming something of a habit of ours, isn't it, Monika?' Father Taylor asked.

'Is that some tactful way of saying that I'm taking up far too much of your time?' Paniatowski wondered.

'No, no, not at all,' Father Taylor said hastily. 'I meant that it was becoming a habit in the nicest possible sense of the word.'

'And what sense is that?'

'It's a rather *cosy* habit, if you see what I'm getting at.'

Yes, she did see what he was getting at, Paniatowski thought. It was becoming a cosy habit because, in many ways, he was a cosy *man*.

She could almost picture him – after a hard day's work in some office or other – sitting in his favourite armchair in his pleasant suburban living room. He would be wearing worn carpet slippers and an old cardigan – which was going at the elbows, but which he could not bear to throw out – and he would be listening happily while his children, gathered around at his feet, described their day's adventures to him.

'Why did you become a priest?' she heard herself saying.

'I thought I'd already answered that question the other night.'

'Maybe you did.'

'Well, then?'

'And maybe I wasn't entirely convinced by what you told me.'

'I assure you, Monika, I—'

'Or it could be that I'd like to hear it all again, just to make certain I heard it right the first time.'

Father Taylor hesitated for a moment, then said, 'I suppose the simplest way to explain how I came to be what I am is to say that I became a priest because I felt – I believed – that that's what God wanted me to become.'

'So you had no choice – no free will?'

'We all of us always have a choice. What would be the point in striving to become virtuous, if we didn't have the free will to choose not to be?'

'What made you so sure that this was what God wanted you to do?' Paniatowski asked.

'The gifts He appears to have bestowed on me.'

'Like what?'

'Even when I was very young, people seemed to have this urge to confide in me.'

'So you're a good listener. That doesn't mean—'

'And more than that, they took what I said in return very seriously. I had the power to comfort them – to lighten their burden. There was a time – in my teens – when I saw it more as a curse than a gift. But gradually I came to see God's purpose working through me.'

'In other words, you became a priest simply because you had a talent for it?' Paniatowski asked. 'In much the same way as you might have become a concert pianist if you'd had a natural aptitude for the piano?'

'Are you mocking me now?' Father Taylor asked, looking hurt.

Paniatowski shook her head, vehemently.

'No, I promise you, I'm not,' she said.

'Then what *are* you doing?'

'I'm trying to understand how a man like you could turn his back on a normal life. You *should* be married! You *should* have children. Even if they weren't your own. Even if you had to adopt them!'

'If it had been God's plan for me to fall in love before I entered the priesthood, then that is what I would have done,' Father Taylor said, simply.

'And once you had entered the priesthood, it was no longer possible?'

'If I feel any stirrings – and I have already confessed to

you that I do – I know it is only God's way of tempting me.'

'He must be a very cruel god, then.'

'No, He is a infinitely loving God, and He only does it to help me to strengthen my faith.'

They had strayed on to very dangerous ground Paniatowski realized – and it was all her fault.

'I have a problem you might be able to help me with,' she said, trying to sound more businesslike. 'And before you jump to any conclusions, Father Fred, it's professional – it's not about God at all.'

Father Taylor smiled. '*Most* things are about God,' he said, 'but if you wish me to keep Him out of the conversation, I promise to try my hardest. What is it you want to know?'

'Say that there were three men cut off by the weather on a mountainside, and that before their rescuers could get to them, one of them had already died,' Paniatowski began.

'Is this some sort of moral theoretical question, or is it real?' Father Taylor asked.

'It's theoretical,' Paniatowski lied.

'I see. Well, in that case, do carry on.'

'Say that when the rescuers do get there, one of the men who's survived is speaking in Latin. Why would he be doing that?'

'What is it he's saying?'

'I don't know. But he's not a classical scholar, or anything like that. He's an accountant and—'

'Are we *sure* this a theoretical example?'

'Does it matter if it isn't?'

'I suppose not. Is this man a Catholic?'

'He is.'

'So you think that he was speaking what, for want of a better phrase, we might call *church* Latin, do you?'

'Yes, I do.'

'And you're wondering what particular piece of church Latin might have come to his mind in the situation you describe?'

'Exactly.'

'Well, I suppose he could have been saying a prayer for the soul of his dead friend.'

'I don't think that was it at all.'

'No?'

'No. From the way he was described to me, he seemed to be more concerned about himself than his dead friend.'

'Then he could have been praying for forgiveness. Perhaps he felt responsible for his friend's death.'

'Responsible *how*?'

'I can't say. It would be impossible to say, without knowing more details. But perhaps – and this is *only* a suggestion – he felt guilty because he was the one who had come up with the idea of the expedition in the first place.'

'I don't think it *was* his idea.'

'Then I'm at a loss.'

'Is it possible that he felt guilty because he could have done something to *prevent* the friend's death, but chose not to?'

'Certainly,' the priest said.

Paniatowski stood up. 'Thank you, Father.'

'Are you going so soon?' Father Taylor asked.

'Well, yes,' Paniatowski said. 'You answered my questions – at least as far as you're able to – so I won't take up any more of your time.'

Father Taylor stood up, and placed his hands on her shoulders.

'Is that truly the only reason that you came here tonight, Monika?' he said. 'To ask me your theoretical questions which we both know were not really theoretical at all?'

'Yes. Well, mainly.'

'Are you sure about that?'

'Of course I'm sure.'

Father Taylor's hands ceased to merely rest on Paniatowski's shoulders, and instead began to grasp them. She could feel his fingers digging into her flesh with an urgency which demanded the truth.

'Look into my eyes – look *deeply* into them – and tell me again that you're sure,' he said.

Monika raised her head, so that their eyes met. 'I'm sure,' she said, unconvincingly.

And before either of them really knew what was happening, they were kissing one another.

Beresford still felt a desperate need to talk to Sergeant Paniatowski, and on the way to the pub he had been racking his brains for some ruse he might employ to detach her from the rest of the team. It was almost crushingly disappointing to find that she wasn't even there – and more than disturbing

198

to see that the only person who *was* actually sitting at the usual table was also the one person who he really didn't want to talk to at all.

He was already backing towards the door when Woodend spotted him, and gestured that he should join him.

Beresford walked reluctantly over to the table and sat down in the chair opposite the chief inspector's.

'What's the matter, lad?' Woodend asked. 'You look like you've lost a pound an' found sixpence.'

'I don't think I'm cut out for CID work, sir,' Beresford blurted out. 'I don't think I'm cut out for it all.'

There! He'd said it! It was finally out in the open!

Woodend shook his head slowly from side to side.

'Oh dear, it's the old crisis of confidence raisin' its ugly head, is it? Don't worry, lad, we all suffer from that now an' again.'

'That's easy enough for you to say, sir,' Beresford told him. 'When you have any doubts, you've got a rock-solid track record to reassure you. *You* can always remind yourself that you've arrested more murderers than I've had hot dinners. But what have I got?'

'You've had your own modest successes, even if you don't quite realize it yet.'

'Like what?'

'Well, for example, bringin' Thelma Hawtrey into the picture. Why did we go an' see her in the first place? Because of what you'd learned about her husband's death from the people in the factory!'

'But I didn't *want* us to go and see her,' Beresford pointed out. 'I didn't think Thelma could possibly have had anything to do with Pine's murder.'

'An', as it happens, you were quite right about that. But if we hadn't gone to see Thelma, we'd never have found the spot on which Bradley Pine was murdered, would we?'

'So if I helped the investigation at all, it was purely by accident,' Beresford said glumly.

'Half the time, *any* progress we make comes about as a result of a lucky accident,' Woodend told him. 'We stir up the pot, an' see what floats to the surface. Sometimes what bobs up is of no earthly use, but if we don't keep stirrin', we'll never get anywhere.'

'I don't think I'm even a very good stirrer, sir,' Beresford said.

'Of course you are. Tell me a few of the things that you've found that I probably don't know about yet.'

'I don't see that'll do any good, sir.'

'Humour me!'

'Well,' Beresford said, reluctantly, 'I found out that Alec Hawtrey had two children by his first wife, a boy and girl.'

'Which was news to me.'

'But is it news that's going to be of any use?'

'We won't know until we've finally closed the case. Were they a happy family before Thelma came along?'

'I think so. I saw this picture of them on their holidays. They all looked as if they were having a good time. Except for the son. He seemed miserable. Not, that's not the right word. What he seemed was *troubled*.' Beresford paused. 'Honestly, sir, I don't think this is doing any—'

'Tell me more.'

'Whatever happened later, Mr Hawtrey must have really doted on his first wife in the early years of their marriage, because he built this huge elaborate house for her, and—'

Woodend chuckled. 'Oh, aye. That house! "Tara"!'

'Sorry, sir?'

'"Tara". It's what other people used to call the house. An' they didn't necessarily mean it as a compliment.'

Beresford looked at him blankly. 'Tara?' he repeated.

'Aye, you know, after the house in *Gone with the Wind*?'

'I'm sorry, sir, I still don't—'

'You've never heard of a film called *Gone with the Wind*?'

'No, sir. When was it made?'

'Round about 1939, I think.'

'That was an awfully long time ago, sir.'

Woodend sighed heavily. 'Sometimes you do make me feel very, very old, lad.'

'I'm sorry, sir, I didn't mean to—'

'Oh, for God's sake, don't go apologizin',' Woodend told him. 'Anybody who says they don't envy you for your youth is a bloody liar – but that's their problem, not yours.' He paused to light up a cigarette. 'They pulled that house down in the end. I was sorry to see it go.'

'Why? I thought you said it was a bit of a joke.'

'Well, I suppose it was, in an way.'

'Well, then?'

'But it was rather like the odd characters you sometimes come across in the pub – they can irritate the hell out of you when they're there, but you quite miss them when they've gone. Still, that's progress for you. The town planners – in their infinite wisdom – decided that the people of Whitebridge needed a new road much more than they needed a good talkin' point, and so they . . . so they . . .'

'What's the matter, sir?' Beresford asked, slightly alarmed by the change that had suddenly come over his boss.

'"Tara" was pulled down because – like a lot of other properties – it stood in the way of the new Whitebridge to Accrington dual carriageway,' Woodend said. 'An' I may be wrong about this, but when I think about exactly where it was, I get the distinct impression it must have been very close to that lay-by we found Bradley Pine in!'

Thirty-One

The visiting room in HM Prison Saltney was large and square, and the table in the centre of it looked as lost as a small island in the middle of a vast ocean. It was perhaps not quite as depressing as the interview rooms back in Whitebridge Police HQ, Woodend thought, but it certainly ran a damn close second.

The door to the corridor swung open, and one of the prison officers escorted Dr Pierson into the room. The doctor had been incarcerated for a little over two years. He had the unhealthy pallor of someone who is rarely out in the open air, but otherwise looked better than might have been expected in a man who had seen his whole life disintegrate.

Pierson sat down opposite the chief inspector, and said, 'Have you got a cigarette, Charlie?'

Woodend slid a full packet across the table. 'You can keep them, Doc,' he said.

'So you think you can bribe me with a few fags, do you?' Pierson asked, but even as he was speaking, he was sliding the cigarettes into the pocket of his prison overalls.

'What makes you think that I was offering them as a bribe?' Woodend wondered.

Pierson shrugged. 'What else could it be, Charlie? This is the first time you've ever been to see me, and you wouldn't have come now if you hadn't wanted something.'

'Do you blame me for that?'

'Blame you for what? For wanting something? Or for not coming to see me before now?'

'For not coming to see you before now.'

Pierson thought about it. 'No, probably not. We wouldn't have had much to say to one another if you had come. We could hardly have reminisced about old times, could we, when the "old time" that really stands out in both our minds is the one when you arrested me?'

'Given what you'd been involved in, you didn't leave me much choice about that, did you?' Woodend asked.

'No, I suppose I didn't,' Pierson agreed. 'When all's said and done, you were only doing your job. But *you* can't blame *me* for wishing that you hadn't done it quite so well.'

'Why don't you tell me about the autopsy you performed on Alec Hawtrey?' Woodend suggested.

'Alec Hawtrey,' Pierson mused. 'So that's what this is all about. As I recall, Hawtrey fell off a mountainside in a blizzard, and broke his leg. His death was the result of exposure.'

'Was it really exposure which killed him?'

'Yes, it was.'

'You're sure about that?'

'I know I've often lied to you in the past, Charlie, but please believe me when I say that, this time, I'm telling you the truth.'

I do believe you, Woodend thought. I don't want to – because that means we've been following another false trail – but I *do*.

'Why did Marlowe go to all that trouble of ensurin' you were the one who carried out the autopsy?' he asked.

'You'll have to ask Henry that.'

'I'm askin' you.'

'I suppose it's possible he did because he had no faith in the Cumberland medical examiner.'

'Now you *are* lyin' aren't you?' Woodend asked.

'Maybe yes, and maybe no. But *if* I am lying, what are you prepared to offer me for telling the truth, Charlie?'

'What do you want?'

'My freedom!'

'Come on now, Doc! You know I couldn't get you released at this stage in your sentence, even if I wanted to!'

'Then perhaps I'd be willing to settle for something a little more modest. A cell that I didn't have to share with anyone else would be nice. I'd also like unlimited supplies of the finest old malt whisky. And if you could round off the package with a promise of gourmet meals which have been cooked especially for me in the finest restaurant in the area, you just might have yourself a deal.'

'Aye, there should be no problem with any of that,' Woodend said. 'An' while I'm at it, why don't I see if Brigitte Bardot, Elizabeth Taylor and Sophia Loren are free at the moment – because I'm sure if they are, I can arrange for them all to visit you on the long winter nights.'

Dr Pierson smiled wanly. 'In other words, you can't get me anything at all that will make my life in here a little pleasanter,' he said.

'Got it in one,' Woodend agreed. 'But I promise you this – if you committed any illegal acts durin' the course of the autopsy on Hawtrey, I'll personally guarantee that you won't be prosecuted for them.'

Pierson laughed. 'All that boils down to is a promise that if I put my head in the noose, you won't pull the handle and open the trapdoor. But why should I even think of putting my head in the noose *at all*?'

'Because it's the right thing to do.'

'And do you seriously think I *care* about "doing the right thing"?' Pierson asked, with derision.

'Yes, I do,' Woodend said seriously. 'I was talkin' to the Governor before I came to see you , an' it seems you've been an exemplary prisoner.'

'Well, of course I have. If you want to earn time off for good behaviour, that's exactly what you have to be.'

'He also told me that you've often volunteered to work extra hours in the prison hospital.'

'Why wouldn't I? The hospital's a pleasant place. Certainly a great deal more pleasant than my cell.'

'An' you've been holdin' classes – teachin' some of the worst educated prisoners to read. Now why, I ask myself, should you have bothered to have done all that?'

'Because it helps to fill in the time?'

'I don't think so. I think you're doin' it because you're tryin' to redeem youself.'

'Redeem myself!' Doc Pierson repeated with a contempt which didn't quite ring true. 'What kind of language is that to use about me? I'm not a Catholic, you know.'

'Doesn't matter whether you are or whether you're not,' Woodend said firmly. 'You don't have to belong to the Church of Rome to understand that you've done wrong in the past, an' to want to try an' compensate for it in any way that you can.'

'And are you saying that my telling you what happened at that autopsy will be part of the redemption process?'

'Yes, I think it will.'

'Why should it be?'

'Because it'll be one more secret that you'll no longer have to keep locked up inside yourself – one less weight of wrong-doin' that's pressin' down on your shoulders.'

Pierson laughed again. 'Perhaps you should have become a priest instead of a policeman,' he said.

Woodend shook his head. 'There'd have been no chance of that. I didn't have the Latin, you see, and you'll never get anywhere in the priesthood if you don't have the Latin.' He paused for a moment. 'So are you goin' to tell me what happened, Doc?'

'Why not?' Pierson asked. 'If for no other reason, it'll be worth it just to see the look on your face when you finally learn the truth.'

The house was located on the cliff-tops, in a seaside town about sixty miles from Whitebridge. It was not quite grand enough to have been called a mansion, but most of the people with whom Rutter rubbed shoulders would have thought all their dreams had come true if they'd had the title deeds to it in their own pockets.

Its present owner had lived there for fifteen years. She had bought it with the money she'd been awarded in the divorce settlement which had left Alec Hawtrey feeling so poor that, in the end, he'd had no choice but to take Bradley Pine into the business as his partner.

The first Mrs Hawtrey was in her late fifties, and was inclining towards becoming stout. She had resisted the temptation to dye her hair – which was now almost white – but it was well cared for and recently permed. She was wearing a sensible tweed skirt, a plain blouse and strong walking shoes – and she had insisted that Rutter accompany her in her daily stroll along the cliffs.

They stood quite close to the edge for a while, watching the seagulls swoop over the sea, then the first Mrs Hawtrey turned to Rutter and said, 'It is truly remarkable how long bitterness can linger, isn't it? It's sixteen years since the divorce, you know.'

'Yes, I'd worked that out for myself,' Rutter said.

'You'd have thought, wouldn't you, that we would have been able to build ourselves a new life during all that time? But the sad truth is that none of us have quite managed it.'

'None of you?' Rutter repeated. 'None of who?'

'Oh, I'm sorry, I wasn't being very clear, was I? I meant myself and the children. I suppose that if you asked other people's opinion of us, they'd say we *had* changed, but believe me, the change is only on the surface. Both children lead their own independent lives now, and I'm very highly thought of as a result of the hard work I've put into several local charities. But there's something missing in all of us, you see – and that something is Alec.'

'I understand,' Rutter said, though he was not entirely convinced that he really did.

'If Alec had died – I mean, if he'd died back then, rather than thirteen years later – it might have been different.'

'How?'

'We'd still have been grieving for him even now, of course, but I think that sense of loss would have been a much easier thing to bear than this feeling of betrayal which still clings to me like a thick layer of dirt. We were such a happy family, you see. His life was built around us, and our lives were built around him. Other people called our house "Tara" – in a sneering sort of way – but we didn't care, because we all loved it. And then Alec became involved with that woman – and he simply deserted us.'

'Do you blame her entirely for what happened to your marriage?' Rutter asked.

'Oh no, I don't blame her at all.'

'Really?'

'Really! I'd know her for years before it all happened, you see. In fact, since she came to us from the orphanage, as little more than a child. That was Bradley's doing. Being an orphan himself, I think he felt sorry for her.'

She really didn't know the half of it, Rutter thought. She had no idea of the *planning* that had gone into the destruction of her idyllic life.

But he said nothing – because it would have been incredibly cruel to tell her the truth now.

'Even in those early days,' the first Mrs Hawtrey continued,

'I could clearly see that she was nothing more than a scheming little bitch – pardon my French, Inspector Rutter, but it happens to be true – and I always thought she'd try to get her claws into some poor unsuspecting man eventually. I just never imagined that man would be my loving husband.'

'But *still* you don't blame her?'

'No, I promise you I don't. I happen to believe in free will, and whilst I'm sure that she used all the pretty little tricks she could to win him away from us, Alec could have resisted the temptation if he'd really tried.'

Just as I could have resisted Monika *if I'd really tried*, Rutter thought.

And he didn't even have any of the excuses that Alec Hawtrey had, he told himself. Monika hadn't been anything like a 'scheming little bitch'. And he hadn't been going through a mid-life crisis which had made him feel the need to have his vanity massaged.

'I'd like to ask you about your husband's friends, if I may,' he said, pulling his thoughts back to the main purpose of his visit.

'His friends? I saw nothing at all of Alec in the last thirteen years of his life. So I have absolutely no idea if he made any new friends or not – though I rather suspect that he didn't.'

'It's his old friends I'm more interested in,' Rutter told her. 'Friends he'd known for so long that they'd become almost like brothers to him.'

'Can I know why you're asking that particular question?' the first Mrs Hawtrey said thoughtfully. 'Does it, in some way, have anything to do with Bradley Pine's death?'

'We think it may.'

'And what way might that be?'

'We think that there may still be people around who were very fond of your husband and blame Bradley Pine for his accident,' Rutter said, picking his words very carefully.

'So what you're actually saying is that you think that Pine's murder may have been a kind of revenge killing?'

'It's a possibility we're certainly not dismissing.'

'If you don't mind me saying so, I think you're barking up the completely wrong tree,' the first Mrs Hawtrey told Rutter. 'Alec simply didn't have close friends like that.'

'Everybody has at least *one* close friend.'

207

'Not my Alec. He worshipped his father and he loved the spring mattress business – and from quite an early age that seems to have been more than enough for him.'

'Until he met you.'

'Until he met me. You can't even imagine what our courtship was like. He was so shy and awkward – characteristics his son has inherited from him – and I almost went into shock when he plucked up the nerve to propose to me. But he *did* propose and I accepted, and we had the lavish wedding which his father insisted on.' She paused, and frowned. 'I think it was the wedding which really brought home to me just how isolated he'd been.'

'Why was that?'

'Well, there were quite a lot of my friends there, but very few of his – and even the ones of his who did turn up were really more like acquaintances. So, you see, Alec simply wasn't the kind of man who inspired that kind of loyalty. The only person who'd ever have cared enough about him to avenge his death was me, and since the betrayal, even that's not true.'

'Thank you for being so open with me, Mrs Hawtrey,' Rutter said. 'I know it can't have been easy for you.'

'Actually, it was easier than I thought it would be,' the first Mrs Hawtrey told him. 'You're a good listener. In that way, you quite remind me of my son. Are you shy, too?'

'Shy?'

'You are! I can see it now. I suspect that's why you decided to become a policeman.'

'Do you really think that "shyness" is a word most people would ever think of applying to bobbies?' Rutter asked, wondering, even as he spoke, why he should have suddenly started to sound so defensive.

'Not to all policemen, no, but certainly to some. I would imagine that your work gives you both a sense of certainty and a sense of purpose that would otherwise be lacking. It forces you to be a part of the world, whereas your natural tendency would be to withdraw.'

She was talking total bollocks, Rutter thought. So why had her words made his stomach turn over?

'If you'll excuse me, I think I should be getting back to Whitebridge,' he said hurriedly.

He shook hands with her, and began to walk away.

He had only gone a few yards when she called after him, 'Will you be writing a report on this meeting?'

He stopped, and turned around. 'A report? Yes, I suppose so. But I don't imagine it will be a very long one.'

'It doesn't matter how long or short it is,' the woman said. 'When you write it, don't refer to me as you did just now?'

'I beg your pardon?'

'You called me Mrs Hawtrey.'

'Yes?'

'For years, I thought of *myself* like that. But it wasn't true. Even if the Catholic Church refused to recognize the divorce – even if we were still married in the eyes of God – I wasn't Mrs Hawtrey any longer. At best, I was Used-To-Be Mrs Hawtrey. So I finally cut myself adrift from the past, and reverted to my maiden name. That probably seems like nothing to you, but for me it took a great deal of courage. So when you refer to me in the report, please use my maiden name, which is the name I go by now, even if it does mean putting "Mrs Hawtrey" in brackets after it.'

'I'd be glad to,' Rutter said. 'But I don't know what your maiden name is?'

'Don't you?' the woman asked. 'Well, I suppose there's no reason why you should.'

And then she told him what name she would prefer him to use.

Thirty-Two

Henry Marlowe was standing in the back room of a village hall – the latest in a long string of village halls which the strategists behind his election campaign were requiring him to visit.

The caretaker – who seemed inordinately proud of the place – had informed him it was known as the Green Room, since it was where the 'actors' changed when the village put on one of its entertainments.

And what pathetic spectacles *they* must be, Marlowe thought sourly, picturing half a dozen overweight middle-aged women thumping around the stage and fluffing their lines.

Once he was in London, he'd go to *real* plays in *real* theatres, and return to Whitebridge as little as possible, he promised himself.

He looked around him again. When the 'Green Room' was between productions, it seemed to serve as nothing more than a general store room for all kinds of unwanted junk. There was a sink – with a mirror above it, and a tap which at first gurgled and then reluctantly released a thin stream of water – but there were no chairs, since these had all been taken into the main hall.

It was a sordid little space at best, Marlowe thought, and he really had no wish to be there.

He'd been booked to address the Women's Institute. He didn't want to face them. In truth, he couldn't see why he should have to face them. He was the Conservative candidate – why didn't they just vote for him?

His political agent, Bill Hawes, had failed to see his point of view on the matter.

'So what if you have to humiliate yourself by rubbing shoulders with the riff-raff once every four or five years?' he'd asked. 'In between elections, you're in clover, aren't you?

You've got a job which is comparatively well-paid, yet requires no more work than you're prepared to put into it. You've an expense account which most businessmen would give their personal assistants' right arms to have. And companies will be falling over themselves to offer you directorships. Isn't all that worth having to crawl on your belly for, just once in a while?'

'But the WI!' Marlowe had complained.

'Oh, they're a bunch of scatty old bags, who I'd probably end up garrotting myself if I had to spend too much time with them,' Hawes had admitted cheerfully, 'but they can usually be trusted to put their cross in roughly the right place, if they're handled properly.'

And so there he was – in this run-down village hall, practising sincere expressions in the mirror over the sink, and wondering if it was too early to uncork his hip flask – when the door opened and Woodend walked in.

'What precisely are you doing here, Chief Inspector?' Marlowe demanded, irritably.

'I just came to wish you the best of luck with the meeting, sir,' Woodend said.

'Is that right?' Marlowe asked, unconvinced. 'And you will be voting for me come election day, will you?'

'No, I'm afraid I just couldn't quite bring myself to do that, sir,' Woodend said.

He looked around for somewhere to sit, upended an empty milk crate, and lowered himself on to it.

'Why are you *really* here?' Marlowe asked.

'I'm really here because of Alec Hawtrey,' Woodend replied, lighting up a cigarette and inhaling deeply. 'I was quite convinced, for a while back there, that Bradley Pine had murdered him, you know.'

'That's a quite ludicrous assumption for anyone – even you – to make!' Marlowe said.

'Thanks for the vote of confidence, sir,' Woodend said dryly. 'But there's more.'

'More?'

'I was also convinced that Bradley Pine knew some nasty little secret of yours, an', because of that, he was able to blackmail you into helpin' him to cover up the murder.'

'How dare you even have such thoughts?' Marlowe

demanded. 'I'm a chief constable! I'm *going to be* a member of parliament. It would never even occur to me to become involved in a sordid cover-up.'

'Now that's not strictly true, is it?' Woodend asked mildly. 'You didn't cover up a murder, but you did cover up somethin' sordid – somethin' pretty horrific, in fact – that Pine did on that mountainside.'

'I must tell you that I have absolutely no idea what you're talking about!' Marlowe said hotly.

'What made you do it?' Woodend mused. 'The only explanation that I can come up with is that you saw it as no more than a natural extension of the mutual back-scratchin' that you Golf Club types have made a way of life. But it was a rather *big* favour he was askin' on that particular occasion, wasn't it?'

'I've heard quite enough of this, Chief Inspector Woodend. I don't know where you get your—'

'Of course, your lot never do anythin' without expectin' somethin' in return. So what were you expectin' from Pine? That he'd support your application to be the next Tory candidate? Because if that *was* what you were after, he let you down quite badly, didn't he?'

'I should never have trusted the man,' Marlowe said bitterly. 'I should never have taken him at his word.'

He was talking to himself, rather than to Woodend. In fact, in his anger at the dead man, he seemed almost to have forgotten that the chief inspector was even there in the room.

'I don't see you had much choice *but* to take him at his word,' Woodend pointed out. 'After all, it wasn't the kind of deal that you could ever have put down in writin', now was it?'

'Deal? What deal?' Marlowe asked, suddenly conscious of the other man's presence again. 'There was no *deal*. And I can assure you that there was absolutely no *cover-up*.'

Woodend shook his head slowly – and almost mournfully – from side to side.

'That really won't wash any more, you know,' he said. 'You can go on denyin' it till you've turned blue in the face, but I talked to your old mate Doc Pierson earlier this mornin' – an' so I'm never goin' to believe you.'

'You talked to Pierson? And he told you . . .?'

'He told me everythin'.'

'What Pine did wasn't a crime, you know!' Marlowe said. 'They'd never have locked him up for it.'

'Possibly you're right, though I think I could find half a dozen lawyers who might disagree with you,' Woodend replied. 'But that's not really the point, is it, sir? Even if it wasn't strictly a *criminal* act, it would have ruined him socially. It wouldn't have done much for his business, either. People tend to be a bit squeamish about havin' dealin's with a man like that.'

'What was so wrong with it, when you look at it objectively?' Marlowe asked. 'Strip away all the sugary emotionalism behind it, and what are you left with? The fact that Bradley Pine found himself in a difficult situation, and did no more than he needed to do to ensure his own well-being!'

'That's certainly one way of lookin' at what happened,' Woodend agreed. 'But since I'm not one of the élite of Whitebridge society – like you are, an' Pine was – I don't think I'd look at it that way myself.'

He stood up and walked towards the door.

'What are you going to do?' Marlowe asked, with a strong hint of panic in his voice.

'Do?' Woodend repeated. 'I'm goin' to do what I get paid to do – which is to try my hardest to find Bradley Pine's murderer.'

'That isn't what I meant, and you know it,' Marlowe said.

'Oh, you mean, am I goin' to tell anybody else what Pierson told me?' Woodend said.

'Listen, Charlie, I'll still have considerable influence in the Central Lancs Constabulary once I'm elected, you know.'

'I'm sure you will.'

'I'll still have a say in who gets promoted and who doesn't. Would you like to be a superintendent? Or even a *chief* superintendent? That can be arranged – as long as you're prepared to keep quiet.'

'There's no need to offer me a bribe,' Woodend told him. '*I* won't tell anybody your nasty little secret.'

Marlowe mopped his sweating brow with his handkerchief.

'Thank you, Chief Inspector,' he said. 'Thank you so much.'

'But whether or not it leaks out from some *other* source will depend, I would imagine, on who killed Pine, an' *why* he killed him.'

213

Thirty-Three

Since his mother appeared to be having one of her more lucid mornings, Colin Beresford had decided to take off a couple of the hours that his recent spate of overtime entitled him to, and spend them with her.

Why bother going into work anyway, he asked himself, when – despite Woodend's pep talk the previous evening – he was far from convinced he was contributing anything of importance to the investigation.

It was true, he argued, putting the case from the other side – as Woodend had done the previous evening – that the chief inspector would probably not have realized, had it not been for him, that Bradley Pine's body had been dumped on the site of what had once been 'Tara' – the old Hawtrey family house.

But how did that particular piece of knowledge help them advance the investigation?

Even if it were more than a coincidence – and that was a long way from being firmly established – neither he nor Woodend had any real idea of *what* it signified.

The inside of his poor mother's head must be a little like this case, he thought. There was so much information – so many memories – floating around in there.

But no structure at all.

No system.

No coherent whole.

'Why don't we look at the old photograph albums, Colin?' his mother suggested.

Why not, Beresford agreed.

Leave it a couple of hours, and all the faces smiling up at her would mean nothing to his mother. So why not grab the opportunity to have her live in the real world while she still could?

She even remembered where they *kept* the albums, he thought, as he watched her open the drawer.

But he shouldn't let that fool him, even for a moment, into thinking she was getting any better. She would *never* get any better. All he had left to hope for was that her decline would not be too rapid.

His mother placed one of the albums on the table, and opened it.

'This was the holiday we all spent in Blackpool, when you were just a little boy,' she said. 'Do you remember?'

'I remember.'

'There's your dad in front of the Tower . . .' Mrs Beresford paused and looked around the room. 'Where *is* your dad, by the way? Has he gone out?'

'Dad's dead, Mum,' Beresford said.

Mrs Beresford blinked, then tried to pretend that she hadn't.

'Of course he's dead, I knew that,' she agreed. 'And there's you, on the sands,' she continued, hastily. 'Weren't you a lovely little boy?'

Beresford examined the faded photograph. The boy in it looked serious – almost brooding.

Had he sensed, even then, what lay ahead of him, he wondered. Could he already see into a future in which his father was dead and his mother was slowly going gaga?

The picture began to remind him of another photograph – though it was not one of him.

And suddenly, he realized why the priest had seemed so familiar!

Woodend had only just got back to his office when the phone on his desk began to ring.

He picked it up, and heard the operator say, 'I have a long-distance phone call from Australia for you. I'm connecting you now.'

Australia?

'Chief Inspector Woodend?' asked a cheery voice down the crackling line. 'G'day! It's Sergeant Archie Boon of the Western Australia Police here. I'm told you've been making inquiries about Jeremy Tully.'

'That's right,' Woodend agreed.

'Then I'm the bloke you need to speak to. He works on one of the farms on my patch.'

'He works on a *farm!*'

'That's what I said. He's a sheep-shearer. An' for a beginner, he's a damn good one.'

'Are you quite sure that we're talkin' about the same man?' Woodend wondered.

'Jeremy Nathan Tully?' Boon asked. 'Moved here from Whitebridge, Lancashire? Used to be an accountant?'

'That's him. What's he doin' shearin' sheep?'

'There's not much choice in the matter, since the sheep can't shear themselves,' Boon pointed out. 'An' old Jerry tells me he quite likes the work. Says he's found peace at last – whatever that means.'

'D'you mean to say you've already talked to him?' Woodend asked.

'Talked to him? I've done more than that. I've *interrogated* him.'

'You done *what?*'

'Interrogated him. But not like you might have done over there in the Old Country – shining bright lights into his face and tapping your truncheon menacingly against your trouser leg.'

Woodend grinned. 'You've been watchin' too many old films, Sergeant,' he said.

'You're probably right,' Boon agreed. 'Anyway, since he's one of my closest neighbours – which means he only lives a couple of hours drive from where I live – I thought I'd better leave the lamp and truncheon at home, and interrogate him the *Ozzie* way.'

'An' what way's that?' Woodend wondered.

'I turned up at his place with a case of beer, and suggested he light up the barbie and throw a few thick juicy steaks on it. We had a real good chin-wag once he'd done that – especially after we'd drained a few tinnies of the amber nectar.'

'What did you talk *about?*'

'Mainly about why he came to Oz. Seems he had a bit of a rough time up a mountainside in old England. Must admit, I didn't know you even had mountains over there.'

'They probably don't look much in comparison to yours,

but we're used to them,' Woodend said. 'And I know what happened on the mountainside, so you can skip that bit.'

'Oh, all right,' Boon agreed easily. 'Well, after he came down from the mountain, he was having trouble sleeping, and when he did fall asleep he had these terrible nightmares. He's a Catholic. Did you know that?'

'Yes, I did.'

'Anyway, he went to his priest, and confessed. I don't understand how these things work – not got much time for religion myself – but I think that was supposed to make everything all right again. Only it didn't work out like that. He was still getting the sweats and the trembles. So he went to see the priest again, and the priest suggested that he moved to Oz.'

'The *priest* did?'

'Yeah, that's right. He told Jerry he should put his past behind him – get as far away from England as he could, and make a new start. And you can't get further away from England than Oz. Turns out it was a real beaut of an idea, because he has no trouble at all sleepin' now.' The sergeant chuckled. 'Course, that *could* have something to do with the fact that he's shearing sheep from dawn till dusk.'

'Did he happen to tell you the name of the priest who gave him this advice?' Woodend asked.

'Can't say that he did. But he did tell me that it was a very *young* priest.'

Paniatowski crossed herself awkwardly and self-consciously. 'Bless me, Father, for I have sinned,' she said.

'You shouldn't have come here, Monika,' the voice hissed from the other side of the grille.

'Isn't this the right place to talk about what happened last night?' Paniatowski asked.

'Yes, but—'

'Well, that's why I'm here.'

'—but not with *me*.'

'I want to know if I did wrong,' Paniatowski said firmly.

'We *both* did wrong,' Father Taylor said. 'But though I know there are no degrees of difference within mortal sin, I still believe that I did more wrong than you – and that I will burn in hellfire for eternity as a result.'

'Not if you confess! Not if you get some other priest to absolve you from your sins!'

'I *can't* confess,' Father Taylor said, agonized.

'Why?'

'Because there can be no forgiveness without true repentance – and I cannot bring myself to repent.'

'So what will happen to *us*?'

'That is in God's hands.'

'Don't give me all that crap!' Paniatowski said angrily. 'You still have your free will, don't you? You can still go where you want to, and be with who you want to be with.'

'Perhaps you're right about that – for the moment,' Father Taylor said. 'But I don't think it will be the case for very much longer.'

'Why?'

'Because events – circumstances – are closing in on me.'

'And just what's that supposed to mean?'

There was the sound of two sets of men's footsteps, crossing the floor of the church and approaching the confessional.

'In the name of the Father, Son and Holy Spirit, I absolve you of your sins,' Father Taylor said.

Though he spoke hurriedly, it was not with the uncertain voice of the man she had been with the previous evening, but with the authority of an ordained priest of the Holy Catholic Church.

'But I can't be forgiven, because I don't repent *either*!' Paniatowski said angrily.

'You will repent,' Father Taylor told her, sadly. 'And perhaps sooner than you think. You have to go now.'

'I don't *want* to go!'

'You must,' Father Taylor insisted.

There were tears in Paniatowski's eyes as she stepped out of the confessional, but through those tears she still managed to see Charlie Woodend and Bob Rutter standing there.

And suddenly, everything Father Taylor had said to her started to make sense.

Thirty-Four

'This is all a complete waste of time, you know,' Father Taylor said, quite calmly, as he looked at Woodend across the table in Whitebridge Police Headquarters' Interview Room B.

'*Why* is it a complete waste of time?' Woodend asked. 'Because you're innocent of the crime with which you're charged?'

'No. Quite the contrary. Because I'm guilty of it. I killed Bradley Pine, and I'll willingly sign any confession that you care to put in front of me. Isn't that enough for you?'

'No, it isn't,' Woodend told him. 'The Crown Prosecution Service will want a comprehensive report, which means that I need you to flesh out some of the details for me.'

Father Taylor laughed. '*Flesh* out some of the details!' he repeated. 'Is that really what you said? Don't you think that's a rather macabre use of the word under the circumstances?'

'Possibly it is,' Woodend agreed. 'But then I've found this whole investigation a little macabre, because we don't get a great many cases of mutilation in Whitebridge.' He paused for a moment. 'Would you like to give me a full statement now?'

'No, I wouldn't. I've said all I intend to say.'

'Come on, help me out a bit here,' Woodend cajoled.

Father Taylor folded his arms across his chest, and kept his mouth tightly closed.

'Then how about this as an alternative suggestion?' Woodend said. 'I'll tell you everything that I *think* happened, an' if I'm goin' wrong at any point, you'll let me know.'

Father Taylor considered the suggestion for what seemed to Woodend like a long time. 'You do understand that there are some things I can neither confirm nor deny,' he said finally.

'Yes.'

'Then if what you propose will bring about an end to all this in the shortest possible time, please go ahead.'

'An hour or so before Bradley Pine was murdered, he paid a visit to St Mary's Church,' Woodend said. 'He knelt down in one of the pews an' prayed for a while, and then he took confession with Father Kenyon. By the time he left the church, you'd already gone yourself.'

'That is correct.'

'You cycled up over to Thelma Hawtrey's house in Upper Bankside – which is a good two miles from your church. Once you got there, you hid your bicycle, and waited in the bushes for Pine to arrive. Is that right?'

'Yes.'

'What did you use as your murder weapon?'

'A large spanner.'

'Where did you get it from?'

'The church boiler room.'

'*When* did you get it?'

'Just before I cycled to that woman's house.'

'So, if you took it with you, you must already have been planning to kill Pine when you left the church?'

'Yes.'

'How did you know where to lie in wait for him?'

'I'm not sure I understand the question.'

'Yes, you do. Bradley Pine could have gone off in any direction once he'd left the church – so what made you so certain that he would be going to see Thelma Hawtrey?'

'That is one of the things that I cannot say.'

'Ah, I see! You knew where he'd probably be going because you learned of his affair with Thelma in the confessional. Was it Thelma herself who told you? Or was it Jeremy Tully?'

Father Taylor said nothing.

'You killed him in the driveway of Thelma's house, then you put your bicycle in the boot of his car. You might have been planning to put his body in there as well – I don't know about that – but anyway, there was no room. So you squeezed the corpse on to the back seat, instead.' Woodend paused to take a drag on his cigarette. 'What happened to the bike, by the way?'

'I threw it into the canal.'

'Why?'

'I thought there might be some forensic evidence on it which would link me with the crime.'

'I see.'

'And once I'd safely disposed of it, I told Monika that it had been stolen from outside the church, so I'd be covered if there were any questions about it later. Isn't it terrible?'

'Isn't what terrible?'

'The way that we use other people – even the people that we love?'

'We're gettin' off the point,' Woodend said awkwardly. 'You killed him, and then you put his body in the boot—'

'And drove out to the lay-by on the dual carriageway,' Father Taylor supplied.

'And drove out to the exact spot where your home had once stood, Mr Hawtrey,' Woodend corrected him.

'Taylor,' the other man said firmly. 'My name is *Taylor*.'

'But you were born—'

'When my mother changed her name back to what it had once been, she changed mine and my sister's as well.'

'Mr Taylor, then,' Woodend agreed.

'And I would be grateful if you call me *Father*. Whatever I might have done, I was anointed as a priest. The hands were laid upon me, and I will be a priest until the day I die, whether I wish it or not.'

'All right, Father Taylor it is,' Woodend agreed. 'When he was making his confessions to you, Jeremy Tully didn't know you were Alec Hawtrey's son, did he, Father Taylor?'

'Nobody knew, except for Father Kenyon. I went away from here as a boy, and came back as an adult. Besides, when people look at a priest, it is only the cassock they see, not the man inside it. Except for Monika. *She* saw the man.'

'Why take the body to the lay-by?'

'I'm truly not sure,' Taylor admitted.

'But you have your suspicions?'

'Perhaps, in some strange, unexplainable way, I thought I was doing it for my father.'

'Because it was Bradley Pine – using Thelma as his instrument – who broke up your family? You did *know* all about that, didn't you, even if your mother didn't? It's another one of those things you learned in the confessional.'

'I have nothing to say on the matter,' Father Taylor told him.

'Pine destroyed the father you'd known as a child, and turned him into someone else entirely. So it somehow seemed appropriate to place Pine's body on the spot where that other man – that other father – had lived before the Fall?'

'Again, my lips are sealed.'

'You didn't blame Thelma, in any way, for what happened?'

'Mother said we shouldn't, and Mother was right.'

'Because Thelma was no more than Pine's creature?'

'My father must bear a part of the blame,' Father Taylor said, side-stepping the question. 'And so . . . and so must I!'

'You think it was partly *your* fault?'

'Yes.'

'Why?'

'Because I wouldn't listen to him.'

Young Fred is sitting in the garden of the house which has always represented a picture of true happiness in his mother's mind, but is now a reality – because his father has had it built out of love for her.

He is thinking about how confusing life is for most people, and how – even at his age – they seem to want to confide their confusion in him.

Why should that happen, he wonders.

Perhaps it is because he's more of a listener than a talker. Perhaps it is because of something else entirely – something he doesn't even understand, yet feels himself in the grip of.

But whatever the reason, it is beyond doubt that he has the gift of being able to help guide these unhappy people through all the complexities of their earthly existence.

He looks up to see his father standing there. They have never spoken much – it is hard to overcome your own shyness with someone who is also very shy – but Alec plainly wants to speak now.

'It's a horrible thing,' he says.

'What is?'

'Getting old.'

'You're not old, Father!' Fred tells him.

'But I'm older than I once was,' Alec says. 'My body aches in places it never used to. I don't have anything like the same amount of energy I had ten years ago.'

'Of course, you don't. That's the way that—'

'There are things I can no longer do – and other things which are starting to slip away. I feel the urge to reach out for some of those things that are still within my grasp – while I still can.'

'You shouldn't worry yourself about such matters,' Fred says. 'A gradual decline, as we get closer to our graves, is no more than the human condition as God intended it to be. Ashes to ashes, dust to dust.'

His father looks at him strangely, as if seeing him as he really is for the first time. 'Don't you ever worry about anything, Fred?'

'Of course I do. Everybody does.'

'And how do you deal with it?'

'I go to church, and pray for guidance.'

His father nods. 'I used to think I was a good Catholic myself,' he says, 'but I seem so unworthy when I compare my faith to yours.'

'We're all unworthy,' Fred tells him.

Alec pulls up a chair, and sits down next to him. 'I want to talk about love,' he says.

'All right.'

'Love is a very strange thing. I love your mother with all my heart—'

'I know you do.'

'—but I no longer feel the same passion for her that I used to.'

'As you said yourself, you're getting older.'

'But the passion's still there within me, Fred, even if your mother can't arouse it! I can feel it whenever I—'

Fred gets to his feet so quickly that the chair he has been sitting on goes flying off behind him.

'I have to go,' he says, in a complete panic. 'There are matters I must attend to. Now!'

'Please, son, I need to explain,' his father says, with an agonized expression filling his face.

But Fred is already striding back to the house.

'You mustn't blame yourself for that!' Woodend said, horrified.

'Why mustn't I? If I'd stopped and listened to him, our lives might have turned out quite differently. Through me –

through my words and encouragement – he might have found the strength to resist temptation.'

'You were just a kid at the time!' Woodend protested. 'You can't possibly be held responsible.'

'When I first came back to Whitebridge as a priest, I used to dream that one day my father would walk into my church and ask for forgiveness,' Father Taylor said wistfully.

'Ask forgiveness from whom?' Woodend wondered. 'From his confessor? Or from his son?'

'It wouldn't have mattered which of those two he chose to talk to. He would have said he was sorry for what he had done, and I would have said I was sorry for what I had *not* done. But he never came. And then he died, and so I knew he never would. But I still loved him. And I still wanted his forgiveness.'

'What about Pine? Did you hope he'd confess to you, too?'

'Yes.'

'About how he'd used Thelma to get what he wanted? Or about what happened on that mountainside?'

'Once more, I cannot say.'

'But if he had chosen to confess to you, do you think he might still have been alive today?'

'It's a possibility.'

'What was it that finally drove you to kill him?' Woodend wondered. 'What was the straw that broke the camel's back? Was it seein' his face in the paper nearly every day – bein' constantly reminded that the man who'd committed so much evil was goin' on from triumph to triumph?'

Father Taylor maintained his silence.

'An' which of his evils did you most hold against him?' Woodend continued. 'Was it destroying your parents' marriage? Or was it what he did to your father on the mountain?'

'I killed him. That is all you need to know.'

'Given that you smashed in his mouth, an' slit open his stomach, I'm inclined to believe it was the latter.'

'There is nothing I can do about what you choose to believe.'

'Bradley Pine didn't kill your father, as I once thought he must have done,' Woodend said, 'but it's more than possible that he lived on *because of* your father. It must have been very hard for you, seeing him leading a full and happy life, sleeping with the woman who he'd used to break up your parents' marriage – and knowing all the time about the pain and misery he must have caused your father in his dying moments.'

'Do you still expect me to break the seal of confession? Even now?' Father Taylor asked.

'No, I don't,' Woodend replied. 'You've given me ample proof that you'd never do that.' He paused to light up a fresh cigarette. 'My chief constable, Mr Marlowe, doesn't really see the harm in what Bradley Pine did,' he continued. 'As far as he's concerned, the man needed food to stay alive, and if that involved cutting the flesh off a dead man's arm and eating it, then that was what he should have done, however repugnant it might sound to other people.'

Father Taylor had fallen silent again, though now tears were beginning to appear in his eyes.

'But Mr Marlowe's not bein' entirely honest about the matter, is he?' Woodend asked. 'He's deliberately overlookin' certain important facts – because that way he can avoid facin' the truth. But *we've* both faced the truth, haven't we, Father Taylor?'

Tears had begun to stream down the young priest's cheeks, but still he said nothing.

'You know it because of what Jeremy Tully told you in the confessional,' Woodend continued, 'an' I know it because my sergeant questioned the witnesses who were at the scene. An' *what* do we know? We know that when Pine took his knife an' sliced into your father's arm, the blood spurted every-where. Because his heart was still pumpin' it round! Because your father might have been dyin' – but he certainly wasn't dead.'

Thirty-Five

Woodend and Beresford sat at the team's usual table in the public bar of the Drum and Monkey.

'Now do you see what I mean about stirrin' up the pot an' seein' what floats to the top, lad?' Woodend asked. 'Most of the stuff you learned at the factory *was* a waste of time, as you suspected it might be, but if you'd never gone there, you'd never have seen a photograph of young Fred Hawtrey – on holiday with his mum an' dad – on the wall of the boiler room. An' if you'd never seen the photograph, you'd never have realized that Hawtrey an' Taylor were the same man.'

'Inspector Rutter came up with exactly the same information from talking to the first Mrs Hawtrey,' Beresford pointed out.

'That's true,' Woodend agreed. 'But he might not have done. We could have decided we didn't need to talk to her at all. Or she might never have mentioned her maiden name to Inspector Rutter. That's why we need as many spoons in the pot as possible – as long as they're good, solid spoons. An' that's what you are – a good solid spoon.'

'You're very kind, sir,' Beresford said.

'I'm very practical,' Woodend replied. 'I need men I can rely on, an' once I've got them, I try not to let go of them.'

Beresford checked his watch, and then drained his pint. 'I think I'd better be going,' he said.

'It's my round,' Woodend said. 'Why not let me buy you one for the road before you go?'

'That's very kind of you, sir,' Beresford replied, 'but I'd better not.'

'If it's your mam you're thinking of, I don't imagine she'd begrudge you an extra half-hour in the pub, tonight of all nights,' Woodend said.

The second the words were out of his mouth he realized

226

he'd made a mistake. And from the black look Beresford was giving him, it was clear the remark had not gone unnoticed by him, either.

'What's that supposed to mean?' Beresford demanded. 'That you think I'm tied to my mother's apron strings?'

'No,' Woodend said heavily. 'It means I know about your mam's condition – an' I know that you're doin' your best to try an' look after her.'

'Who told you?' Beresford asked.

'That doesn't really matter, does it?' Woodend said soothingly. 'The important thing is that you didn't want me to know – an' you're far from chuffed to learn that I do.' He paused for a moment. 'Why *didn't* you want me to find out, lad? It can't be because you're ashamed of her, can it?'

'Of course not,' Beresford said angrily. 'She can't help it, any more than she could help having cancer.'

'So what is the problem?' Woodend wondered.

'I don't want you making excuses for me!' Beresford told him.

'Pardon?'

'If I do something wrong, I want you to give me a first-class bollocking for it. I don't want you holding back, because of what I have to put up with at home. I don't want you making *allowances* for me!'

'What you really mean is, you don't want me to start *pityin'* you,' Woodend said.

'Maybe that is what I mean,' Beresford agreed.

'You're doin' neither me nor yourself justice, lad,' Woodend told him. 'Pity's somethin' that's reserved for people who can't handle what life throws at them, an' from what I've seen of you, you're not one of them. You'll cope with your mam's deterioration – probably better than I would have done in your place.'

'And if I start to screw up the job, because of the pressures at home?'

'I tell you, just as I've had to tell Bob an' Monika in their time.'

'Honestly?'

'Honestly. I'll have no choice in the matter, because the job's got to be done, an' if you can't do it, somebody else will just have to take your place. But there's no point in worryin' about somethin' that hasn't happened yet, now is there?'

Beresford was silent for a moment, then he said, 'We seem to have spent so much time talking over my problems that I could have had that pint you offered me after all. But now it really *is* time I went.'

Woodend nodded, sympathetically. 'I can't do anythin' to make what goes on at home any easier,' he said, as Beresford stood up and turned towards the door, 'but what I can do is offer you a job that'll at least distract you while you're at work. Think about that, when you're making up your mind whether you'd rather direct traffic or track down murderers.'

On the previous occasions when Monika Paniatowski had walked through the main door of St Mary's Church, she had done so warily, and perhaps a little deferentially. There was no evidence of deference this time – she strode in as if the church counted for nothing, and she was all that mattered.

'I've come to collect a few things that Fred Taylor might need,' she told Father Kenyon.

'Things?' the old priest repeated. 'What kind of things?'

'Toiletries. Tooth brush, nail brush, electric razor . . . all the stuff a well-groomed man will need when he's banged up in gaol.'

'Did they have to sent *you*, of all people, on this errand, my child?' Father Kenyon asked, pityingly.

'You've got it all wrong,' Paniatowski told him. 'Nobody *sent* me. I'm here because I *wanted* to do it.'

And to prove to myself that I could, she added silently.

The priest nodded, almost as if she'd spoken those last words aloud, and he'd heard them.

'Give me a moment to deal with matters here, and then we'll go together and get whatever you think Father Fred will need,' he said.

'You don't seem the least surprised that he's been arrested,' Paniatowski said.

'Don't I?' Father Kenyon asked.

'You haven't even asked me *why* he's in gaol.'

'That's true,' the priest agreed. 'I haven't.'

'But then you don't *need* to ask, do you? He'll have told you all about it when he made his confession. Isn't that right?'

'What a man says in the confessional is between him and his God,' Father Kenyon said.

228

'What about what Pine said when he was in that holy box of yours?' Monika demanded. 'Did he confess to you that he'd eaten living flesh in order to save his own miserable life?'

'I must answer as before,' the priest said calmly.

'Mind you, that probably didn't shock you half as much as it would have shocked most people, did it?' Paniatowski said. 'Eating living flesh is what you're supposed to be doing every time you take Communion.'

'You are very bitter, my child, and I can understand that,' the priest said gently. 'But I hope and pray that what has happened will not turn you against the Church.'

'You are joking, aren't you?' Paniatowski asked.

'I never joke where matters of faith are concerned.'

'I've tried your religion twice, and it hasn't worked out for me either time,' Paniatowski said. 'It doesn't get another chance.'

'My child—'

'Listen, I really don't need any of this,' Paniatowski said. 'In fact, there's only one thing I really need – and that's a bloody drink. So if you want to make sure that Fred gets his stuff, you'd better take it to the station yourself.'

She turned, and began to walk towards the door.

'However you may feel about Him, God will always give *you* another chance,' the priest called after her. 'And another. And another. That, above all else, is what makes Him God.'

'Well, the next time you talk to Him, tell Him I don't need another chance,' Paniatowski called over her shoulder. 'Tell Him I've decided to go it alone from now on.'

When Paniatowski arrived at the Drum and Monkey, she found her boss sitting there alone.

'Bob's just rung to say he's still got a bit of private business to wrap up, but that he should be here shortly,' Woodend said.

There was a vodka already waiting for her on the table, and Paniatowski downed it in one.

'So that's what he calls it, is it?' she snorted, as the alcohol hit her nervous system. 'A bit of private business!'

'Is something wrong?' Woodend asked.

'Why should anything be wrong?' Paniatowski demanded. 'Does something always have to be *wrong*?'

229

'No, but you sound a little—'

'Can't we forget Bob Rutter for a while? Can't we talk about something else for a change?'

'I wasn't aware we *did* normally spend that much time talkin' about Bob,' Woodend said mildly. 'But if you want to change the subject, that's fine with me. What shall we talk about?'

'I don't know. Anything at all, as long as it's not Bob-bloody-Rutter! How's the election going?'

'Not all that well – at least for Henry Marlowe,' Woodend said. 'He's withdrawn his candidature, which was probably very wise, considerin' that what he did on that mountainside will soon be public knowledge.'

'So who'll blow the whistle on him? You?'

'No, not me.'

'Then who?'

'Father Taylor's defence lawyer. When it comes to the sentencin', he'll put forward what Bradley Pine did to Taylor's dad up that mountain as a mitigatin' factor.'

'Fred will never allow that. He can't – because it was told him under the seal of confession.'

'But the man who *made* the confession can say what he likes, and I'd be very surprised if I don't see Jeremy Tully – the reborn Australian sheep-shearer – up there in the witness box.'

'Do you think Marlowe will go to gaol?'

Woodend shook his head. 'Not unless the age of miracles has finally come to pass. He's got too many friends in high places – friends who follow the same code as he does, an' will understand that he only did what was necessary to protect one of their own. They won't exactly pin a medal on him – that would be too much, even for them – but if you ask me, all that's likely to happen is that he'll get a slap on the wrist an' then be given his old job back.'

'Which won't be good news for you,' Paniatowski said. 'He's bound to hold you responsible for his having to withdraw from the election.'

'Of course he'll hold me responsible,' Woodend agreed. 'He holds me responsible when a stray dog craps on his front lawn. But I'll get by.' He lit up a cigarette. 'Now we've exhausted the subject of local politics, do you want to tell me what's been on your mind ever since you walked in here?'

'No.'

'I really think you better had, Monika. It's doin' you absolutely no good at all keepin' it bottled up inside.'

Paniatowski sighed wearily. 'I stopped on the way here to buy a packet of cigarettes. There's a café just next to the off licence I went to. I just happened to look in through the window and I saw Bob. He was sitting at one of the tables – with Elizabeth Driver.'

'Was he, now?' Woodend said, thoughtfully. 'Still, it probably doesn't mean anythin'.'

'Yes it does. They seemed very . . . close.'

'What are you sayin' exactly? Did he have his hand up her skirt or somethin'?'

'No, he didn't.'

'Well, then—'

'But it's only a matter of time before he does.'

'This investigation's been a big strain on you, lass, an' I think you're overreactin' a bit,' Woodend said.

'Am I?' Paniatowski demanded. 'Why do you think she changed her hair colour from black to blonde?'

'I don't know.'

'Because Maria's hair was black!'

'I still don't see it.'

'Then you're a fool! Now that Maria's dead, she's become some kind of saint in Bob's eyes, and Driver knows she can never compete with her, however much she tries. But I'm still alive – so I'm fair game.'

'Come on, lass,' Woodend said uneasily.

'Don't you see what she's offering him? She's offering another version of me – but without the guilt.'

'Do you want him back?' Woodend asked gently.

'No!'

'Truthfully?'

'I *want* him back – of course, I do – but after all that's happened, I know I can never have him. What I *really* don't want is for Elizabeth Driver to have him – because she'll destroy him.'

'You could be quite wrong about the whole thing, you know, Monika,' Woodend said.

'I'm not wrong! And before too long, you'll see for *yourself* that I'm not.'

* * *

231

Elizabeth Driver had tried to talk Rutter out of going for an end-of-investigation drink with Woodend and Paniatowski. She had done so for no other reason than to see how strong a hold she had over him, but she had not been too disappointed when her efforts failed, because it was still early days yet.

Alone again, now that Rutter had gone, she was on the phone, talking to her literary agent in London.

'I've had a wonderful idea for a book,' she said. 'I'm going to base it on one of the regional police forces.'

'That's not a very good way to go, if you're aiming at it being a blockbuster,' the agent cautioned. 'It might sell well in the area where it's set, but that's about the extent of it. Most people – and Londoners especially – aren't really interested in how the police work in other parts of the country.'

'But you see, it *won't* be about how this police force works,' Elizabeth Driver said.

'No?'

'No! It'll be about how it *doesn't* work – and it will be sensational!'

'You might have trouble getting enough information to fill a whole book,' the agent said, still dubious. 'Police forces tend to be tightly-knit, and, as you know from your own experience, they're very good at keeping reporters like you at arm's length.'

'Not this time,' Elizabeth Driver said confidently. 'This time I've got a man on the inside, and he'll give me everything I need.'

'What rank is he?'

'An inspector.'

'Not bad, providing he has contacts in the higher ranks.'

'He does. His *chief inspector* thinks he's wonderful, and would never dream of hiding anything from him.'

'And does this inspector of yours know exactly what it is you're planning to do?'

'Of course he doesn't,' Elizabeth Driver said. 'He hasn't got a bloody clue. And he'll continue to have no bloody clue – at least until the whole thing collapses in on him.'